FURY'S MAGIC

A FURY UNBOUND NOVEL
BOOK 2

YASMINE
NEW YORK TIMES BESTSELLING AUTHOR
GALENORN

A Nightqueen Enterprises LLC Publication

Published by Yasmine Galenorn
PO Box 2037, Kirkland WA 98083-2037
FURY'S MAGIC
A Fury Unbound Novel
Copyright © 2016 by Yasmine Galenorn
First Electronic Printing: 2016 Nightqueen Enterprises LLC
First Print Edition: 2016 Nightqueen Enterprises
Cover Art & Design: Ravven
Editor: Elizabeth Flynn
Map Design: Yasmine Galenorn
Map Layout: Samwise Galenorn

A Nightqueen Enterprises LLC Publication
Published in the United States of America

ACKNOWLEDGMENTS

I dedicate this book to Mandy M. Roth, who has helped me learn to believe in myself as I shift from traditional publishing over to indie. You're truly a wonderful friend and talented, successful woman.

I also want to thank my agent, Meredith, for backing me up, Samwise, my beloved husband, who supports me constantly. Thanks also go to my assistants, who trust that I can make a success of this. To the women in my urban fantasy group, who have helped me learn along the way. And thank you to my readers, as I make this shift—thank you for coming along on the ride with me.

If you wish to contact me, you can do so through my website at Galenorn.com.

Brightest Blessings,
~The Painted Panther~
~Yasmine Galenorn~

Welcome to Fury's Magic

"Please contain the spirits and prevent them from attacking the men. Prevent them from leaving the ship until we banish them. I need to examine this chest and figure out how to exorcise them." I wasn't sure how much power the Psychofágos wielded, but with luck, it would be enough to keep the spirits in check.

"As you will." He turned and with a loud rumble, drew the spirits to him as though he were a magnet. They struggled, anger oozing off them like mist off dry ice, but they couldn't break free. Their wrath was so palpable it made my skin itch. Yeah, they would hold a grudge, all right.

When I was satisfied they were firmly bound by the demon's stasis field, I turned to see the lid of the chest fly open on its own. Oh hell, I had wanted to get the men off the boat first, but apparently whatever was in the chest had other ideas.

Breathing deeply, I slowly edged forward to peek inside. There, in the center, affixed to the bottom, was a bottle. In that bottle were the skeletal bones of a hand, clutching a talisman. Even through the glass, I could recognize the symbols etched on the disk. They were the runes of Ares, and around the hand scuttled several eternity beetles.

"Don't open that bottle, or we're all dead." I stared at the spell, understanding now. The ghosts had been part of the crew of the sunken ship, and they were forever bound to wage a war long over.

Map of the Seattle Area
Post-World Shift

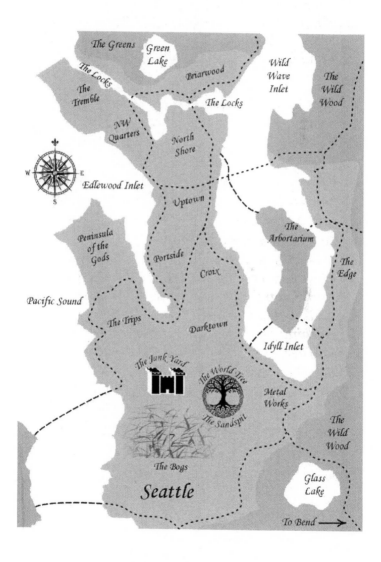

The Greens

Green Lake

The Locks

Briarwood

Wild Wave Inlet

The Wild Wood

The Tremble

The Locks

NW Quarters

North Shore

Edlewood Inlet

Uptown

The Arbortarium

Peninsula of the Gods

Portside

The Edge

Croix

Pacific Sound

The Trips

Darktown

Idyll Inlet

The Junk Yard

The World Tree

Metal Works

The Sandspit

The Wild Wood

The Bogs

Seattle

Glass Lake

To Bend →

The Beginning

The end of civilization as we knew it arrived not with a whimper, but with a massive storm. When Gaia—the great mother and spirit of the Earth—finally woke from her slumber to discover the human race destroying the planet through a series of magical Weather Wars, she pitched a fit. The magical storm she unleashed change such as never before had been seen. The resulting gale ripped the doors on the World Tree wide open, including the doors to Pandoriam—where the Aboms—chaotic demons of shadow and darkness—live, and the doors to Elysium, where the Devani—ruthless agents of light—exist.

In that one cataclysmic moment, now known as the World Shift, life changed forever as creatures from our wildest dreams—and nightmares—began to pour through the open doors.

The old gods returned and set up shop. The Fae and the Weres came out from the shadows and took up their place among the humans. The Theosians began to appear. Technology integrated with magic, and now everything is all jumbled together. Nothing in the old order remained untouched. The world might appear to be similar to the way it was, but trust me—under that thin veneer of illusion, nothing has remained the same.

Chapter 1

My name is Kaeleen Donovan. They call me Fury. I walk in flame and ash, on a field of bones. Some nights I think I'll burn to a crisp under Hecate's moonlight. Other nights, I sit on the roof and play with the starlight, soaking up as much beauty as I can to sustain me when I'm facing the Abominations who rise from the depths of Pandoriam.

"Are you sure you're up for this?" I held up my sword. Xan was perpetually sharp so I never needed to hone her edge, but she asked for a good polish every now and then. The ornate blade vibrated in my hand. She was growing stronger. Every time I used her, the energy sang. At times I felt I could almost hear her speak, but the barrier between us hadn't quite broken open yet. Although Hecate wouldn't tell me what the sword's full potential was, I knew that I hadn't tapped into her full nature yet, but it was just a matter of time.

Tam lounged on the sofa, one foot propped up on the seat while the other hung over the edge. Leaning back, he read on his tablet. Without looking up from his book, he said, "Yes, I want to go. Quit worrying about me."

"All right, but remember, I asked." I went back to shining my blade, although I wasn't about to stop worrying. I knew very well that Tam could hold his own. After all, he was one of the Bonny Fae. And not just one of them. He was their Prince. The Lord of UnderBarrow. But I'd still feel responsible if he got hurt. My lover and friend, his health mattered to me, and the fact was, we were headed into a dangerous situation. Hauntings were seldom easy. If the ghosts were chill, then most people left them alone. It was only the nasty ones that they called me about.

Jason let out a snort from behind the counter. "You're both nuts. Why on earth do you want to go prowling around a boat filled with ghosts?" He was mixing up a batch of *Dove's Love*, a powder designed to calm volatile situations. We sold far too much of it here at Dream Wardens, Jason's magical consulting shop. Sales of the powder were very good. The fact that it was needed so often? Not so good.

"Because it's a job? Because Hecate found it for me? Because I need the money?" Finally satisfied that Xan was as clean and sparkling as I was going to get her, I slid her back into her sheath and set the blade to the side. "We should head out. The ghosts are more active once the sun sets." I glanced out of the store window. The light had waned and dusk already was stretching its hand over the skies. We were well into October, and daylight faded by four.

Tam abruptly closed his tablet and stood, stretching as he yawned. "Then we shall go. Jason, do you need me anymore today?" He was tall and lanky, with long black hair that curled to his waist, and his eyes were silver, ringed with black. Not only striking to look at, Tam had a natural magnetism and charm that exuded from every pore in his body.

And he has good hands, I thought. *Very good hands. And lips. And...*

"Not right now, no." Jason put an end to my reverie. He, too, was tall and ruggedly good-looking, with wheat-colored hair and vivid green eyes. Where Tam wore his hair loose and flowing, Jason gathered his own back into a braid. His nose had an unusual curve to it, like most hawk-shifters' noses.

Jason had let me set up my own little business in a corner—the Crossroads Cleaning Company. I took on exorcisms and psychic cleansings, offered tarot readings, and I threw the bones for those who wanted oracular advice. Hecate had strengthened my gifts in those areas, and while business waxed and waned, I usually made a decent living. But it had been awhile since I'd had a job like this one, and I was trying to remember what I needed as I gathered together my tools.

I opened my bag to make sure that all my ritual tools were there. Hecate had given me a sacred crystal skull that allowed me to focus my energy toward the dead, and I had several different powders and sprays: *Rest Ye Well* powder to quiet spirits, *Exorcism* oil to evict ghosts from their possessed victims, holy water from Hecate's sacred fountain, graveyard dust and Crossroads dust. A leather sheath held my dagger with a bronze hilt and a crystal blade that was to be used for magic only. Also in the bag were a clapper-bell to drive the dead away and other assorted goodies.

"I think I'm ready." I looked around to make certain I hadn't forgotten anything else.

"Before you go, Tam, how's the new database coming along?" Jason pushed aside a ledger, frowning. Our old inventory database had crashed. It hadn't been built to handle the volume of business Dream Wardens was fielding. Tam was working on a new one that promised to be bigger and better than we needed. Software for the shop to grow into.

Tam was the shop's techie, which seemed oddly out of place given his Fae nature. He loved gadgets and all things concerned with computers.

"Let's just say the new software coming out of Mage-Tek blows the old programs we were using out of the water. It's going to take awhile to transfer all the information, but once we finish that, finding and tracking inventory and spell components will be a breeze. The program is vox-enabled, which means we all need to password code it by voice as well as by thumbprint." Tam shrugged on his leather duster. He was wearing a pair of black jeans that hugged his butt in the most delightful way, and a V-neck shirt that showed off his waistline.

"How long do you estimate until you finish the conversion?" Jason dusted his hands after pouring the last of the powder on the scales. He measured powders out using an archaic weights-and-measure balance. Jason loved antiques. Tapping the mixture into a plastic bag, he slapped a label on it, then tossed it into a basket with the rest of the pouches. "Done. This should hold us on *Dove's Love* powder for a solid month."

"I figure another week and we should be good to go. That is, if nothing else interferes. Ready, love?" Tam turned to me.

I still blushed when he called me that, especially in front of Jason, but I was slowly getting used to it. "Yeah, I don't think I've forgotten anything."

I was dressed for Hecate's work, with my black leather jacket, warm blue turtleneck, black leather shorts, and ankle boots that I could easily run in. I slid Xan's scabbard over my shoulder and made sure my dagger was firmly in place, strapped to my left thigh. Pulling on fingerless gloves that had a nonslip grip on the palms, I headed toward the door.

"We'll call you if we're going to be late."

Jason closed up the shop one evening per month and we ate dinner at his place. I suspected these family-of-choice evenings were more important to him now than ever, given the recent death of his fiancée. Eileen's death had hit him harder than he wanted to let on. But we never said anything. He made it clear he wasn't ready to talk about how it had affected him.

"Thanks. I'm making spaghetti, so be there. And take it easy," he called out as we slipped into the dark Seattle night. "Don't let the ghosties bite you in the butt."

I'm Kaeleen Donovan but they call me Fury. I'm a Theosian, a minor goddess. Yoked to

Hecate from birth, my primary job is to seek out and destroy Abominations that come in off the World Tree. Secondary are psychic readings and cleansings, and whatever else Hecate might have up her sleeve for me.

My mother was brutally murdered when I was thirteen. I landed, quite literally, on Jason's doorstep and he took me in. He looked around my age—thirty—but he was actually well over two hundred. Most shifters and Fae are exceptionally long-lived. I will be too, given my nature, but I'm still young and still new to the world compared to Jason and Tam.

My mother and father were human, but on the way home from work one night my mother wandered through the Sandspit and got engulfed in a cloud of rogue magic. She was pregnant with me at the time. Boom, in that one moment my DNA changed, and that's what turned me into a Theosian. When I was born, the hospital sent my parents to the Seers. They ordained that I was to be handed over to Hecate for training. Since birth, I've been under her leash, bound to her by oath and by blood. If I dishonor her, she could have me destroyed. But I genuinely like Hecate and I think she feels the same about me. We work well together, most of the time.

Hecate is a goddess of the Crossroads, of the dead and of magic. And so I do a lot of my work out on the Crossroads where life and death intersect, and where dimensions and worlds meet and blend. My magic is that of flame and lightning, of energy so white-hot that it can blind.

Not long ago, my friends and I ended up in a tussle with an order of rogue magicians. The Order of the Black Mist is bent on unleashing the

Elder Gods of Chaos on the planet. We managed to thwart their plans, but Lyon and his cronies are still out there, and I have a queasy feeling in the pit of my stomach that we're not done with them.

It's not easy, being a minor goddess. Belonging to the Elder Gods is even harder. But every day I learn a little more about myself. All too often, those lessons come at the tip of my sword, when I'm facing down the evil determined to make our world its home.

As we exited the building, we passed Hans, who was on his way in. The brawn of our shop, he kept the riff-raff and bogeys out of the store. A Theosian like me, he was yoked to Thor and looked the part. Muscled and bald, he was bad-assed to the bone, and was wearing a knit cap and earmuffs against the chill. His girlfriend Greta was with him. A Valkyrie in training, she had been born in Scandnavaland, in the city of Bifrost. Her family had emigrated to the Americex Corporatocracy when she was little.

"Colder out here than Gaia's tit," he said, blowing on his hands as we stopped to say hello. His breath froze into puffs in front of his face and he stomped his feet on the sidewalk. It was cold enough to snow. We'd had one good snow the month before, but it had melted off. Now, though, we were into mid-October, and winter was targeting us for a good pummeling. "Where are you headed? Done for the day?"

"No, we're on our way to Portside. We'll see you at Jason's in a few hours. At least, I hope we will. With luck, the job won't take more than a few hours."

"What did she stick you with today?" Hans had a skewed view of Hecate. She frightened him. Given that he hung with the Norse, it seemed odd to me she shook him so much, although once he confided to me that Hecate reminded him of Hel—the Norse goddess of the dead. And Hel scared the hell out of everybody.

"A haunted fishing boat. Tam's coming to keep me company."

"Well, that, and to keep the sea dogs from panting all over you. And before you say it, yes I know you can hold your own. But you're going up against ghosts. You don't need to be distracted by idiots itching to unzip those leather shorts of yours." Tam snaked his arm around my waist. He was more possessive than I had thought he would be, but not in a creepy way.

"Um hmm," I said, shoving my hands into my pockets. My legs were freezing, but I couldn't wear pants, not and still leave easy access to my whip. The flaming brand wove down the outside of my right thigh and leg, brilliant ink glowing in the night. But one touch and it would come off in my hand. A weapon of fire and electricity, it was one of Hecate's gifts to me. She had inked it onto me herself the night she gave me the name *Fury*. And that had been a furious night, indeed.

"It's the truth." Tam kissed my nose.

"Are you sure you don't just want to keep an eye on who's ogling my butt?" I asked, smirking.

Greta let out a snort. "That sounds more like it."

Tam grumbled, but then he laughed. "Well, maybe I don't like the thought of them ogling you. But that's my prerogative, isn't it?"

"It is at that, I suppose. Anyway, let's get a move on. It's freaking cold tonight." I turned to Hans and Greta. "See you at Jason's."

"Will do." And with that, they gave us a quick wave and slipped through the door.

An icy blast of wind rushed through the Market and I zipped up my jacket as we headed toward the Monotrain station, grateful that it was only a few blocks away from Dream Wardens. From there, it would be a quick ride down to Portside, which was located on Edlewood Inlet, which flowed off of the Pacific Sound.

Down was an accurate description, given the steep grade of the streets. Located over a series of fault lines, the district was pleasant enough. At least I hadn't been called to go to Uptown or North Shore. Portside might be mostly made up of Weres and Shifters, but I didn't feel out of place there like I did in the human-centric districts of the city.

The cold might be clamping down on the city, but it hadn't stemmed the swarm of activity. The Market in Darktown was running full tilt, a colorful, whirlwind array of vendors hawking their goods. Mouthwatering aromas wafted from the food stands as we passed by. This was prime time—the dusk till dawn shift change over in the Metalworks. Factory and line workers from the various plants stopped to pick up quick, easy meals on their way home after hauling eight- to twelve-hour shifts.

My mouth watered but I steadfastly ignored the stalls. It wasn't a good idea to load up on food before clearing out ghosts. A full stomach clouded the sight and weighed down the energy. The smells of bread and meat and roasting vegetables mingled with that of fragrant oils, the char of smoke, and body odors emanating from the crowds who wandered through the Market. I had learned to tune out the noise over the years, but the scents weren't so easy to ignore.

Darktown was a gritty place. Ruins from the World Shift still dotted the district, although last month's earthquake had taken down some of the shakier ones that had survived Gaia's wrath. The sky-eyes patrolled but they never dove too close. There were too many chances of someone trying to steal it or smash it down. The Devani didn't enter here either, although the Conglomerate had given them a lot more freedom the past few weeks. We were hearing reports from Croix, especially, where the golden soldiers roamed the streets, looking for any infractions.

The Devani were brought in off the World Tree, ruthless and brilliant in their golden breastplates. I had never seen one close up, and I never wanted to. They weren't human. Far from it, although they looked like beautiful golden-haired men and women with perfectly structured muscles. But the Devani were ruthless, and true to their masters at all costs. If they had emotions, it was hard to tell. In one sense, the Devani were the opposite of Abominations. Order and law versus chaos and anarchy. But the Devani steered clear of Darktown, and word was they never went out on the Tremble.

A bogey wandered by. I could tell he was from the Junk Yard. Bogeys had a feel to them. Dangerous and rough, like feral dogs, they were as likely to cut you as look at you. He gave us the once-over, but I turned slightly and pointed to my whip on my leg. He quickly glanced the other way and hurried along. I was known in Darktown, and a lone bogey wouldn't bother me unless he was sky-high on Methodyne or Opish.

"You wear your authority well," Tam whispered with a laugh. "I think that's what makes them so afraid of you, once they realize who you are."

"I think it's more than that," I said. "I've actually been thinking about this for a while. I protect Seattle from Abominations. Most come in through the World Tree. They're hungry when they come off the tree, and they're looking for food. So the most likely victims? People down here in Darktown and the Junk Yard. I stop the Aboms from feasting on the bogeys just as much as I stop them from hurting everybody else. I think the bogeys give me a grudging sort of respect for that. I know the Nancies and the play-girls do."

Tam suddenly pushed me toward the brick building we were near. "Sky-eye. Freeze."

We froze as the drone hovered overhead. In crowded areas it didn't matter so much, but I always tried to hide from the sky-eyes when I was easy to single out. I lived off-grid, and the Conglomerate would be furious if they found out. All Theosians were supposed to be chipped. The government kept an eye on us and too often those of my kind ended up vanishing, especially if the Corporatocracy decided our powers were too useful or too dangerous. Or both. In fact, if they thought us both too useful and too dangerous, it was like we were the pot of gold at the end of the rainbow.

When I was thirteen, Tam had removed my chip and altered it, a painful but necessary act. I still registered as having one, but Tam had hacked into its grid and falsified the information. But if the Devani got hold of me, it wouldn't take them long to figure out that I was running on fake identification.

The sky-eye scanned the sidewalk, its ray of light sweeping over the concrete. Then, with a sudden lurch, it picked up speed and zoomed off toward the center of Darktown.

I let out a sharp breath. "It won't be back for several hours. Let's go. There's the platform." I pointed up the block toward the Monotrain platform. The trains ran through the city, a hundred feet aboveground, speeding from station to station. Though they were more erratic in Darktown, and they wouldn't go into the Junk Yard, overall the mass transit system worked well.

We took the elevator to the waiting platform. Usually I opted for the stairs. It was too easy to get caught in an elevator with a bogey. And a lot of times, the cars were so old and creaky they stalled out on their way up. But Tam's presence gave me a little boost of self-confidence. Truth was, what I did was lonely, hard, dangerous work. It felt good to have somebody else there with me, taking chances and risks by my side.

The next car was due in five minutes. We made quick work of the time by huddling together on one of the covered benches before boarding the train. Then, with a silent *whoosh*, we were off, headed to Portside to meet with a boatload of spooks.

Chapter 2

Portside was a tidy district, even though it was down on the docks. PortCom, the primary corporation in charge of shipping and transportation along the West Coast, employed hundreds of workers. The economics trickled down to the shop workers selling everything from souvenirs to one of a kind homemade gifts, to the fishmongers who sold the catch that the fishermen hauled out of the waters. There was a brisk feel to the district, and Portside was a haven for tourists who felt safe enough to stroll along the docks in the afternoon, or on a lazy evening after a leisurely dinner.

After Gaia brought about the World Shift, fishing once again emerged as a viable industry after having been diminished for so long due to overfishing, though the trade was heavily regulated. With the freeways blown to smithereens in so many areas and trucking limited, ocean liners and cargo ships once again ruled the seas.

At one time, great airliners had filled the skies but now the aeronautics industry was quite a different thing. Very few traveled via sky-high-lines. Mostly government workers and the über rich. But hot air balloons were all the rage, and drones were used for surveillance and local deliveries, but mostly the government was focused on engineering interstellar travel into a viable reality.

As Tam and I wove through the crowds, I was surprised to see so many people out and about. In the Metalworks, the factories ran all day and all night. In Darktown, the Market was filled from sunup to sundown, but outside of the grittier districts I had assumed that the districts kept shorter evening hours. Apparently, I was wrong.

"Have you been in Portside often? I seldom ever make it over here." There really wasn't much reason for me to visit the west bay, especially with the sky-eyes so active, not to mention the Devani. The last thing I needed was a run-in with either one.

"I've been here plenty of times, but I usually come for the fish." Tam grinned, pulling me to him and planting a kiss on my lips.

I smiled, suddenly feeling shy. He was so generous with his affection that I wasn't sure how to handle the attention. But every time I looked in his eyes, the warmth made me melt, and I wondered how I had overlooked him all of these years. I'd had a crush on Jason for a long time, mostly hero-worship I realized now, but when his fiancée had been killed reality crashed in. While it hadn't been a magnificent love match, he felt guilt over Eileen's death. That was enough to enshrine her into sainthood in his heart. Jason didn't love me the way I thought I felt about him. He made it clear that he saw me as a good friend. Though the realization was bittersweet, it went a long way in helping me let go of the fantasy.

We passed through the Fish Market, which was still open. A long, covered array of stalls offered up fish and shellfish. I seldom ate seafood. The array looked incredible, but fresh fish was usually out of my budget. I stuck to the cheaper cuts of meat, bread and cheeses, local greens, and occasionally fresh fruit when it was in season.

The briny smell of the fish mingled with the saltwater scent of the air. A bumper spread of bloom had drifted in on the inlet, and the combination of the algae and brine and fish set me to thinking about taking a ferry somewhere. I loved being on the water. I could almost taste the salt on my tongue.

"I love the smell," Tam said. "It smells like a home that I left long ago. One that will never be the same again."

"How far back are we talking? To what you call Eire?"

He nodded. Now that we were together Tam often spoke of a time before the World Shift and the Weather Wars when the Tuatha de Dannan—his people—lived on an island called Eire. As for me, I was still trying to get used to the idea that I was dating a man who was thousands of years old. I asked him how he dealt with it and he told me that the Fae perceived time differently. That it took on an entirely different meaning.

"The Bonny Fae are bound to the water, you know. The ocean and the forest are where we draw our strength from. Take us away from either and we wither."

One thing I had learned over the past few weeks was how much the wild meant to Tam and his people. While I was managing to adapt to UnderBarrow, I was never fully comfortable underground. But when we headed over to the Wild Wood I felt free, like I had broken out of jail. Most of my time had been spent in Darktown but I was quickly getting used to the vast expanses of unbroken forest.

"I don't know if I could ever leave the coast. I can't imagine living in the Mid-Lands. It's too flat and vast, with too many unbroken stretches of land. Lakes just aren't the same."

"No, they aren't." Tam looked around. "So, where's Queet?"

I snorted. My soul-bound spirit guide was conspicuously absent. "He told me he'll meet us at the boat. He mumbled something about some task Hecate wanted him to do, though he didn't say what. He's been deep in the grumblers lately, and I haven't felt like asking him much of anything. To be honest, I'm ready to ask Hecate to talk to him, though I don't want to get him in trouble. He didn't ask to be stuck with me."

"Stuck with *you*? I'd say you were stuck with *him*. But you're right, Queet's a good sort, despite his glum nature. So, where is the boat?"

"Portside, Dock 53, Slip 84. She's called the *Fanta Verde* and her captain is scared out of his wits. Captain Varga called me this morning. He asked for help at the temple and they referred him to me. Hecate has a way of engineering jobs when I need them, but a boat filled with ghosts sounds a little out of my league. I'm used to dealing with spirits on a singular basis."

"You go after Aboms every week. Of course you

can handle this."

"I think you have more confidence in me than I do." I pressed my lips together, wondering if my bag o' tricks would be enough firepower against a multiple-haunting. I could haul ass on the hardest of ghosts, but it was never easy, and taking on multiple spirits was a tricky pursuit. Neither fit my idea of fun.

The rhythm of the evening had settled in. People hurried home for dinner, stopping at the vendors to pick up food. The play-girls had slid out of the woodwork looking for Joe-boys, and the Nancies were cruising the streets in search of their own customers. Portside had far fewer bogeys than Darktown, but there were still the sketchers—the ones who weren't all there, who weren't Broken, but were likely to go off on you if you crossed paths.

The crowds grew louder as the boys of the Fish Market started their routines. Throughout the day, they put on shows to amuse the customers. Strong and bare-chested, they tossed fish from one to another like it was a game of keep-away. The glistening scales slid against their clean-shaven chests and then off again, to the next one, as though they were dancing with the huge silvery creatures. The displays worked. People bought more fish than they could afford. Nearby, a flautist, a drummer, and a guitar player thrummed away on their instruments, keeping up a cheery, bouncy beat that was as mesmerizing as the dance itself.

As we passed the main market, I was struck by how calm the atmosphere was compared to Darktown. We had entertainers and vendors, but there was always an underlying current of danger. Here, people laughed and had a good time. The mood was lighter.

We came to the edge of the street where a winding path snaked down at a steep grade, leading through the rubble toward the ports. Ten blocks over we could have caught the Monotrain down to the water, but I wanted to conserve time and energy. Ten blocks might not sound like much but in Seattle the city blocks were long, and the hike, a tiring one. We'd cut our time in half by taking the shortcut. Although treacherous—the chance of tripping was high and the downward grade, steep—we'd arrive at the docks a lot faster. We eased our way around the heaps of rubble. The narrow path leading through the dirt had been compacted by thousands of footsteps, and it was so hard it might as well be rock.

Tam and I focused on keeping our footing. The rubble actually proved to be helpful. The blocks of stone provided an easy way to brace ourselves as we picked through the piles of dust-laden debris. Here and there, signboards had remained intact, reminders of a time long gone. The words were faded and no longer readable, but the signs made me think of the people who had walked this path when it was still vibrant and thriving. At times, I thought I could hear whispers riding the wind, but then I'd listen and they'd fade to nothing.

After a few minutes, I paused. Something felt off, but I couldn't pinpoint what. I closed my eyes, casting around to see if I could sense what was wrong.

"Damn it, I wish Queet was here."

"What's wrong?" Tam asked, his voice soft.

"I'm not sure. Give me a moment." I leaned against one particularly large chunk of rubble. I lowered myself into trance and brought up my

Trace screen. Maybe there was an Abom in the area. But after a few moments, I eased back. Nothing. But something was bothering me. I just didn't know what. My alarm bells were ringing loud and clear.

"There's someone following us. An outlier, just out of my range of hearing and sight."

"An Abom?"

"None around. But this is a hunter, and he's stalking us, I believe." I opened my eyes. "I searched for a magical signature, but whoever it is, he's intent on keeping himself cloaked. The energy feels familiar, but I can't pinpoint it to any specific person or event." I tried once more to no avail. "Nope. All I know is somebody's there."

"Do you want to call Hecate?"

I thought about it for a moment, then shook my head. "There's nothing she could do. She's not going to come running every time I have a feeling in my funny bone, nor do I expect her to. Let's just deal with the ghosts and get our butts back to Darktown."

A gloom settled over me. While Portside was a lovely place, the feeling of being watched left me unsettled. I hoped to hell it wasn't the Devani following us, though I had no reason to think they would, except the golden boys made everybody nervous. And they had been far more active lately, though they were still avoiding Darktown and the Junk Yard.

The street curved steeply around the remains of an ancient building, and from there, it turned into a series of steps. The winding staircase stopped just short of a quarter mile, which meant about two thousand stairs, with landings on which to rest every hundred steps or so. Below, we could see the panorama of the port lights. Thank gods the stairs were also lighted.

"We're definitely taking the Monotrain back up," I said.

Tam laughed. "The stairs are no bother to me, but I admit, in this weather? With this chill? I welcome the comfort of the train."

We fell into a silent rhythm as we descended the stairs. That was one thing I appreciated about Tam. We could be together, and yet be in our silence. I didn't feel like I had to be constantly on, or that I had to entertain him. We had our moments of chatter and talk, but even this soon after coming together, we had discovered our ability to connect without words.

I looked out at the silent water. The fog was rolling in at a good clip off Edlewood Inlet. It would blanket the ports by the time we got there. The clouds had socked in and if we didn't see snow by midnight, I'd be surprised. I huddled my shoulders against the cold. At least my legs were warm from all the walking.

There weren't any other people on WaterEdge Stair, a surprise to me. Then again, this wasn't the place to find easy marks. Most tourists took the Monotrain down to the water, and on a night like tonight, finding anybody out on a pleasure walk was going to be iffy. Anybody here would have business, and would mean business. And so we continued, silent, with only the soft fall of our feet on the concrete steps to keep us company.

By the time we reached the bottom, I let out a groan, bending over to stretch my hamstrings.

"Remind me to go to the gym tomorrow. I haven't been this week and I'm paying for it."

Being bound to Hecate in the capacity I was, I

had to frequent the gym four to five times a week to keep in shape. Aboms were tough, and I had to be in top form to fight them. I was strong, though I wasn't ripped like some of the muscle-bunnies who frequented the gyms. But I could spar with the best of them and usually win my match.

"I know one set of muscles you can't exercise there." Tam gave me a lascivious grin.

I swatted him, and he pulled me in for a long kiss. Breathless from his touch, I murmured, "Tonight, if we're not too tired after evicting the ghosts, maybe you can train me."

"I love being your training partner," he whispered. "Now, let's go take care of your clients and get you some cash, so we can get the hell out of here."

My breath still in my throat, I shook my head to clear my thoughts and bring my focus back to the present. "Right. Onward."

Picking the pace up to a jog, I headed toward Dock 53, which was another quarter mile down Shipside Street. The fog had, indeed, come in and now it wove around the street and docks like a living shroud, enveloping everything and everyone it passed. I had done a map search and knew the relative position of where to find the *Fanta Verde*, but even so, the mist skulked along our knees, rising to obscure the way. Everything seemed convoluted. It would be so easy to get lost in the rolling clouds.

We finally reached the correct dock and turned off Shipside, heading down the narrow walkway that led to the pier. The ghostly silhouettes of tall ships and ocean liners buttressed both sides of the wide wooden walkway, the fog steaming around them, covering the water's surface.

"This is a perfect night for assassins and thieves to cloak themselves in the shadows," Tam said, his voice soft.

"Thank you so much for that comforting thought," I tossed back. But truth was, the thrum and hustle of dockworkers made me feel safe enough. Thugs seldom hung out on the piers, not with the round-the-clock shifts that went on. The wooden walkway echoed faintly with our footsteps, the fog muffling sound. Here and there, we caught fragments of conversation that filtered out from the boats, and the sounds of crates and boxes and barrels being moved around, and the grinding sound of the forklift motors reverberated through the shrouded night.

Finally, we came to Slip 84, which was to the left, and turned down the narrow walkway leading to the ship's side. The *Fanta Verde* was a moderately sized fishing vessel with a ten-man crew. About one hundred years back, the Aqualinia Corporation had discovered a way to convert seawater into energy, and so most big liners and fishing vessels no longer used agroline, instead opting for the expensive but cost-saving Waterthresher motors. This eliminated a great deal of fuel consumption, and oil spills were a thing long past, and meant that no boat with a Waterthresher motor would ever be stuck out of fuel.

Tam and I stared up at the massive boat. She wasn't big by the standards of some of her surrounding sisters, but she was still as big as one of the medium-size ferries. A man was standing on the plank that led on board.

"Fury?" he asked as we emerged from the fog.

"I'm Fury and this is my associate, Tam. You

must be Captain Varga?" I held out my hand.

He nodded, taking my fingers in his as he gave me a firm shake. "Pleased to meet you both. I'm glad you could make it. I'm afraid I'm going to lose my crew if you can't take care of these ghosts. If not to another boat, to the sea. These haunts are dangerous, Fury."

I stared up at the ship, my senses on high alert. Even from here, I could feel the spirits, and they weren't restful or good-natured. "How long have you had this problem?"

"Since we visited Dutch Vista. It's a fishing town in Alaska."

"Isn't that part of the Canadian Empire?"

"Not exactly. Dutch Vista is located within the Canadian Empire, but they allow a couple of Americex fishing ports to rent land there. Dutch Vista is one of them. We pulled into port to offload some fish and pick up a new deckhand. When we left a few days later, we had a boat full of ghosts. They've been wreaking havoc ever since, and my crew's exhausted." He removed his hat and wiped his brow. "Honestly, if we can't get rid of them, I'm not sure my crew will survive the next run."

"That was one cargo you didn't need." I rubbed my chin. "So, tell me, what did you take on? Anything besides a new crew member who might have had ghosts attached to it?"

He let out a disgruntled sigh. "Not during the on-load. But..." The way he stretched out the word told me that there was something he wasn't sure about revealing.

"I need to know everything in order to proceed."

The captain grimaced, then slowly capitulated. "All right, if it will help. We were less than two days away from Dutch Vista when one of the men spotted something bobbing in the water. It was a metal chest. There was nothing to indicate where the chest might have come from, so we sent a probe down—a subscope. We found a ship on the bottom, a very old ship."

"How old?"

"From what we could tell, it came from the time of the Weather Wars. We couldn't dive for it, but we filed a salvage claim. And we hauled the chest aboard. I decided to wait until we were back in port before opening it. But the ghosts arrived that night, and they've flooded the ship ever since. There are five or six of them and they're making life a living hell."

A ship from the time of the Weather Wars could mean several things. It could have been just a regular ship like a cruise ship or a fishing vessel. Or, it could have been far more dangerous.

"Did you manage to find out which ship it was? Are there any records?"

"We haven't had any word yet," Captain Varga said. "But I know what you're thinking and I'm pretty sure you're right. The subscope showed that the ship possessed a row of guns on both sides. It was a war vessel."

As I had feared. War vessels lined the bottom of the oceans, and most had gone down in battle. "Did you see any evidence of how it sank?" Chances were the evidence could have easily rusted away during the intervening centuries, but Captain Varga gave me a solemn nod.

"The scope showed that one entire side of her hull had been blasted open. But Fury, it wasn't an outward attack. That ship exploded from the inside by the looks of the hole. I think her own men took her down. She had to have gone to the bottom quickly. The hole was huge. And there are bones down there, plenty of them. A ship that big could easily carry a crew of five or six hundred."

As what he was saying sank in, my mood plummeted. We were dealing with a lot of unknown factors, none of them promising. I turned to Tam.

"All right, let's go on board. Captain Varga, it's time to open the trunk and see what we have in there."

Without further discussion, he turned and led us on board.

Chapter 3

As we crossed the plank, it occurred to me
that I had never been aboard a real ship. Ferries,
yes, but a ship that sailed out into the wild ocean?
Never. I jumped the short distance from the plank
down to the deck of the boat. The water rolled
beneath us, making it difficult to stand at first,
but I finally got my sea legs. The waves churned,
frothing in the inlet, and I could only imagine what
they must be like out on the ocean proper.

Tam must have been thinking along the same
lines because he said, "The Ocean Mother's
restless, isn't she?"

Captain Varga nodded. "That she is, man. That
she is."

Under the lights of the ship, it was easier to
see him. He wasn't a terribly tall man, but he was
broad shouldered, and stocky. He was wearing a
white shirt beneath a waterproof vest, and gloves.
His pants looked to be waterproof as well, and
wide galoshes covered his feet up to his knees.

Varga had skin the color of freshly tilled soil, and his hair was a salt-and-pepper mix of tangled braids. His eyes shone in the night like a cat's and that's when I realized that he wasn't fully human, although I didn't know exactly *what* he was.

I had barely taken two steps aboard when something shoved me from behind and I went stumbling against the rail, hard, bruising my stomach muscles.

"What the hell?" I whirled, expecting to see somebody there. Neither Tam nor Varga were near enough to have touched me.

"Ghost. They're bullies, among other things. We've had hell to pay out on the ocean with the men trying to fish and bring in a run. Almost lost one of my crew to a squall when one of the fuckhead ghosts knocked him overboard." Varga's voice took on an edge that sent a chill through me. The captain was *not* happy.

"So they're not just a nuisance. They're actually dangerous." Most ghosts that I dealt with were relatively benign, but now and then I got hold of one that was more than just a scare-'em-up spook. It wasn't that there weren't plenty of deadly spirits out there, though. I had just lucked out until now.

"They're dangerous, all right. The minute we pulled into port, two of my best deckhands threatened to quit if I didn't get rid of the haunts. So I petitioned Poseidon and he turned me over to Hecate." At that moment, his eyes flashed again and I knew. Captain Varga was a Theosian, like me. And he was bound to Poseidon, which made us temple-mates, so to speak.

"That's why she recommended I take the job. I had no idea."

"That I'm a Theosian? I don't tell a lot of

people. My men don't even know. Poseidon's tasks are odd and varied. I don't have one specific job. Mostly I fish. But when he sets me out on stormy seas, we usually navigate just fine." A glint in his eye told me there was something else that he wasn't telling us, but common courtesy prevented me from asking.

Theosians were often reticent about their powers, and with good reason. The government insisted on chipping us at birth, when we were first categorized. They didn't bother to give a reason. They didn't have to since they were the ones in power. But every Theosian knew why they kept tabs on us.

Tam had altered my chip when I was thirteen and first landed on Jason's doorstep after my mother was brutally murdered. While I appeared to have the requisite tracking during cursory scans, the information on them was garbled enough to prevent anybody from figuring out who I really was unless they did a detailed search and put all the pieces together. That wouldn't happen in a normal scan or cop-and-stop, but if the Devani hauled me in on any charges, that would be it. They'd find out who I was, and that I was wearing an altered chip. Considering it was a capital offense, there would be no hope for me. So I kept out of range and out of sight as much as possible.

I glanced around the deck of the ship. Large pots lined one area of the boat. Crabbing pots. So the *Fanta Verde* braved the north seas, still as dangerous an occupation as it had ever been. A door led below deck, and the wheelhouse rose over us, lit from within.

"Do you mind if we poke around? Does your crew know we're aboard?"

"They do, and be my guest. The chest is down below, in the galley. I figured you'd want to take a look at it."

Cooperation in jobs like this was king, and I was grateful Captain Varga understood that.

"It will help a lot if we know which ship it came from. There are some historical documents left from that time. But if the ship was blown out of the water, it doesn't matter who did it or who was on it. That sort of end would leave a lasting impact in the astral zone over the area of water in which she sank. If the ghosts were soldiers, they're probably still fighting a war that's been over for hundreds of years." Chances were the ghosts saw the men of the *Fanta Verde* as the enemy, which was going to make it a lot harder to clear them.

I headed toward the door leading below. Tam followed, and after him, Captain Varga.

The staircase was steep, but at least there was a railing. After the WaterEdge Stair, these steps seemed as simple as skipping stones. As I turned left into the galley, a group of five men looked up from where they had gathered around the table. The booth could seat at least fifteen. Rough and ready, most looked to be true seamen, weathered by salt and wind with brine for blood. Their leathery faces reflected the years spent out in the elements. But to a man, especially the youngster of the group, their faces mirrored fear.

"Gentlemen." I gave them a cursory nod, my focus moving to the chest. It was large, all right, with a thick stream of energy oozing from it. Long fingers reached out, hunting. Whatever was inside that chest was sentient. Shivering, I tore my attention away from it as Captain Varga introduced us.

"Boys, this is Fury, and her partner, Tam. They're here to oust the ghosts." Captain Varga motioned for them to scoot over so we could sit down.

But as I approached the table, a miniature lightning fork sparked off the chest, surging toward my shoulder. I darted to the side just in time. The bolt drove past me toward the wall of the galley where it drove a hole deep into the wood. The boat groaned and the smell of char filled the air as the captain rushed over to make certain there was no fire.

"Crap." He poked at the hole. "There don't appear to be any embers," he said, turning back to the table. "But what the hell was that?"

I glanced over toward the stove, where one of the men was preparing dinner.

"Watch the flames on your stove. These spirits mean business. That bolt could have done some serious damage, though I doubt it would have killed me."

Tam edged over to the chest. "The bolt came from the lock. Whatever's connected to this chest is sentient." He picked up one of the forks on the table and prodded the side. The tines clinked against the metal. Nothing. He poked it again. Still nothing.

I took a step toward the chest and the energy swirled up, a viscous green mist taking the shape of a serpent. It coiled, staring at me. I backed away again and it dissolved.

"Well, it sure doesn't seem to like me." Musing, I glanced around the galley, looking for the other ghosts. "Where is everybody on the spooktacular level? Where do the ghosts seem to congregate?"

"They tend to hang out in here," one of the men

said. "They vanished a few minutes ago. One was trying to scare Jesse."

"That's me," the cook said. "Damned near made me drop a dozen eggs. Freakin' ghost poked me in the back as I was whisking them up to make scrambles and toast." Jesse turned around, a wary look on his face. "I don't like talking about them. But I can tell you, I'm tired, miss. I'm tired of trying to keep one step ahead of them."

A suspicion tugged at the back of my mind. "Tired? More than usual?"

"A lot more."

"He's right, ma'am." One of the younger deckhands doffed his hat and gave me a congenial nod. "I'm always up and ready for work, but I've had the hardest time getting a move on lately. It's like I've got heavy weights around my ankles. And I'm so tired. I can't seem to get enough sleep. We run short shifts in the bunk as it is, but I'm having a hard time falling asleep. I feel like I'm being drained. And when I do sleep, I have horrible nightmares." The young man blushed. "I don't like admitting it, but I feel like an old man. I could fall asleep right here."

It was one of the first times anybody had ever called me "ma'am," but he seemed very young and very afraid. I wouldn't put him out of his teens, provided he was human. And I was pretty sure he was.

I slid into the booth next to the boy. "What's your name?"

"Reggie."

"Well, Reggie, how old are you?"

"Seventeen, ma'am." He glanced over at Tam, then with a hesitant smile, said, "This is my second season on the *Fanta Verde*."

"He's a good deckhand, too," Captain Varga said. "We took him on after his parents were killed by the Devani in a raid on their place. It was a false alarm, but that didn't stop the freaks from using their bog-dogs to kill." He said all this softly, and Reggie did his best to keep a blank expression. But when he blinked, slowly and only once, it was enough to reveal the pain and heartache still present.

Tam let out a soft sigh. "They're getting worse, too. Ever since the quake hit, they've been out on extra patrols. We'd all do well to mind ourselves and watch our steps."

"That's for certain." I steered the conversation away from Reggie's parents. I looked around at the others. "Are all of you tired like Reggie is?"

They nodded, one by one.

I was about to say something, but a faint mist rising up from the chest caught my attention. Then, with a sudden rush, it lashed out, racing through me. I shivered, chilled to the bone.

"Tam?"

He gave me a slight nod. "I felt it, too."

Closing my eyes, I pulled up my Trace screen. No Aboms, but with a flash, my Sight opened. Hecate was queen of phantoms and spirits, and she had given me the gift of seeing ghosts and spirits.

The next moment I opened my eyes to see the galley filled with misty forms. They were a sickly, mottled color. Vaporous, they weren't quite human, yet not purely nebulous, fog-forms. They hovered around the men, cords running deep into their crown chakras, draining them of energy. The steady pulse running through the etheric veins showed the flow of energy to be a one-way. At this rate, the ghosts would drain the men of their life force before long.

Trying to ignore the ghosts—who didn't appear to know that I could see them—I asked the men, "How many of you have been attacked by the spirits?" Draining energy was bad enough but that the ghosts were attacking the men was even worse.

One of the more grizzled deckhands spoke up. "The name's Ethan, ma'am. Last night, I woke up thinking my cabin was on fire. I saw flames everywhere, but as I cleared my door, I realized that I didn't smell smoke. I managed to shake away the visions, and the fire disappeared. To be honest, I thought I was going crazy."

Ethan looked to be an old geezer, but I'd lay even odds that he could take on a bog-dog and win. Leather-skinned, weathered, and wiry, he'd probably be working on the deck until he keeled over from old age or a heart attack.

"We need to open this chest." I motioned to Tam, who slipped over to my side. In whisper-speak, I said, *I can see the ghosts, and they're draining these men. Chances are when we open that chest, things are going to get dicey. Should we send them off the ship?*

"Perhaps." Tam's voice was so low the men seemed to take no notice. "What do you think will happen to the ghosts when the men leave the room? Will they follow, if they're attached?"

"There's only one way we're going to find out." Bringing my voice back to normal level, I said, "You. Sir? With the coffee mug? Can you do me a favor and step out of the galley for a moment? I want to check on something."

He looked confused but obliged. The moment he left, the ghost followed him, still attached.

Damned life-sucking leeches.

"All right, come back in," I called out.

He returned, giving me a quizzical look, but I kept my mouth shut as I tried to puzzle out the best course of action.

We couldn't risk a sudden surge of attacks when we opened the chest, but I needed to keep the ghosts here. Somehow, I had to separate the men from the ghosts before we proceeded.

I set my bag on the table and opened it. During spring and summer, either the ghosts were more friendly or they got lazy, but as autumn swung toward winter, haunting season would ramp up again. Over the past few years I had noticed that while ghosts were always around us, they tended to come out more during the melancholy weather. Maybe it had something to do with the introspection that came during the darker months, or perhaps there was just less interference in the astral currents. One way or another, my business always picked up come September. I'd have to ask Hecate about it. If anybody knew why, she would.

I spread out a black velvet cloth, embroidered with a pattern of a triskelion of serpents, before I set the crystal skull in the center. Readying the powders and waters, I rested the dagger parallel in front of the skull, with the bell to one side.

Looking around, I called for Queet.

Nothing. Damn it, he was supposed to meet us here. Where the hell was he?

"What's wrong?" Tam asked, again keeping his voice low.

"Queet's not here. Usually, he can hear me when I summon him."

"We'll have to start without him, then."

"Yeah, I know." I could do this without Queet,

but I preferred having him around for backup. I swallowed my grumpiness, trying not to let my mood affect me, and gave Tam a nod. He took up watch, standing next to me as I leaned my elbows on the table and stared at the skull.

The crystal flared to life from the center, right behind the eyes. The sockets began to glow with a faint blue fire. Out of the corner of my eye, I kept watch on the ghosts. The moment I tapped into the skull's power, they straightened and looked my way. Time to get the show on the road before they realized what I was about to do.

I picked up the dagger and began to cast a circle around the room, intoning the Casting Chant in a loud, clear voice.

> *"By Hecate's Might, By Hecate's Will,*
> *With her magic, this room I fill.*
> *By broom and cauldron, chalice and blade,*
> *A circle of protection shall be made.*
> *From the magic of the Crossroads I call,*
> *A darksome force both strong and fell.*
> *Psychofágos, come from the source,*
> *And surround these shades with your force."*

The ghosts immediately left off draining the sailors and rushed toward me as a dark, shadowy figure rose in the center of the circle. The sailors let out a collective gasp. They could all see the Psychofágos as he formed in front of me.

The demon rose up seven feet tall, gleaming black with golden eyes and short bat-like wings. He could fly, but the wings were purely for show. Bowing abruptly, the Psychofágos rumbled, "Command me."

I swallowed hard, corralling in my fear. Hecate

ruled over the realm of the Psychofágos. Demons, they corralled spirits and, when necessary, fed on them. Since I worked with the dead, Hecate had given me the power to summon them when in need, but I used it rarely and judiciously. Demons were extremely touchy and they remembered any slights, intended or not. But the Psychofágos could help me contain the spirits. I could send the men to safety while we figured out how to de-ghostify the boat.

Grateful the demon was the same one who always came when I summoned the Psychofágos, I returned the bow with one of my own, a sign of respect and gratitude. Demons weren't much for small talk, which was actually a blessing. Somehow a conversation about the weather didn't seem like proper chitchat for the demon-brigade.

"Please contain the spirits and prevent them from attacking the men. Prevent them from leaving the ship until we banish them. I need to examine this chest and figure out how to exorcise them." I wasn't sure how much power the Psychofágos wielded, but with luck, it would be enough to keep the spirits in check.

"As you will." He turned and with a loud rumble, drew the spirits to him as though he were a magnet. They struggled, anger oozing off them like mist off dry ice, but they couldn't break free. Their wrath was so palpable it made my skin itch. Yeah, they would hold a grudge, all right.

When I was satisfied they were firmly bound by the demon's stasis field, I turned to see the lid of the chest fly open on its own. Oh hell, I had wanted to get the men off the boat first, but apparently whatever was in the chest had other ideas.

Breathing deeply, I slowly edged forward

to peek inside. There, in the center, affixed to the bottom, was a bottle. In that bottle were the skeletal bones of a hand, clutching a talisman. Even through the glass, I could recognize the symbols etched on the disk. They were the runes of Ares, and around the hand scuttled several eternity beetles.

"Don't open that bottle, or we're all dead." I stared at the spell, understanding now. The ghosts had been part of the crew of the sunken ship, and they were forever bound to wage a war long over.

Chapter 4

"What the hell is that? How are those beetles still alive?" Captain Varga's gaze fluttered from the beetles to the talisman. "*Ares...*" he breathed, his eyes wide.

"Yes, Ares. And the beetles are eternity beetles. When placed under the right magical geas, they will live for thousands of years without food or water."

Tam shifted, looking uncomfortable. "Fury, the bottle is a war talisman. It binds the ghosts to the chest. Whatever the case, I can tell you right now that these spirits are no longer sane. They've been under a curse so long that it's all they know. Their forms are mere shells, conduits for the energy of the curse."

The bottle was flickering. I stared at it for a moment, then turned to the Psychofágos. "Are there any more spirits on board, or are these it?"

He shook his head. "There are five ghosts aboard. These five. I sense there were more connected to the chest but they never made it to the surface."

"Can you eat them?" I hoped for a "yes" but didn't expect one. Somehow, that would make everything too simple and with our luck lately, the Fates obviously weren't handing out *simple* as an option.

"No, I can neither break the curse nor devour the spirits. You must destroy the talisman, and you'd better hurry. They're strong and I can't hold all of them for much longer. Fury, *they spread their infection*. Destroy them now, and the men aboard this ship won't progress further. Wait much longer and as the spirits drain the life force from the men, the men will fade and become a part of the band that connects these unfortunate souls."

A plague bottle. I had heard of such spells, but I had never come across them. They were considered extremely wicked magic, and usually showed up during times of war and rebellion.

I snapped my fingers. "A magical plague that infects the soul, of course. It makes sense."

"What do we do?" Captain Varga asked. "I need to protect my men."

I glanced over at the Psychofágos. "If the men leave the ship now, will the ghosts follow them?"

"No, I've broken their hold on the men for the moment, but I won't be able to hold them much longer."

Turning back to Varga, I said, "Get your men off the ship, *now*. The spirits aren't fully attached to them at this point. You and your men go and let us attend to this."

The captain smiled softly at me. "I cannot leave my ship, girl. But my men can."

"Why not? I'm not planning on sinking your

ship, so you don't have to worry about being here to go down with it." I didn't want to argue, but I'd drive him off the ship myself if I had to.

The captain motioned to his men. "Go. Leave everything as it is for now. Don't forget to take Trey. He's still in his bunk." When they hesitated, he barked out, "Go on, damn it. I don't want to see you back aboard until we call for you. *That's an order*. In fact, I suggest you boys take the night off. Have a drink. Go to a movie. Do something fun. Spend the night in a hotel and charge it to the boat."

The men shifted, looking decidedly uncomfortable, then trudged out of the galley. The ghosts strained against the Psychofágos, trying to follow them, but the demon held them fast, though he was grimacing.

As the men filed out, Reggie glanced over his shoulder.

"Be careful, okay?" Even though the question was aimed at his captain, he was looked straight at me.

I nodded at him, and he vanished around the corner. After a moment, Tam dashed up the stairs, then returned a moment later. "They're off the boat, though they look confused."

I turned back to Varga. "What didn't you want to say in front of them?"

"As I told you before, they don't know I'm a Theosian. But there's more to it than that. I *can't* go ashore. Or rather, I can, but I'm bound to the sea. If I step off that plank onto land, I'll turn into one of Poseidon's stallions. The men don't know that either. They think I'm just a little queer in the head. They're a good group and they know better than to pry. That's one thing about the sea and fishermen. We keep to our business unless it might affect the boat."

I had no clue what to say. On one level, I wanted to see the captain transform, because Poseidon's horses were incredibly beautiful and it just seemed like such a cool thing. But that wasn't the most diplomatic thing to say and it wasn't my place to out him to his men.

"If you stay, you run the risk of being attacked when we take the spirits on."

"I know, and I'm willing to take that risk. Tell me what you need me to do and I'll do it. I can't leave port with the ghosts still aboard."

Tam cleared his throat. "My magic generally doesn't affect the dead, but I do know that talismans of this sort are best destroyed with fire. The spell was bound to the sea. Fire will be its natural enemy."

I leaned closer, attempting to get a good look at the talisman. The skeletal hand suddenly jerked, one bony finger pointing toward me. The beetles scurried around it, and I could hear the scuttling sound as their feet met the glass.

I jumped back. "Cripes. The hand's still alive."

Tam let out a long breath. "I think I can wager a guess who those bones belonged to."

I darted a sideways glance at the ghosts. They were still struggling against the Psychofágos. "The more info we have the better, but hurry. The spirits are getting agitated."

"During the Weather Wars, the magicians were beholden to the kings. I know, I lived through that time, although my kind removed themselves from the world at large. The magicians were bound to the will of whoever was in charge. My bet is that the hand belonged to one of them."

"One of the *magicians*? That seems wasteful." Killing a magician to bind one spell seemed like overkill to me.

"Yes. For the talisman to survive all this time, it would need a powerful source of energy. And I seem to recall that the magicians who helped bring about the Weather Wars often found themselves on the sacrificial end. First, the king would command a powerful spell to be cast, usually by his right-hand magus, the elite among magicians. Then, to feed the spell, another magician— someone considered expendable—would find his life forfeit. His life force would be drained into the talisman, and his bones kept with it as an anchor. This would power the spell for hundreds of years, or longer."

The Weather Wars had been a gruesome, tumultuous time. That my boyfriend had actually lived through it still boggled my mind, but I tried not to think about that.

"Then the hand still contains some of the magician's essence," Captain Varga said. "What will happen if we break the bottle?"

I contemplated the glass. "My guess is that if we break the bottle, the energy will pour out all at once and we'd all be targets. If the Psychofágos says it's a plague bottle, then you *know* it's a plague bottle. The demons may not have our best interests at heart, but the contract with them guarantees they won't lie to those who work with them. No, he's right. The men on the original ship were infected. Whatever sort of energy is bound into that talisman, it caused the sailors to die and then turned their spirits into a raging band of warriors who cannot rest."

"How did it end up on the bottom of the sea?

Plague weapons were aimed to spread infection as far as possible. Why would the attackers sink the ship after they infected the crew?" Captain Varga suddenly snapped his fingers. "My best guess is that the crew fired their guns into the side of the hull themselves."

Tam rubbed his chin. "I'd say you're spot-on about that. They must have recognized what was going on. Before the spell could drain all of the men, the ones still in their right minds sank the ship to keep from spreading the plague. Ten to one, they're also the ones who locked the bottle in the chest and took it to the bottom of the ocean with them. Something, a rogue wave or a giant fish, must have disturbed the chest, allowing it to float to the surface. When you found it, a few of the spirits who had been infected were still attached to it."

The captain reached out to touch the sides of the chest. "Those men sacrificed themselves to save others. I only hope most drowned before the plague infected them. Better to journey into the afterlife than stay chained to a sunken ship at the bottom of the ocean."

I tipped my head to one side, contemplating our options. "We can't get rid of the ghosts without destroying the plague bottle, so we'd better focus on—"

"Do something now," the Psychofágos interrupted. "I can't hold them much longer."

The ghosts were straining harder against his hold, and it was apparent that the demon was having trouble keeping hold of them. One spirit almost slipped away but the demon tightened his grip on the etheric cords and the spirit lashed around, his eye sockets burning. He gnashed at the

Psychofágos but the demon was able to ward off the blow.

"We could just dump the bottle back in the ocean," Tam said.

"We can't do that. Especially not while we're in port. Somebody would surely find it and then the plague would run rampant through all the boats on the dock. Damn it, I know how to deal with most spirits and Abominations, but this, I'm not so sure." I stopped, thinking maybe we could shove the bottle through one of the portals on the World Tree, but that wasn't an answer, either.

"*Fire*. I keep thinking fire. The spell is bound to sailors and the sea. So it's water based. Fire has to be able to break it. It's the only thing I've got that has a hope in hell of working. *Rest Ye Well* powder won't work until they're freed from the curse. So I'm thinking, zap the hell out of that bottle with my magical fire and it might disrupt the spell."

There wasn't much else we could try. We didn't have time to go hunting down a historian who might be able to give us the lowdown on plague bottles created during the Weather Wars.

"All right, I say go for it." Captain Varga looked gung ho, though his voice quavered a little. But he set his jaw and gave me a steely nod.

"All right," Tam said. "I'm in. What do you want us to do, Fury?"

I motioned overhead. "Carry the chest up top to the deck. If things get out of hand, we dump it over the side." Turning to the demon, I asked, "Are you ready? You'll need to come topside with us."

"I'm there."

At that moment, a familiar presence breezed in and I found myself feeling both relieved and pissed off. "Queet! Where the hell were you?"

I was detained. He didn't sound happy. *But I'm here now. What are you up to? Oh, for Hecate's sake, what the hell are you doing with that?* He started to point toward the chest, then noticed the demon. *And you had to call up a Psychofágos? What's going on?*

Both the captain and Tam glanced over in his direction but said nothing. Very few could see Queet unless he wanted them to, but Tam was one of the Bonny Fae and Captain Varga a Theosian, which made a world of difference in how they viewed the spirit world.

"Long story short: We have a plague bottle on our hands from the Weather Wars. I need to destroy it. I was thinking fire."

Queet nodded. This time he spoke loud enough for Tam and Varga to hear. "Those spirits are bound to that bottle, but you can't just break the bottle. You'll need to melt it and ash the bones inside. Which means using an exceptionally hot fire. I know you can do it. You caused a blast that hot when you propelled yourself out of the Carver's lair."

If Queet noticed me cringe at the name of my mother's killer, he didn't let on. Instead, he continued. "The question is, can you consciously cause a fire to blaze that hot? You have to be sure. It must consume the bottle, the beetles, and the bones."

"The three Bs, huh?" Even I didn't laugh at my attempted joke. I let out a long, slow breath. Could I create a fire hot enough to incinerate everything in the chest? In the past, I'd proved I had the ability, but I had never consciously attempted to create a blaze that hot. It had always been a subconscious force.

The thought terrified me. To be able to work with flame was an incredible gift, but I realized that I was afraid. What if, once I unleashed my full ability, I wouldn't be able to master control over it? The old saw about not being able to put the genie back in the bottle rang true in my heart. Mustering up my courage, I let out a long, slow breath to steady myself.

"I have to do this. We can't take a chance on hauling this thing over to the Peninsula of the Gods. There are too many ways for it to go wrong." But a soft voice, deep in my heart, whispered, *You've got this.*

"Take it topside. I can do this." I followed Captain Varga and Tam, who took a handle each and cautiously carted the chest to the deck. Grateful it was dark, I asked them to wrangle one of the crab pots onto the lift, so we could set the chest on it and tip it over the side if necessary. Captain Varga motioned for us to get out of the way and then manned the crane, quickly and deftly bringing one of the giant cages onto the lift. The automatic locks set it into place and he jumped down, a remote control in his hand.

"I can use this to ping it to flip the pot if necessary," the captain said. He and Tam lifted the chest onto the pot and steadied it.

Glancing around, I pointed to the various ropes and rags strewn around the deck.

"Get everything that might catch fire out of the way. I promise, I'll try to avoid burning down your boat, but I'm afraid I can't guarantee it." I flashed the captain a wry smile.

He returned it with a forced laugh. "Well, if you can't solve this and get the ghosts off my deck, we might as well burn it down. That would create a

53

fire hot enough, I think."

"Yes, well, we'll save that for a last-ditch solution."

I asked Tam to stand behind me, far enough to keep him from being a target, yet close enough so he could jump in to help. Given he worked with water magic, if the fire broke too high, he might be able to bring the waves up and over the railing to swamp it.

Captain Varga crossed the deck without question when I asked him to relocate himself. He was good at following orders, unlike some men, though I was pretty sure it was all relative. He ruled the boat, but right now, the ghosts had usurped his rule and therefore, he stepped down to let me take care of it. That was a mark of wisdom, Hecate once said: Knowing when to call in an expert. Nobody was good at everything and you had to surrender the helm at times in order to regain your authority.

Queet moved over by Captain Varga. What I was about to do wouldn't harm him, but he was leery of the bottle. "I don't know what effect that spell would have on me since I'm already a spirit, but I don't really want to find out."

The Psychofágos took up a spot near the bottle. Whatever happened with it wouldn't affect him. "I believe you will want these spirits near enough to the talisman so it can drag them back to it, regardless of what happens." He was struggling to keep them under control. They strained at the etheric harnesses with which he had leashed them. "Fast, Fury. Move fast."

I nodded. We were out of time. I had to do something. I sought deep inside, searching for the spark that burned constantly in my soul. A fire that never felt quenched, it drove me on.

And then, with a bolt of clarity, I knew what to do. I slapped my hand to my leg, against the hilt of the tattoo, and the whip came to life, forming an ethereal weapon in my palm. Gripping the handle, the smooth knot of energy provided a firm hold. I raised the whip overhead and circled it, listening to the crackle as the thong of fire whipped rhythmically around my head.

Center...find the connection, feel the anger in the whip, the fury that rages as it churns through the air over my head... Find the fire that gives the thong form, find that primal force that creates the white-hot lightning.

Something sang out inside—a clear note formed by the white-hot fork of lightning that sparked to life. A mass of flames flared to attention as I brought the whip up, reveling in the sheer destructive power that flowed through my veins. I was the enforcer. The punisher. I was the lightning and fire that raced through the whip. I was the strength of Hecate, bound in ink and flame and ash. *I was Fury.*

And then, as the power peaked, I brought my whip to bear, triumphantly lashing the tip toward the chest. I envisioned the glass melting, burning everything inside it and attached to it to a fine wisp of ash. My whip connected with the bottle and the next moment, a blinding flare lit up the boat, so brilliant that I had to close my eyes. The boat rocked as thunder cracked all around us, rolling over us like a wave.

Captain Varga dropped to his knees, holding his head. Tam reeled, but he managed to stay standing. The Psychofágos didn't appear fazed at all, but the ghosts he was holding broke free and went spinning around the boat like crazed dogs, shifting and turning into long, gaunt figures that bore no resemblance to the humans they had once been.

Still luminous and lit by the fire of the divine, I rose up, feeling fierce and wild and absolutely feral. One of the ghosts careened toward me but I lithely jumped to the side, using my blur-speed. Queet whipped past, standing in front of me with arms raised. The frenzied ghost changed direction, skidding as he took new aim and once again barreled toward us.

I screamed for Queet to get out of the way, but he stood fast. As the ghost reached him, Queet blazed, flaring up with a radiant plum-colored light. The ghost put on the brakes, then began to backtrack.

The next moment, all of the ghosts set to howling like wounded wolves, and I turned. The bottle had melted. The bones were disintegrating. The beetles were a pile of dust. As the last of the bones vanished, dropping the now-unrecognizable lump of metal that had been the talisman to the ground, the ghosts faded. They slowly dissipated and, one by one, vanished into oblivion.

I lowered my whip, spent and dripping. I was clammy with sweat, relieved and yet terrified. I had never expended that much energy before, save for once. And *that* memory had forever remained blank. But now, the radiant scar of electricity buzzed through me and I was high on the power.

Always before, my whip had been the conduit. But this time, my body had channeled the energy, bringing it into the whip. The lightning had driven through me, leaving me numb and yet blazing. I had called down the lightning, and the lightning had answered. I grinned, crazy in love with the bone-charring jolt that had filled every vein full with liquid gold.

Panting, still revved from the jolt, I stared at the chest, which was glowing from the heat of the blast. Everything was gone. The ghosts, the curse, the skeleton's hand. The Psychofágos vanished without another word. Like I said, he wasn't into small talk.

The chest itself was distorted, barely recognizable. Any energy that had been attached to it was gone, cleansed by the divine fire. I looked over at Tam, who was making sure the captain was okay. Captain Varga might be a Theosian, but that flash could have knocked anybody onto their knees. A moment later, he shakily stood, using Tam's shoulder as a brace.

I was still shaking. My entire body felt like it was vibrating. "Are you both all right?"

They nodded. Tam caught my gaze and moved closer, reaching out to barely touch my arm. He began to ground me, bringing me back to my body.

Captain Varga let out a shaky breath. "Are they gone?"

"They are. And they won't be back." I toed the misshapen chest. "Get rid of the chest tonight. Call Hecate and she'll send someone over to collect it and to bless your boat. I don't have the energy to do that tonight. Meanwhile, I think you're good to go. You can head back out to open water tomorrow, but in the future, I'd refrain from hauling anything like this aboard. There were lots of weapons lost during the Weather Wars. Some of them are very dangerous."

I was thinking of the Thunderstrike, an artifact we had recently managed to corral when the Order of the Black Mist decided to try to use it.

"How can I thank you?" Captain Varga leaned against one of the railings, a look of relief washing across his face as the tension in his shoulders eased and he let out a long breath.

It warmed my heart to help him. The man had a shine to him that made me want to cuddle up and watch movies with him, or just snooze away on a lazy day. Perhaps it was because he was a Theosian, but I had the feeling it was deeper than that. My gut told me here was a man we could trust and turn to.

"Pay my fee, and don't get yourself in trouble again. And touch base when you're in port. While you might not be able to walk ashore, we can come out to you. Or if you want to spend some time in a field, running, we can probably work out transportation for you."

A soft light in his eyes told me that was the right thing to say. "It's been a long time since I've had the pleasure of racing through a meadow, with the wind in my face. I might just take you up on that. Meanwhile, let me get you a cash card." He slipped below deck.

I nodded to the chest. "What do you think, guys? Should we leave that with him?"

"It's devoid of energy," Queet said. "There won't be a problem as long as he puts in the call to Hecate."

Tam slid his arm around my waist, cautiously avoiding Xan's scabbard. "Love, we need to go home as soon as you get paid and rest. You need food."

Nodding, I leaned my head against his shoulder, relishing the scent of cinnamon and apples and freshly mown grass. I was suddenly

aware of my body, and everything ached from head
to toe. I was also starving, and I wanted nothing
more than to drop into bed with some sugary treat,
then fall asleep when my belly was full.

Captain Varga returned, handing me a cash
card worth five hundred. It was two hundred more
than the agreed-on price. I started to argue but he
wouldn't hear any protests. After bidding him good
night, we took off, heading toward the Monotrain.

I could hardly wait to get back to Jason's
and get some food. I was drop-dead tired and
whispered a quick prayer that the Aboms would
keep themselves at bay until morning. Queet was
silent, but I could feel him near.

Less than half a mile from the Monotrain,
we stumbled into a crowd of late-night revelers.
Rowdy and drunk, they were protesting something
though I couldn't read the reader-signs from
where we were.

Fury, you need to get out of here. Queet
whispered loud enough so both of us could hear.
*Something's going down and you don't want to be
here. I don't know what, but the energy is poised
to become very ugly, very quickly.*

Tam and I began to skirt around the mob
when a noise made everyone in the crowd freeze.
Collectively, we turned. A low hum filled the air,
and the marching of feet.

Crap. I knew what that hum meant. *Every*
person in Seattle did. It meant *Turn around
slowly, hands in the air, or risk becoming
somebody's target.*

Sure enough, the Devani surged out from
between two buildings. Their golden skin gleamed
from behind armor equally as blinding, and their
brilliant turquoise eyes fastened onto the crowd.

Weapons raised, they began to move forward.

Chapter 5

"Oh hell," I whispered. "My chip. They'll find out about my chip."

"Hang on. We'll get you out. Just play it calm." Tam gently reached out to place his hand on mine. I wound my fingers through his, but then let go and readied myself to run if we needed to.

"Queet, tell Hecate what's happening." I wasn't sure what she could or would do, but I'd feel much better if she knew.

Without a word, Queet vanished. Once again, I was grateful for my grumpy spirit guide. He may not have signed up for the job, but he had my back.

The Devani marched closer. They were trigger happy, and the golden boys trained their weapons on us. The Devani were natural enemies of the Aboms, but really, when you got down to it, the soldiers from Elysium were just as terrifying as the creatures from Pandoriam. And the Devani had the backing of the government.

The golden boys had come in off the Seattle World Tree only a couple hundred years ago. Before that, the Conglomerate relied on humans and Otherkin for their police and military forces, but in the Devani, they found their perfect conscripts.

They came from the realm of Elysium, the golden-skinned warriors with turquoise blue eyes. Straight shouldered, they were clone-like. It was difficult to tell them apart, save for whether they were male or female. Even among themselves, they communicated by what linguists decoded were series of numbers and sounds. The Devani showed no emotion. There were no recorded instances of a Devani crying, or offering help in anything but a military fashion. In fact, they were so ruthless and focused that at first humans thought they were robots or AI. But all it took was one skirmish where blood was drawn for that theory to be dismantled.

When that first brutal battle ended, with humans barely managing a win, the Devani had lay down their weapons and acknowledged their loss by pledging to serve the victors. Which apparently meant anyone who lived on this side of the World Tree who had authority.

Their actions rocked the world. Their loss had been a fluke, only through some backhanded strategies pulled by our forces. Everything was recorded in the history books. Humans played dirty, and they played to win. The Devani marched to a rigid code. The two systems were vastly different and the Conglomerate had used those differences to wrangle control. Now the Americex Corporatocracy was the most feared nation in the world. Apparently the Devani had only shown up in our corporatocracy. Sadly, the people of our nation feared the police as much as the rest of the world did.

So, the Devani's authority grew as the Conglomerate relied on them more and more. And the Devani's ethical code was slowly bending to match that of the government's. Which meant that the Devani were learning how to buy power.

I kept my eyes on the approaching soldiers, raising my hands. Their stunners were supposed to be set on incapacitate, but that rule was often "accidentally" overlooked.

The woman next to me was weeping. I glanced over at her. She was human, and a young boy stood next to her, eyes wide. He couldn't have been more than ten or eleven years old.

"What's happening?" I lowered my voice but did not move, my hands firmly in the air.

Her hands were upraised too, as were her son's. "We were staging a peaceful protest against the Restructuring Law that's being enacted."

I had heard of the Restructuring Law. It was brutal. If a citizen fell into arrears on their mortgage, or if they couldn't pay their taxes, their rights would be terminated until they managed to pay off their debt. They weren't forced out of their home, but anybody who belonged to their immediate family was subject to involuntary government service at slave wages and the money would then be applied toward the back debt.

The only exceptions were children still in Under School, those who were infirm or disabled to the point of not being able to work, and those who were already employed.

"I already pay most of my wages to them. We barely have enough to eat or to pay our rent. If they pass the law, the interest alone will swamp us. My children will inherit a crushing load of debt. And my son won't be able to continue studying beyond Under School. His life will be mired down because my husband died and left us in a hole so deep that I don't know how to get out of it." Tears streamed down her face. "I just wanted to protest how unfair it is. That's all."

I glanced over at the Devani. They were poised, weapons at the ready. Mist rising from the sewer grates began to cloak the area as the clouds socked in. The atmosphere was so thick I could barely breathe, and I could feel the fear that was beginning to build. Fear had a way of taking on a life of its own.

I leaned toward Tam, cautious to keep my hands where the Devani could see them. I had faced a lot of Abominations in my time, but this was more frightening than any of them.

Usually, the Devani order the crowd to disperse. Tam's whisper-speak was at the lowest range, but I managed to catch it. *I wonder why they haven't done so yet.*

Maybe... A horrible thought crossed my mind. Were they now refusing to give the crowd a chance to surrender? Protest wasn't against the law, but the laws could change daily.

I didn't have a chance to finish my thought because one young man, probably no older than fifteen, threw a bottle at one of the Devani closest to him, and the storm broke. The Devani waded into the crowd, their stunners buzzing. Their victims writhed on the ground, screaming from the painful jolts of electricity running through their bodies. Stunners could kill, but apparently this time, they were set to disable rather than destroy.

Tam pushed me to the side as one of the soldiers headed our way. "Run, Fury. You can run at blur-speed. Get out of here while I distract him."

"Not without you—"

"Your chip, Fury. I don't have any. I'm not required to have them. I'm safer than you are." He gave me another push, his gaze holding mine for a moment. "Go, love. I'll be there shortly."

My heart was telling me to stay, but my head was wrapping around the realization that he was right. I raced away at blur-speed and then, as I hit the intersection in the middle of the street, I raised my arms and clasped my hands over my head, transporting to the Crossroads. The last thing I saw before I vanished was the soldier taking Tam down with the stunner.

The mist rose around me as I landed in the world between worlds. The Crossroads bordered a number of realms and dimensions, and the deities associated with the Crossroads were legion. Although I had seen several of the others out here—including Papa Legba—my business here was always with Hecate.

I always arrived at the same place when I shifted over. I would end up in a barren juncture where three roads intersected, in a barren field that stretched beyond the horizon, dotted only with a few scattered trees and boulders, and a bench here and there along the road. I always landed in the center of the intersection, next to a low cauldron that rested in front of a signboard. I had read the sign so many times that it was burned into my memory.

> *STAND AT THE CROSSROADS*
> *STATE YOUR CLAIM*
> *TO SEAL THE DEAL,*
> *STRIKE THE FLAME*

I dropped to my knees, resting my hands on the ground as I reached out, trying to summon Queet. "Queet, are you near? Can you hear me? I'm on the Crossroads."

Nothing.

Exhausted from the evening and worried about Tam, I dragged myself to my feet and wandered over to a nearby bench, slumping down on it. I couldn't go back to Portside right now. If I appeared in the middle of the skirmish, they'd catch me. I'd have to head for Jason's house instead.

Fury? I'm here. His whisper-speak faint, Queet appeared by my side. He looked translucent, which wasn't a good sign. His energy field looked wavy, like bad reception on the viseo.

Are you all right? Something was wrong with him. *You don't look so good, Queet. You look faded.*

No, actually. Hecate will tell you. I'll be all right, though. I just need a little rest. But I told her what was happening. She told me to tell you to go to Jason's place. Text her once you're there. She gave me this for you.

He handed me a talisman. It looked at ethereal as he did, but when I held out my hand, he dropped it into my palm and it landed, solid as I was.

"A Transfer charm. Oh, thank the gods. I need this." The talisman would allow me to step off the Crossroads to a destination other than the one I had entered from. And that would save my butt. I was about to thank him, when Queet vanished.

Now even more worried—both my lover and my spirit guide were in trouble—I hurried toward the exit. I always saw it in my mind as a flickering arrow of green energy, like an EXIT sign in a shopping mall. Holding the talisman tightly, I visualized the intersection in front of Dream Wardens and then shifted. As the mist and fog of the Crossroads swirled around me, I felt myself sliding through the layers that divided realities. Then, in one long blink, I was standing in the middle of the street in front of Jason's shop. The Market Square clock was chiming nine p.m.

I raced up the stairs tucked away between Dream Wardens and Up-Cakes and, not bothering to knock, barged into Jason's apartment over the shop. Hans and Greta were in the living room, and Hans leapt to his feet, reaching for his dagger, but stopped when he saw it was me.

"Fury, what's wrong?" The burly Viking's words drifted off as he homed in on my face. "What happened?"

Greta had also jumped up. Six feet tall, her long golden hair was bound into two thick braids. She was amazingly built, so statuesque and muscular that one look would be enough to scare any perv looking to bother her. But her eyes glittered, a startling blue, and her expression was far more gentle than one would expect from a Valkyrie in training.

"Jason? Jason, get in here!" I gave the pair a nod as I stripped off my scabbard and leaned Xan against the wall.

Jason entered the living room, a pan of noodles in hand. "Fury? Are you that hungry?" He stopped when he saw my face. "What's going on? One moment." He darted back in the kitchen and returned without the food.

"Has Tam checked in with you in the past twenty minutes?"

They all shook their heads.

"No, should he have? What happened? The ghosts get the better of you?" But the flippant tone on Jason's tongue died as I shot him a withering glare.

"Damn it. Damn it to hell." I slowly eased myself down into one of the recliners and pulled out my phone, checking to see if Tam had managed to text me. Nothing. I quickly sent Hecate a text before continuing. Then, the adrenaline suddenly leaving my body, I collapsed against the chair, looking at the others mutely.

"Fury, what's going on?" Jason knelt beside me. "What happened out there? Seriously, did one of the ghosts hurt Tam?"

"No." Not wanting to verbalize it, I let out a shuddering breath. Putting something into words always seemed to make it real, but I had to tell them. "I think they caught him. I think they arrested him."

White as rice, Jason abruptly sat down on the

footstool next to me. "Oh, crap."

"How do we find out? *I* can't go to the precincts and ask. I'm afraid to call him because what if they *do* have him in custody and use that to find me? Or what if he escaped and I call, and he's hiding and they find him because they hear the phone? He never keeps it on vibrate." I realized that I was starting to melt down. Now that I was actually with friends, it was safe for me to fall apart.

Jason wrapped an arm around my shoulder. He looked over at Hans. "What do you think? You have contacts in the precincts. Can you find out what's going on?"

"I'm on it." Hans stood, his face a blank canvas. But his voice was roughshod, holding every fear I was feeling. "I'll be back. I have to watch how I step with this one, because though I trust Gregor as far as I can, the fact is you never really know the truth about anybody unless you've linked blood with them. And even then, people can turncoat you. But if the Paggymen have Tam, I'll do my best to find out." Hans had no love for the authorities and delighted in using the street slang for them. He turned to Greta. "Stay here, my Strudel. I'll be back for you as soon as I can. Do what you can to help."

"Of course," she said, kissing him lightly. "Go and Thor be at your back, Dumpling." She reached up and stroked his bald head lightly. "Remember, you owe me a wedding."

And with that, Hans was off, out the door, just as Shevron, Jason's sister, entered, carrying two large pink boxes that she slid on the table. Pastries for dessert, no doubt, from Up-Cakes, her bakery next door.

"What's the hurry?" She looked at Jason, then

at me and then Greta. "What's going on? You all look like you're headed to a funeral."

I filled her in on what had gone down and she muttered a sharp curse. "Those damned Devani will be the death of us yet. One day, the Conglomerate is going to look around and realize they've handed over the reins to that lot, and guess who's going to be in charge of us then? They should just ship them all home to Elysium and bar that portal. The Devani are dangerous. Mark my words."

Greta wandered over to the box and opened it, removing the apple pies that Shevron had brought. The scent of cinnamon and apple filled the room. "Jason, finish plating up dinner. We can't do anything right now but wait, and Fury needs food. Look at her. She's pale as a sheet. Not only was she out on the Crossroads, but she dealt with a bunch of wayward ghosts." She paused, turning to me. "I can feel the residue around you, and you need to cleanse yourself. The residue gunk oozing in from the astral is wearing you out."

"As much as I hate sitting here while Tam might be in danger, I think you're right. There's nothing we can do without more information. We'd probably just make things worse." Jason headed back into the kitchen.

Shevron set the table. I wanted to help but I was exhausted and afraid, and the combination made me want to curl up in a ball and close my eyes until Tam was home safe and sound. I drew my feet up beneath me on the sofa and stared at my phone, willing Tam to call, but by the time dinner was on the table, we still hadn't heard anything.

Hans returned just as we were dishing up the

spaghetti and garlic bread. As he let himself into the apartment, I started to rise, but he shook his head.

"Sorry, Fury. I don't have any news. My contact wasn't able to find out what happened. He doesn't have clearance. Apparently, the event isn't listed on the general blotter as anything but 'an incident' and there's no file linked to it, which means it's all hush-hush. None of the Paggymen who were at the riot with the Devani are talking. And of course, there's no way in hell the Devani who were there will say anything to anybody."

I sat down again, returning to my food as Hans joined us at the table. I forced myself to eat. Even though I had no appetite I knew that Greta was right and it wouldn't do Tam or me any good if I didn't keep up my strength

Shevron pushed back her plate. "I don't mean to change the subject, but I have a problem. Jason, I'd like you to talk to Len." Len was Shevron's fifteen-year-old son. He was half hawk-shifter, although the shifter side had bred true for the most part but in his case, his human side was very evident. He was generally a really good kid.

"What's going on?" Jason frowned. "And why me?"

"He loves you, and he looks up to you as a role model."

"What's he gotten himself into?" Jason was all about family. The Cast stuck together, and the families making up the Cast stuck together. Hawk-shifters were a tight-knit group. A lot of the shifter clans were.

Shevron grunted. "Have you heard of a vampire named Kython?"

Jason shook his head. "No," he said, looking at

the rest of us. But neither Greta, Hans, nor I had heard of him either.

"Kython's popular up in the NW Quarters. He lives on the edge of the Tremble and is head of a cult called the Kythonic Dreamers. And Len is far too interested in them. I'm afraid he may be getting ready to run away and join them. The damned vamp appeals to youth, especially those who feel alienated. And like it or not, Len feels outside the Cast since his father wasn't a hawk-shifter. I try to remind him he's a full member, but a few of the old biddies are very vocal about blood lines and they talk where he can overhear."

"Crap. He's getting interested in vampires? That's a deadly road to walk. I'll have a chat with him and see if I can detour him from any stupid ideas. You might want to put him into Celsa's boot camp."

I frowned. I had been around hawk-shifters over half my life now and had never heard of Celsa. Apparently, neither Greta nor Hans knew who they were talking about, either, because they looked just as puzzled.

Shevron leaned forward, her eyes glittering as she scowled at Jason. "You really think I'd subject my son to Celsa's vision of how a good little hawk-shifter should act?"

"You have to admit, his program works." If I didn't know Jason, I would have thought he was angry with her, his voice was so sharp. But hawk-shifters could be ruthlessly logical and yet not mean to upset their friends. It was just their nature.

"His program works because he scares the hell out of those kids. I won't do it." Shevron suddenly deflated, slumping back in her chair. "Not unless it's the last option I have. Leonard is very sensitive. It's his father's blood. I don't like to admit it, but truth is, he isn't fully Cast. He can't ever hope to be, not with his inability to control his emotions. I don't want to see him hurt. I don't want to see him broken, Jason."

Jason relented. "Yeah, I know, sis. I'll see what I can do. Maybe he'll still listen to me. I'll have a talk with him tomorrow, okay?"

Shevron nodded, and we finished our meal in silence.

Chapter 6

Shevron dropped me off at home. She had driven over to Jason's in order to avoid dealing with the Monotrain. We didn't even bother with a pretense of talking. Neither one of us was in the mood to discuss the two main problems we were facing. I was more than grateful that hawk-shifters weren't gabby by nature. Shevron had taken over as my surrogate mother when I landed on Jason's doorstep, and she had always been there for me but now she was facing her own concerns. I wasn't about to put even more weight on her shoulders by using her as a dumping ground for my own fears.

Shevron dropped me off, waiting to make sure I got in the building. As I headed through the secure door, I waved and she pulled away from the curb.

Security building though it might be, the Kings Cross Apartment Building didn't have an elevator, necessitating a four-floor climb. But the building sat on the edge of Idyll Inlet, and though my apartment was a small suite—one

bedroom, narrow living room, bath, and a tiny
kitchenette—the view made it worth the rent and
the inconvenience.

As I let myself in, then coded the locks that
barred my front door, I held my breath, praying
that Tam would be there. Or Queet. Or both. But
I was disappointed on all counts. The apartment
was empty, and the tiny slice of the world I called
my safe haven suddenly felt cavernous and lonely.

I shoved the leftover pie in the refrigerator
and checked my messages again. Nothing except a
note saying my rent was a week overdue. Wearily,
I went to the front panel next to the door where
the locks were located and slid the cash card
that Captain Varga had given me into the pay-
slot, tapped in the amount to deduct, and within
seconds, rent was taken care of and the landlord
off my back until the next month.

Tired, but feeling at loose ends, I opened the
curtains and turned off the lights. The view looking
out over the inlet always calmed me. My element
was fire, so water helped me relax, tempering the
constant feeling of heat that ran through my body.
It was like I was a live wire, and water temporarily
disrupted the circuits so I could rest.

Finally, out of options, I sat on the ottoman,
facing the window. I debated calling Tam, but
reluctantly decided against it. Even though he had
encrypted my phone, the Devani weren't stupid
and they could probably trace it back to me. So I
did the next best thing. I called Hecate.

She didn't answer, so I texted her again,
begging her to get in touch with me as soon as
she could. Another five minutes, and I knew that
watching the water wasn't going to do it tonight. I
wouldn't get any sleep without help.

I trudged into the bathroom, popped three tabs of Sleep-Eze for six hours of uninterrupted sleep. Feeling like a traitor for not sitting up waiting for word of Tam, I crawled into bed and hugged his pillow tightly to my chest. His scent was on it, and as I drifted off to sleep, it almost felt like he was embracing me.

The alarm went off at six. Squinting, I floundered for it, then gave up and used the vox control to turn it off.

"All right, shut up! Alarm, off." As I pushed myself up to a sitting position, I yawned and grabbed my phone to see if Tam had called during the night. *Nothing*. But there was a text from Hecate, telling me to get my ass down to the temple as soon as I woke up.

"About time," I muttered, tossing my phone on the bed.

A quick rinse-off later, I dressed in leather shorts, a warm turtleneck, and my duster. A glance out the window showed a dusting of snow, and the slow drift of lazy flakes gliding down. Snow meant my sturdy ankle boots with skid-proof soles. Then, fastening Xan's scabbard over my back, I shifted until the sword was comfortable, then strapped my dagger and sheath around my left thigh. Locking the door, I headed out into a world turned white overnight.

"Coffee. Hot and strong." I blew on my fingers as I stopped by the coffee stand opposite my building. "Damn it, I forgot my gloves."

Coffee Guy—I didn't know his name and asking him would invite too much familiarity—handed me a large cup. "Winter's brewing. Fingers gonna freeze."

"Yeah, but what are you gonna do?" Giving him a wave, I headed for the Monotrain platform. The train bound for the Peninsula of the Gods was just pulling in. I slid Xan off and and rested the scabbard between my feet, leaning the hilt against my shoulder as I struggled to drink my coffee without spilling it.

"You're a Theosian, aren't you?" The voice interrupted my thoughts.

I looked up to see a ratty-looking bogey staring at me from the opposite seat. Actually, he looked like one of the Broken rather than a bogey. He seemed more sad and vague than scary.

"Yes, I am." There was no use denying it. We all had an aura about us and while not everybody could place us at first look, eventually most people figured out we weren't human. I flashed him a smile.

The man was wearing a threadbare jacket. His jeans were grungy and beneath the jacket, he was wearing a wrinkled plaid shirt. His cap was pulled down over his ears, and his shoes had holes in the toe box. The soles were probably worn through, as well.

He returned the smile with several missing teeth. "Do you live around here?"

I nodded. "Yeah, I do. You?" It never hurt to chitchat with strangers on the train unless they were batshit crazy. Never knew what kind of info you might pick up.

"I live at Evermore." He held up a government identity tag that hung around his neck. That explained a lot.

Evermore was an institution. *Facilities*, they

called them now. Rules were in by the shelter's
designated curfew for dinner, stay the night, then
out in the morning after a sparse breakfast. The
"shelters" offered showers, and the barest of a
health ward.

Anybody down on their luck could apply, but
only if they agreed to be chipped and put to work
at any job the Conglomerate saw fit to hand out. In
return, they could stay as long as they liked. The
shelters for men and women were segregated, and
if families applied, their children were thrown into
government foster care. It was a rough life, and
one I wouldn't wish on an enemy.

"What's your name?" I was lonely. Talking
to somebody else would stop me from running
through all the lethal scenarios Tam could have
gotten into.

"Gin. Short for Gino." He paused, then wiped
one hand across his eyes, as if trying to clear away
cobwebs. "I don't always remember my last name.
Guess the tags are good for something," he added,
trying to laugh.

I thought about giving him some cash, but if
the shelter found it on him, they'd take it away.
The poor weren't allowed any real creature
comforts or kindness if they were accepting
government help.

"That coffee?" Gino stared at my steaming cup
with a wistful, nostalgic look.

I cleared my throat. "I don't seem to be all that
thirsty this morning. Would you like my coffee?
I've only taken a few sips and I'm not sick."

"Sure, sure." He reached out with unsteady
hands and I carefully handed him the cup. As he
brought it to his lips, he smiled.

I leaned back, thinking how much I hated

the government. They'd give him Opish free if he wanted, but not a cup of coffee. At least, not outside of the two sparse meals a day.

As I got off the Monotrain and headed for the Peninsula of the Gods, I thought I saw him follow me, but a glance back at the crowd showed no one there. Shaking away thoughts of Gino and his coffee, I plunged through the gates leading into the temples.

The Peninsula of the Gods was protected from everyone, including the Conglomerate and the Devani. The soldiers didn't dare pass through the gates, and neither did the Abominations. The gods ruled supreme and the entire area was considered Sanctuary.

The peninsula was rectangular. At least, the actual campus that sat on the land was. Five tiers deep, staircases led down to the center, stopping at each tier. Elevators on all four sides offered access to those who didn't feel like tackling the steps. Mini-malls with food courts and restrooms offered places to sit. Moving sidewalks encircled each tier, carrying supplicants past all the temples as they made a complete circuit.

In the center of the campus, at the bottom, was a pond into which rainwater filtered, and pumps beneath the pond drew off the excess during the rainy season. The water was then recycled for city use. During winter, the pond froze over to create a fountain of ice. Ice sculptors would create a frozen landscape of beauty to please the gods. Now, the gardens surrounding most of the temples were covered with snow, creating a silent blanket that muffled the sound.

I stopped at the third tier and stepped onto the moving sidewalk. I liked watching over the railing as the sidewalk carried me along. The morning bustle was silent but tangible as priests and priestesses hurried past, bracing against the chill. Theosians were bound to the gods, but we were never given the title of priest or priestess. We were minor gods in our own right, held to service for as long as the Elder Gods wanted us.

At the same time, no Theosian I had ever known had been promoted to Elder God. But then, we were young compared to the Elders, mere glints in their life spans. And we were an accidental creation, collateral damage from the Weather Wars and the World Shift. So much history had been lost in the chaos that it was difficult to know when we had begun to appear.

Passing the Coliseum—the Roman temple—I finally came to Naós ton Theón. I avoided the general admittance line, which seemed longer than usual for a Tuesday morning, and went straight to the entrance for those who worked in the temple. The guardian who was watching the detector motioned for me to place my hand on the scanner, while the priest standing next to him motioned for me to give him my sword. I handed over the sword and my dagger and he ran them through the detector. They came up on his screen and he set them to the side.

"Fury, servant to Hecate. Walk through the detector, please."

I trudged through the arch, watching as the golden light that crackled across the face of the portal changed to green. That meant I was cleared through.

"Any—"

"Nope," I finished for him. "No hidden charms or magic to declare."

"Here are your weapons. Go ahead." They motioned me on. I had met both of them before. By now, most of the priesthood knew who I was.

I strapped my dagger back on and then slipped Xan's scabbard over my shoulder so it was hanging at easy reach across my back. My breath coming in white frozen puffs, I headed into the temple, out of the cold.

Coralie, the receptionist in the waiting room on the floor where Hecate's office was, looked frazzled as I exited the elevator. Her golden hair was caught up in a messy bun, and her one-shouldered toga dress looked a little askew. She glanced up with a fearful glint in her eyes.

"Oh, Fury! Thank gods it's you. Hecate's champing at the bit. You're to go directly back." She nodded toward the hall leading to Hecate's office.

"Oh, hell. She on the rampage?" That could mean a number of things, but so far I hadn't done anything wrong that I knew of.

"Not as much as Zeus." The girl lowered her voice. She leaned forward, glancing around to make sure nobody could hear us. "You wouldn't believe the row he and Hera had. We heard it all through the temple. He stormed out about an hour ago. I'd expect to see some thundersnow sooner or later today."

I grimaced. Zeus and Hera were renowned for their temper tantrums. They routinely had rows that echoed through the temple. "Is Hera still here?"

When the bigwigs were in the building and pissed, it paid to keep a light step and get out of the way.

Coralie nodded. "Yeah, so watch it, though she's on the top floor. She seldom comes down here. But she found Zeus canoodling with one of her Theosians." Her voice dropped and I knew precisely what had happened. Well, not the full details, but whatever the punishment had been extended was guaranteed to be well beyond any my imagination could cook up.

"The girl still alive?"

Coralie nodded. "She probably wishes she wasn't. Hera told her that if she wanted to be Zeus's little bitch, that's what she'd be. She turned the girl into a puppy and dumped her out in the streets. I think somebody managed to sneak out and get the girl...the pup...to safety, but that's pretty much the end of life as she knew it." She glanced at the clock. "You'd better get back there. Hecate was in a pique as well. And we don't need any more hounds around here."

I nodded, heading through the door that led to the divine offices. I often made light of working for one of the Elder Gods, but truth was, it could be terrifying. Theosians belonged to their gods. If our patron chose to destroy us, there was nothing we could do to stop it. No law of the land extended rule over them, and they didn't live by human ethics. Not that humans were much better.

I paused outside the door to Hecate's suite, then knocked and peeked inside.

"Hecate?"

She motioned me in.

YASMINE GALENORN

Hecate was gorgeous. Contrary to popular opinion, beauty could be as terrifying as it was arresting. Hecate's hair was waist length, jet black, and she wore it gathered up in a high ponytail. In her hair, she wore a diadem, a circlet of three silver snakes entwining with a black moonstone nestled in a crescent moon. Horns up, the moon was held aloft by the snakes' heads. It mirrored the tattoo on my neck marking me as Hecate's property. Her black leather pants and indigo V-neck sweater were, as always, meticulous, and a silver belt encircled her waist. But her eyes were what knocked her beauty out of the stadium. They were twinkling periwinkle like the light that divided early evening from twilight.

She looked up from where she was sitting on the edge of her desk. "It's about time. You certainly weren't in any hurry to get here, were you?" She paused, frowning. "You know I don't have all day to waste." With a pause, she set down her tablet. "What's wrong?"

Great. She was pissed. As much as I respected her, the last thing I needed was to be scolded by an impatient goddess. "I had a rough night and took Sleep-Eze to knock myself out. In case you didn't realize it, my boyfriend's missing. I asked Queet to tell you last night."

"You mean Tam still isn't back?" The impatience in her voice shifted to concern.

I shook my head. "No, and we haven't heard a word from him. Hans tried to poke around down at the precinct but his contacts are clueless on this one. It's been hushed up. The last time I saw him, the Devani were using a stunner on him. Hecate, I'm worried sick. This isn't like him. He'd contact me if he could."

She worried her lip for a moment, then motioned for me to sit down. "I'll do what I can. You're right, this isn't like Tam. I'm sorry I was so abrupt. We just have a bad situation breaking and I need you to be in top form."

I grimaced. I didn't want to go fighting. I wanted to go hunt down Tam. But I had a job to do and when the gods said, "Jump," we Theosians jumped.

"What's going on?"

"An Abom was spotted coming in off the World Tree. He's a bad one, Fury. You need to head out hunting before he goes on a feeding spree. He's not in-body, and he's strong. Very strong."

I let her words register for a moment, not wanting to respond. But then, routine kicked in and I straightened my shoulders. "Give me the specs. But what about Queet? I need him. What's going on with him lately?" Technically, I didn't actually need Queet, but it made my job so much easier when he was there.

"He'll be here in a few moments. He's been going through some difficulties, Fury, so try to understand. A psychic leech latched onto him and was feeding off his essence. He was having trouble keeping himself situated, let alone focusing enough to help you. He came to me, as is proper, and I examined him. Queet couldn't see the creature because it was cloaked. I managed to dislodge it and we've been repairing the damage. He's embarrassed about not noticing it, and he didn't want you to know."

I hung my head. "He thought I might use it to tease him, or make fun of him, didn't he?"

"Well, you two don't have the most amiable of relationships, but I paired you off for a good reason. You spur each other on." She flashed me a look that could have read as irritated or amused. I decided I was better off not knowing which.

"If you want the truth, Queet's okay. I like to bug him because he always seems so bent out of shape. Yes, he gets on my nerves and I get on his, but he's helpful and courageous and I'd do whatever I could for him. I won't tease him. I promise."

Thank you. I think you're okay, too, Fury. Queet swept up behind my back, and then settled beside me on the sofa. *I'm feeling much better now.*

I cocked my head. "You know, I wonder if the astrigators we encountered over in Bend a few months ago were responsible. They eat magical and psychic power like candy."

"That could well be. This creature was of a similar disposition." Back to business, Hecate picked up her tablet and scanned it. "Let's get back to matters at hand, shall we? There's a lot I wanted to discuss today, but this takes priority. The Abom came off the World Tree like the others, as I said. By reports, he's not in-body, and hasn't taken over a human vehicle. But he's corporeal, so I'm not sure how or what to believe. Whether he's in-body or not, he'll come up on your Trace screen. He's headed for the Trips and so far, he hasn't taken any victims, so something is up. You need to figure out what he's trying to do, and then put a stop to him. Usually they go on rampages the minute they cross over but so far, he hasn't."

I frowned. Aboms usually waited a few hours before assuming a human vehicle, but during that time, they raged through victims, feeding to grow even stronger as they looked for a suitable host. Aboms usually chose someone exceptionally strong on a physical level.

But there were also Aboms who sought out victims holding positions of power. We weren't sure what their end game was or why they were trying to infiltrate our society. We managed to kill most of them taking that route, but it was always worrisome when the Aboms didn't follow the pattern. And if this Abomination hadn't taken down any victims yet, he was out of sync.

"The Trips? I wonder why. Aboms usually head into Darktown and then try to work their way into Croix and Uptown. Where is he now?"

"Almost to the edge of the Junk Yard. If you head out now, you might be able to catch him before he crosses the district border. But hurry. The Fates are worried about this one."

That she had talked to the Fates about an Abom worried the hell out of me.

"He's that bad, huh?"

"That bad. Let's just say, this one is on our watch list. Some Aboms are easy enough to dispatch. But I fear you may have trouble with this one. He's after something in particular and I don't know what. I want you to trail him for a little bit, unless he goes after somebody, and find out what you can."

The last thing I wanted to do was go on a monster hunt, but Hecate's will was my will, and I was in no position to refuse. "You'll look into Tam's disappearance?" I wanted her assurance. I wanted to know somebody was doing something.

"I promise, Fury. As humans say, cross my heart. I'll do everything I can to find out what happened to him." She walked over to me, leaning down to cup my chin. With whisper-soft lips, she pressed a kiss against my forehead. "I'll get on it the moment you leave this office."

Hecate could be cold as the grave, and as ruthless, but when she was in a mood to be generous, it came through clear as crystal. She gazed into my eyes, her own spinning circles of dusk. She reached out then, to touch the gold-and-ruby *"F"* I wore around my neck. The pendant vibrated with her touch.

"You are mine. You are bound to me. What hurts you, concerns me. I like Tam and I like that you and he have chosen to forge a relationship. I will do what I can to find out where he is. You're one of my daughters, Fury. *And I always protect my own.* At least, to the extent that I am able." With that, she turned and crossed back to her desk. "Go now, and I will text you when I learn anything. Keep me informed on what you find out about the Abom, and I leave it to you to decide when to move against him. Knowledge is important, but saving lives comes first."

With that, she dismissed Queet and me. Before we made it out of the temple, though, a loud shriek emanated from the upper levels. I had heard it once before and I had hoped to never hear it again.

Come on, let's get the hell out of here. I began to speed walk through the hall, though running wasn't allowed in the temple without a good reason.

What is it? Queet seemed downright jaunty now, back to his old spirits.

Hera. She's up in arms. I think Zeus may have returned and we don't want to be around if they're about to launch into each other again. I made sure my voice was low enough so that it wouldn't be detectable to anybody but Queet.

Whisper-speak wasn't just reserved for Theosians, after all, and the last thing I wanted to do was get anybody in power pissed at me. Especially any priestess of Hera or priest of Zeus who might be wandering by.

That hurried Queet up. The moment we exited the temple, I began to jog toward the nearest set of stairs, slogging through the newly fallen snow. Within minutes, we were at the top of the Peninsula and heading back toward the Monotrain. As I raced along, blowing on my fingers, I only hoped we would find the Abom before he managed to find a victim to his liking.

Chapter 7

The Trips was a residential area. My mother and I had lived there when I was a child. A lot of workers who pulled shifts in the Metalworks chose to make their home there, along with those who felt Darktown was too unsafe for family life.

Theosians were only allowed to live in Darktown, the Trips, and Portside within the city of Seattle proper. If we wanted to chance ending life way too early, we *could* live in the NW Quarters, but the gangs there hated us.

And anybody could choose to enter the Tremble, but once in, never out. The Tremble was different. The Tremble made the Sandspit look like a walk in the park. As for Briarwood, the Greens, the Wild Wood, and the Edge, they all belonged to the Fae and the Shifters. Some humans chose to live there, and probably some Theosians, but there were no guarantees and life in the wild had truly become life in the *Wild*.

The Trips was Uptown's country cousin. Tidy,

neat, relatively low crime, the Trips was filled with low-income families who were just trying to make it through life with some modicum of comfort and a relatively full belly. The apartments were weathered but tidy, and the houses showed a lot of wear and tear, but the families took pride in their homes and maintained them as best as they could, overall.

"It's been awhile since I've thought about the Trips," I said, more to myself than anybody else.

But Queet heard me. *I remember, Fury, when you lived here. Your mother and father were into some rough times when you first came along. He had the beginning of blue-lung disease and your mother had a rough time coping. Jason was always there for all of you.*

Jason had known my parents before I was born, but for the life of me, I couldn't remember much about him from when I was little. But then, after my father died, he came around more and the memories were clearer.

Jason helped my mother keep it together when Father died. He was probably the best friend she ever had. I didn't add that the only thing that kept me from losing it during that time were my books, and Hecate. Queet knew, though. He was there, even then.

Shaking off my thoughts, I pulled up my Trace screen. The moment the Abom came within hunting distance, he'd show on my screen.

A thought crossed my mind. *Queet, why are most Aboms male?*

I don't know. You might ask Hecate. But you're right, most of them that come through are male.

We passed through the neighborhoods, my attention constantly focused on the Trace. I had been born with the ability but Hecate had ignited it, putting me to good use. While she supervised my hunt for Abominations, you might say I'd been destined by my rogue DNA to seek them out and destroy them.

Several people on their way to the Monotrain platforms took one look at the sword hanging across my back and quickly shifted to the opposite side of the street, not wanting to get too close. *Big sword equals dangerous woman.*

While I was well known in Darktown, my reputation hadn't spread far into the Trips, and I decided I rather liked it that way. It made me less of a target from freaks on the human side of the equation. While I had sent most of the Abominations right back to the realm of Pandoriam, there were a few not-so-astral critters and people who would be a lot happier if they could ensure I didn't exist.

He was coming from Darktown, and we were moving in from the Peninsula of the Gods. I hoped the Abom would show on my Trace before we hit the border separating the Trips from both the Junk Yard and Darktown. An Abomination loose in the Trips had a lot more chance of harming children than one in Darktown. The kids in Darktown knew to run the second they even *thought* they saw an Abom was near.

Nobody knew quite what the Abominations really were. They weren't exactly demons, but they *were* from one of the lower realms. The shadow realms ran energy on a much lower vibration and the inhabitants had no sense of human mores. They fed on life energy. At times, they fed on flesh as well. They sucked the souls out of their victims, then took on their body like a suit. *A human vehicle*, we called it. A few were even capable of passing for a time and tried to work their way into positions of power, although we weren't sure just what they expected to accomplish.

We made our way through the streets with the flow of people heading off to work. Queet had lapsed into silence as he often did when we were on the hunt. He knew that I needed to focus on my Trace and he was good about not distracting me.

The Trace was like an internal hologram. I could see it in my mind, and whenever an Abom got within range, a brilliant red dot would flare up on a map and a soft alarm would chime. As I closed in on the Abom, the light grew in intensity. When I was close enough, I could even tell how many blocks away he was thanks to my infernal GPS, as I called it.

As we neared the juncture where the Trips, Darktown, and the Junk Yard converged, the alarm started to sound and a faint red dot appeared.

"Got him. He's still in Darktown." I didn't bother with whisper-speak. Nobody around me was paying attention and one more crazy talking to herself wouldn't turn a single head.

Queet grunted. *How far away?*

"About five blocks I'm guessing, by the strength of the signal. He's on the run and moving fast. In fact, he's coming directly at us. I wonder why he's headed for the Trips. Most Aboms stay near the World Tree. They find plenty of food there."

Remember, Hecate wants you to follow him.

"I just wish it wasn't into the Trips, but yeah, I remember. I'll follow him as long as he doesn't go after anybody." I was surprised how fast this one was traveling. He was speeding along, which also seemed odd. Even if they weren't in-body, Aboms tended to meander until they found a target.

You should get out of the way so you can fall in behind without being noticed when he passes by.

I didn't really want to. I honestly thought following him was a bad idea. It was better to take them right out when they came in, before they had a chance to hurt anybody. But Hecate's will was my will, and so I took Queet's advice, slipping into the burrow-lane between two apartment buildings. A man—probably one of the Broken—was further up the lane, urinating against the side of the building. He took no notice of me, just stuffed his dick back in his pants after shaking the last drops off, then zipping up and shuffling in the other direction.

After judging him as mostly harmless, I peeked around the edge of the apartment complex. Of old red brick, the walls were cracked in places with long, narrow fractures that looked fresh. No doubt the quake we'd had a few months ago had opened those up. A string of Wandering Ivy peeked over the top, and the tendrils waved, searching for meat on the hoof. But it was too far up to be a danger.

My attention shifted as the Abom loomed closer. It was almost filling my Trace screen. I held my breath, praying he wouldn't home in on me. Sometimes they seemed to sense me through the Trace. But I began to notice that Hecate was right. He seemed to have a very specific focus. There were plenty of people on the street he could have jumped, but he still hadn't chosen a vehicle. Most Aboms fed as soon as they came through the World Tree.

The flashing light came closer still and suddenly, I could sense his energy signature all around me. He was powerful, definitely. And, there was something else. I closed my eyes, trying to pinpoint what I was sensing. There it was, at the very edge. He was cunning. Beyond cunning. But the next moment, the energy tangled, as though some giant kitten had taken all the threads and snarled them up in a big ball of yarn.

Queet was hovering over my shoulder, but he kept silent.

I held my breath. The Abom was almost upon us. If he noticed me, he might attack. If he was any typical Abomination he would. *One beat. Then another. And yet another.* It must have been only a moment but time felt like it stretched out with no end, before finally the creature passed by, a whisper of power and hunger and shadowy anger.

The residual trail he left behind him struck me as odd. It took me a moment but then I realized that he wasn't alone. Not that he had an invisible friend, but his energy told me that the Abom was working for someone else. There was a Control spell on him that packed a punch bigger than any I had ever seen. The realization that some magician was controlling an Abomination hit me like a sledgehammer. Some idiot had cast a spell on the creature and was using him for...*for what?* Hecate was right. I had to follow him, if only to see if I could figure out who was in control.

I waited till he had moved past us to do anything, though I made sure he was still on my Trace screen. When I was sure he wouldn't hear, I caught my breath.

Queet, this is a bad sign.

Do you think that—

Lyon might have done it? I shivered. Lyon Burkenwald was a powerful magician and the leader of a chapter of the Order of the Black

Mist. A group of magicians, the Order was bent on yanking open the seals to the realm of Chaos and waking the Elder Gods within. They were dangerous and I had already gone up against Lyon once. I didn't want to face him again and had hoped that he might back off once he lost our first major go-round.

Yes. It would be like him, looking to cause havoc.

We can't know for sure, but I'm sure as hell not dismissing it. Come on, we need to follow the Abom.

I swung around the corner of the building. The Abom was far enough ahead and so focused that he paid no attention to me. I picked up my pace, running at blur-speed to keep him as close as possible without risking attracting his attention. Queet, of course, had no trouble keeping up. Ghosts and spirit guides had it one-up on the living when it came to movement, unless they were bound to an area, but that was an entirely different matter. The Abom passed several likely candidates for a meal, but each time as I prepared to intervene, he sailed by, ignoring them.

Finally, we were on the outskirts of the Trips. Shortly after we crossed the border to the Peninsula of the Gods, he abruptly made a left turn, heading into an overgrown area. Wary, I slowed, allowing a little more distance between us. It paid to be cautious here. The ravine divided the edge of the peninsula from Pacific Sound. The abrupt edge overlooked a drop-off that could easily send the unwary or the careless tumbling down into the volatile waters.

But where the hell could he be headed? I didn't remember any suburbs or neighborhoods located back in this area, and there weren't any office buildings, either. It was relatively overgrown brush and a tangle of scrub.

As I slowed my pace, sneaking to a brick wall that ran along the border dividing the districts, a vine dropped down, tapping me on the shoulder, then abruptly started to coil around my neck before I could brush it away.

I grabbed my dagger with my left hand and the vine with my right, and quickly severed the tendril from the plant. With a low crackling noise that sounded suspiciously like a hiss, the Wandering Ivy withdrew and I edged away from the wall. While there were other, more dangerous sentient plants than Wandering Ivy, it had taken over the city. Bramble Lords could be just as deadly, and *much more* painful, given their thorns. But Bramble Lords tended to grow in rural areas. And Stinging Nettlers were another carnivorous plant that had taken over in marshy areas.

The Wandering Ivy made another half-hearted swipe at me, but I just silently held up my dagger and the plant pulled back. I wanted to mutter something nasty to it, but no sense chancing the Abom overhearing me.

The creature turned right at the end of the wall, and I paused.

Queet, go as carefully as you can and tell me if it's waiting just around the corner.

Will do. Queet was off. Within a few seconds, he returned. *No, check on your Trace screen. He's moving again but slowly now.*

I checked my Trace again and, sure enough, the Abomination was on the move, though at a slower pace. I followed, easing up to the corner. As I peeked around the wall, I could see him—a glowing outline of sickly green light. He had stopped in front of what looked to be an abandoned graveyard.

That was odd. What could an Abomination want with a cemetery?

Curiosity waged war with my concern, and I crept closer. The Abom had managed to dig a hole in the ground and seemed to be burying something. *What the fuck?* I was about to send Queet over to find out when the creature suddenly straightened up and turned my way. With a roar, he charged me.

Oh, hell! He wasn't in-body, so Xan wouldn't be much use, but I slapped my right hand on my thigh and the whip came off into my palm. As I gripped the coil of energy, it sang to me with the pulse of fire and lightning. I stepped back, raising the whip for a clear shot as the Abom skidded to a stop in front of me.

He seemed wary all of a sudden.

No, this wasn't just any typical Abomination fresh off the World Tree. He was cautious, or the person controlling him was cautious. He circled to my left. He was starving. The hunger rolled off him in a wave. The Abom needed energy, and he needed it soon. The magician controlling him must have been starving him for a reason.

I eased a step to the right, never taking my eyes him as he moved with me. When Aboms weren't using a human vehicle, they tended to be more of an amorphous shape. Bipedal and yet, rather blobby. They didn't contain their energy well, reminding me of a child's magical Soft-Clay doll, always dribbling bits as it moved around the pottery pit.

The Abom paused again, then lurched forward.

He tried to grab hold of me as a long tube wriggled out of where the back of his neck would be.

Fury, dodge! His siphon!

"Crap!" I lurched into a back bend as the tube lashed out at me.

When not in-body, Aboms attacked by creating a psychic tether to their victims. They would jam their siphoning tubes into their victims' crown chakras, then drain off the life force from both the aura and the body.

I rolled to the side, coming up to lash out with my whip. Unlike Xan, my whip *could* hit victims who weren't corporeal. As the thong unfurled toward him, the fall wrapped around the Abom's neck. The jolt raced over his body, a sparkling net of energy.

He stiffened, freezing for a moment before the attack faded. I pulled back for another blow and struck before the Abom could pull away. Once again, the fall wrapped around his neck, cracking loudly as another net of sparks wove around him. I squinted, trying to find the mark that would allow me to send him back to Pandoriam. Unlike Aboms who were in-body, the soul-hole on their astral forms was harder to find, and I had to hit it square on.

With my left hand, I unsheathed my dagger. *Queet, where's the soul-hole? Can you see it?*

His soul-hole is in his stomach, Fury. You'll have to get close if you plan to use your dagger. Xan would be better.

Stomach? You've got to be kidding. Damn it.

I fumbled, sliding my dagger back into the sheath as I raised the whip for another strike. Once more, I brought my aim to bear, this time lashing toward his chest. Then, while he writhed from the hit, I slapped my whip back on my thigh and reached over my back to slide Xan out from her scabbard. The Abom was still staggering from my last blow, but I didn't have long before he recovered. I brought Xan around, holding her steady at the level of his stomach and braced myself as he charged forward again.

Too late, he seemed to realize what I was doing, but he couldn't stop. He plunged directly onto my sword. As he stared down, as though he couldn't quite believe what was happening, I seized the opportunity and drove the blade deep into his soul-hole. We were face to face at that moment, Xan protruding from his back.

He stared at me, his light fading. Then, with an audible *pop* like a balloon bursting, his astral form flared into a burst of angry reds and rusts, and he vanished back to Pandoriam, leaving me standing there with Xan, facing an empty graveyard.

Breathing hard, I slowly lowered my sword, staring at the ground. The flare was gone from my Trace screen, but I still felt uneasy.

Queet, can you sense anything around?

But I had no sooner asked the question than something slammed into my back, knocking the wind out of me. Surprised, I dropped Xan as I lurched forward, my spine aching from the blow.

Fury! Queet's voice came through loud and clear. *Behind you! Dive and roll!*

I didn't question, just forced myself to move. As I hit the ground, I landed on a sharp, fist-sized rock. Rolling off, I looked up to see three men standing over me. The next moment, one of them kicked me in the side and I let out a sharp scream as his steel-toed boot dug into my flesh. I didn't recognize him, but he sure seemed to know me. He was wearing dark jeans and a hooded sweatshirt, as were the two other men.

"She's a looker—"

"Getchyer mind off her snatch, Bale. We have a job to do." The one who had kicked me sounded all too delighted to continue his task as he hauled off and kicked me again.

I managed to roll onto my hands and knees. As I reached for my leg to activate my whip, the third man grabbed my wrist and dragged me to my feet.

"Now, Fury girl, we don't want you playing with that whip, do we?"

The man identified as Bale caught my other arm and they stretched my arms wide between them. I stopped struggling. I couldn't focus on my magic if I was trying to escape. I lowered my head, trying to ignore the pain as I summoned up what energy I could. I was already tired from fighting the Abom and now, the pain was making it hard to think.

"Lesson one: Stop sticking your nose in where it doesn't belong," the first man said as he sent a punch directly to my stomach. I started to double over, but they forced me upright and my midsection cramped like crazy. Whatever hold I had on my *Flame* went right out the window.

"Who the hell are you?" I managed to ask, praying to stave off another blow while Queet summoned help. I couldn't sense him around and knew that was where he had gone. He always had my back.

"Figure it out, bitch." My main attacker took aim again and this time, his fist connected with my face. Thank gods I was more resilient than the average human. My Theosian nature made me tough. I was harder to kill, but that just meant it would take more blows to do the job.

Jarred from the pain sweeping through every muscle, I sniffled as blood trickled from my nose, the droplets falling on my lips. I could taste their salt on my tongue as I licked them away.

He wasn't going to answer me, so I focused my attention into trying to fluff up my aura, to cushion me from the pain as much as I could. Then another blow hit, and another. I was desperately trying to memorize what they looked like when one last blow connected with my nose. The last thing I remembered was the men letting go of me, dropping me on the ground as they laughed and wandered off. Everything was cloaked in a thick fog, and my body hurt so much that I couldn't find a place that didn't ache. Nothing wanted to work.

"Hurry, Queet," I stammered out, not even sure if I was speaking aloud or not, but then the world went black before I could say another word.

Chapter 8

"Fury? Fury?"

The voice sounded familiar and safe, and I struggled against the fog that held me captive. Trying to move, I let out a long groan as pain knifed through every muscle of my body. I couldn't pinpoint where it originated, but there it was, strong and vibrant and richly colored, turning the fog encasing me a brilliant crimson.

"Fury, can you hear me?"

Once again, I responded to the voice, trying desperately to follow it to consciousness. Finally, I saw the thread. It was gentle blue light in the midst of all the bloody red, and I latched hold of it, journeying past the pain, past the aching that enveloped my body and clouded my thoughts.

"Fury, you're scaring me."

And then I opened my eyes. Well, one eye. The other felt welded shut. I blurrily stared up at Jason, who was kneeling beside me. Hans was on the other side, and they seemed to be checking me over. I felt a prod here or there, but everything hurt and I couldn't be sure if they were poking my bruises or if the bruises were just pissed off and throbbing.

I struggled to form words. "Hurts. Everything... hurts."

"I know it does, love. I know. Come on, honey, we've got to get you to a medic. Can you move at all?" His voice was soft, but the look on his face was dark and clouded. I knew what that look meant. Jason was pissed as hell and wanted to kill. I had only seen it a few times, but the sentiment was unmistakable.

Hans glanced over me to Jason. "We should take her to Sarinka. She's close. She lives on the outskirts of the Trips, only a few blocks away."

Sarinka was a healer who worked in Darktown two days a week, giving out free medical help. The rest of the time, she worked from home. She specialized in healing acute wounds and injuries, and while she wasn't a recognized doctor, she was a certified mender.

"Good idea. Today's one of her days at home, too, so it's not terribly far. I know she's broken a few bones but I don't think her spine was fractured and she's moving her head, so her neck wasn't broken. Why don't you carry her while I grab her sword." Jason eased back. "Unless you think we should bring Sarinka here?"

"We can't be sure. Just to be on the safe side, let me fetch Sarinka. Meanwhile, you keep your guard up. Whoever did this might come back to finish the job." Hans vanished from my field of vision.

"Jason." Breathing was hard, and so was

talking. My ribs felt like kindling. But I wanted to tell him to check the graveyard, to see what the Abom had buried.

"Hush. Not another word."

"But..."

"No, be quiet." He pressed one finger to my lips. "You're hurt, Fury. You'll live, but whoever did this meant to hurt you. You need to lie quietly until Sarinka gets here."

I thought about asking Queet in whisper-speak to tell Jason, but I couldn't focus enough to manage it. Finally, I gave up and slid back into the void that yawned around me.

The next time I opened my eyes—or eye, rather—I was on a soft table, with my head cushioned by a pillow. A cool cloth was draped over the eye that didn't want to open, and the pain in my body seemed muted. I let out a soft groan, relieved to find that the crusted blood on my nose and mouth had vanished. My jaw hurt like hell, but even there, the pain was muted.

"What...where..." Then I remembered. They had been taking me to Sarinka's. Or bringing Sarinka to me. Since I didn't appear to still be lying on the ground anymore, I had a feeling we had found our way to the mender's apartment.

"Fury?" A melodious voice trickled over me like cool rain.

"Yeah, I hear you."

"I'm Sarinka. Remember me?" She leaned over the eye that I could see out of, the deep amber of her skin glowing like late autumn sunlight. We had met a few times before, and she had mended up some bruised ribs after a particularly grueling workout a few months ago.

"Yes, I do. Is this your place?" I was still struggling to breathe without hurting, but it wasn't quite so hard. "What time is it? What day?"

"You're in my home. You were attacked last night. Jason and Hans brought me to you, and we carried you back to my place on a hovstretch." She sounded almost proud and I thought she had every right to be. Hovstretches weren't cheap, and healers who could afford them were doing business at a good clip. The stretchers glided on a thick layer of air, smoothly and without turbulence, allowing the patient a safer, more comfortable ride.

"How roughed up am I?" It was getting easier to form complete sentences. My tongue seemed to be working better and even though my jaw ached, using it loosened up the bruised muscles. I tried to sit, but she gently pushed me back by one shoulder.

"Not yet. I want to make certain you're ready. Your face took a lot of damage." She grimaced. "You're lucky, given the beating you took. I didn't find any broken bones, but I'm pretty sure that's because you're a Theosian. If you were human, my dear, you would be as dead as the bodies you found out in that graveyard." She pulled back my blanket and I shivered. The room felt chilly, and I wanted the warm back.

"I'll just be a moment. I'm going to check out your heart again and see how the All-Heal is working on your bruises." She placed a Vita-Chek directly over my heart and then tapped away on her tablet. At least medical software had come a long way over the past decades. She left it there for a minute and stared at her tablet.

"All right, then. Your heart and lungs are all right, though you do have a severely bruised rib and that's what is causing your difficulty in taking a deep breath. But the bone isn't fractured, so if we wrap you up tight, you should be all right until it heals. I'm not seeing any concussion, which surprises me, but your black eye is a mess. I can speed the healing but it's going to be quite the shiner for a few days."

"I wish Tam was here," I said, my throat on fire. "He could drain some of this out of me." Among his other attributes was the ability to heal with a kiss. Oh, he couldn't bring anybody back from the dead, and he wouldn't be able to save a dying man, but he could heal up a lot of bumps and bruises, as well as diffuse energy drain. In fact, that's how we got started—with a kiss to help me out. The energy had been comforting and had ignited the chemistry that now flared between us.

"Let's sit you up now, so I can wrap those ribs." Sarinka gently shouldered me into a sitting position, with Jason helping her from the other side. I was naked. She had obviously needed to examine me, but I still broke out in a full blush.

Hans winked at me. "Don't be so shy. You're gorgeous, bruises and all." But he turned away to give me privacy, as did Jason, after I managed to hold myself upright.

First Sarinka scrubbed me down so there wasn't a speck of dirt on me, then she bound my ribs tightly with a thin layer of verathane. Verathane was a thin bandage that compressed tightly without adding bulk. "You can take off the bandage as soon as you get into your corsets. They'll provide you with a better layer of constriction. And no lifting anything. I don't want you touching your sword."

I groaned. "What if I need to use it?"

"Use your whip, since you wield it with your right hand. Most damage is on the left side. But I warn you: Using that whip's going to hurt like hell. I'd rather see you off your feet and in bed for at least a week to give those muscles a chance to heal up. I put All-Heal on you, which drastically cuts down on recuperation time, but seriously, girl. You need to lay low for a bit. Especially since it seems you were specifically targeted and this isn't some random act of violence."

I grumbled under my breath.

"What did you say?"

Feeling chastised, I shrugged. "Nothing. Just, I *wish* I knew who those assholes were." I closed my eyes, trying to picture them. Everything right before the attack was muddy. But a few things stood out. One, the words echoed through my head.

"They told me *'Lesson one: Stop sticking your nose in where it doesn't belong.'* So it's somebody I pissed off. I think I asked who they were. They told me to figure it out." Squinting through my one good eye, I frowned. There was something else. Something I had noticed during the fight. Or rather, attack. *They* fought. *I* didn't have a chance to defend myself. "I remember something, but I'm not sure what it is."

"Lie back and close your eyes." Sarinka helped me ease back against the pillow. I wanted to protest that I was okay, that I could sit up without a problem, but the truth was lying down felt good and eased the pain in my head. I let out a soft sigh as I settled back beneath the covers, elevated enough to where my breathing was easier.

Sarinka removed the cloth from my swollen eye, replacing it with another one. "These are soaked with All-Heal and will reduce the swelling in your eye enough so you'll be able to see out of it tomorrow. You'll still look like a major mess, but you'll feel a lot better."

"Good to hear." I leaned my head back and closed both eyes, resting them from the light. I was trying not to freak out, to remain as professional as possible. I had been hurt before but by *Aboms*. This was different. This reminded me all too much of the Carver and what he had done to my mother. Those men had *enjoyed* hurting me. And that's what had frightened me. They hadn't just been doing their job. They had enjoyed every punch and kick.

"We need to know more about who did this." Sarinka brushed the bangs off my forehead, smoothing them back. "Here, you are safe. So let yourself drift back to the fight. Try to remain detached and tell us everything you notice."

I resisted at first, not wanting to dredge up the memories that I already wanted to bury, but this was important. So I took a slow, easy breath, trying not to disturb my ribs, and then softly exhaled in a long stream, willing the images to flow freely.

Then, I was there on the ground again, and the blows were coming fast and thick. I wanted to shout, to beg them to stop. But I tried to calm myself as I remembered that I was safe. These were just images. Just memories.

I examined the men as they were hitting me, looking for any marks that might identify them. They were wearing hooded shirts and loose jeans. It was impossible to see their hair color beneath the hoods. But something caught my eye. I looked past the fists and saw a mark on the chest of each shirt. It was a white circle on black, and inside the white circle were concentric half-circles that were off kilter just enough to confuse the eye, in shades of black, blue, red, and white. It was hard to describe, though there was something terribly familiar about it.

As I opened my eyes, out of the good one I could see Jason tapping away on his tablet. All of a sudden, he let out a curse under his breath.

"Did it look like this?" he asked, holding the tablet up so I could see the crisp design. It was jarring to the eye, precise and yet skewed.

"Yes, that's it. All three of them had that symbol on their shirts. Who is it linked to?"

"The Order of the Black Mist. Lyon sent those men to find you." His voice was raspy.

I did sit up then, forcing my way up and propping myself on my elbows.

"I wondered if that was the case." And then, another memory hit me. "The Abomination. It was doing something in the graveyard. I'm not sure what, but I remember wanting to ask you to check out what it had buried there. But I fainted before I could do so. I was hoping Queet would have told you."

"Queet vanished after he led us to where you were."

I was about to say that he'd been having a rough time lately, but the familiar, raucous strains of my ringtone for Hecate interrupted. Hans silently handed me my purse and I fumbled out my phone. Punching the TALK button, I held it to my ear.

"Hello? Hecate?"

"Fury, where are you? I've been texting you since yesterday."

I paused. So Queet hadn't told her yet? Was he okay? Distracted by all the thoughts running through my mind, I started to shake my head to clear it but that was a big mistake and I let out a groan as a jolt of pain stabbed through my forehead over my left eye.

"Fury, are you all right?" She sounded calm, but I knew her well enough by now to recognize the sound of worry beneath the surface.

"Not entirely. I'll tell you in a moment. What's up?" I wanted to glance at her texts but that would entail putting her on speakerphone and right now, I didn't want to chance anybody overhearing anything that might give me grief.

"I found out what happened to Tam, Fury. I know where he is."

My heart slowed, as I began to battle with a rising flood of fear and worry. "Where is he? Is he alive?"

Her voice bleak, she said, "Yes, he's alive but, Fury, the Devani sent him out on the Tremble. He's been sentenced to a year's exile there."

And, once again, everything went black.

Apparently I wasn't over my shock because when I opened my eyes, I realized that I had passed out. Jason was on my phone, and I could guess who he was talking to. Hans was standing behind the table, watching over me as Sarinka waved a wretched-smelling cloth under my nose.

I managed to sit, the pain in my body a distant cousin compared to the pain in my heart. Jason turned around to look at me. Then, after a few mumbled words, he tossed my phone on the table.

"I had a talk with Hecate. She told me what happened, and I made sure she knew what was going on with you. Queet just showed up in her office. He faded again, whatever that's about, and wasn't able to reach her." His expression was bleak as he turned to Hans. "Tam was arrested by the Devani and sentenced to a year's exile. They chipped him and dropped him out on the Tremble."

The Tremble.

The Tremble was a geologically and magically unstable piece of land, where the impossible became reality, and where normal was a word too distant to understand. Out on the Tremble, it looked as though all the jumbled leftovers of the world had been tossed together by a great whirlwind, reality twisting in on itself. The resulting landscape was a mishmash of optical illusions that were anything but illusion. Nobody lasted out there long without going mad. Not even shifters or Fae were immune to the discord that laced the entire district.

"We have to find him. We have to bring him back." I stared at Jason, willing him to agree. If I had any semblance of a charm spell, I'd be using it now. But I didn't need one.

Jason straightened up. "No question about it. Hans and I will start out tonight."

"No, you won't. I'm going with you." I struggled to stand up, wincing as my ribs let me know they weren't happy at all. But I didn't care. "You aren't going after him without me." I turned to Sarinka. "Is there anything you can give me to help me with the pain that won't cloud my mind?"

She nodded. "Yes, but take it too long and it's habit-forming. Try to hold out for as long as you can before taking the pills. I'll get them for you. I can see that there's no use in ordering you not to go." She vanished into another room.

I turned back to Jason. "I know you're going to try to stop me, but don't. Don't you *dare*. Tam pushed me out of the way. He distracted the Devani so I could escape. He's my... I think..." I paused. I hadn't used the words with Tam yet, nor he with me, but the feelings were there, coiling in my heart, and I knew that they were real. So I simply said, "He's my love."

Hans held up his hand as Jason started to protest. "Let her come. She's Hecate's guard. She's a Theosian. And she's loyal to those she loves." He turned to me. "You'd make Thor proud, Fury. I'd ask Greta to join us, but she has temple duties."

Jason let out an exasperated sigh. "Very well. I can't stop you and I guess I shouldn't. But perhaps we should stop at UnderBarrow before we head out to the Tremble. Maybe his people can give us some help. And we're not starting out till tonight. You need more time to rest. You may have been out of it most of the day and all night, but every hour of rest that you get will help."

Cautiously holding my side, I eased back onto the bed. "All right. We start tonight. First, we'll head to UnderBarrow, and then, we go rescue Tam."

"I have to get back to the shop. I can make us some talismans and charms that may help us deal with the Tremble." Jason pressed his lips together and I could tell he was worried. He had good reason to be.

"Fury can stay here the rest of the day. Pick

her up around four." Sarinka returned, handing me a bottle of pills. "Take one every six hours, at the most. Try to avoid taking them back-to-back. It only takes a few days of regular doses to cause a raging addiction, even among Theosians. But for what you want to attempt, this is the only thing I can suggest."

I stared at the bottle, then set them on the table next to the nightstand. "Do you have some Sleep-Eze? The deeper I sleep before tonight, the better. I need about five hours' worth. So, two and a half tabs."

"I'll get them." She disappeared again.

"I'll stay here, just in case those freaks decide to try a Trace on Fury. Call me if there are any developments," Hans said.

Jason nodded. "Oh, by the way. Hecate told me to tell you to call her before you leave to go after Tam. Apparently, she knows you better than any of us." And with that, he reluctantly headed out the door.

Sarinka gave me the sleeping meds and I stared at them. "Hans, if anything happens, wake me up. Promise?"

He nodded. "I'm here, Fury. And I'll keep watch over you. Sleep now, and rest."

With that, I popped the pills and drifted back to sleep.

Chapter 9

Sarinka had helped me as much as she could. Jason had stopped off at my house and brought me one of my more flexible corsets, and now, I grimaced as I slipped the busks closed. The metal fasteners held the corset snug, and even though at first it made me catch my breath, it also helped to ease the pain.

I felt better. My eye was less swollen and I could see out of it. But Sarinka was right. I wouldn't be using Xan for the next week or two. I'd have to make do with my dagger and my whip, although reaching over my head wasn't going to be a picnic, either. The corset helped, but I was going to hurt like a son of a bitch for quite a while.

"You *have* to be careful. You're so beat up that if you end up in another scuffle, you might break something. Bruised bones break easier." She stood back, eyeing me closely. "I still think you're daft to go running off to the Tremble, but if you have no choice, you're about as healed up as you're going to get for the next few days."

"I have to. Every time I think of Tam up there…" I couldn't finish the thought. I knew what happened to people dumped out on the Tremble. A year's exile was as good as a death sentence.

Reaching out, she brushed my hair back away from my bruised eye. "I know. I see it in your eyes. Well, your eye. Your other eye isn't so pretty right now, but you're not entering a beauty contest. I fixed a small container of All-Heal for you. Rub it on your ribs at night and in the morning. And here's another one of AntiBruise. Use this on your face around your eye. It will help keep infection away. Try to avoid any more blows to the head, or you may end up with impaired vision. You came close this time."

"I know. Trust me, I'm going to try to stay away from any fighting." *At least till I heal up*, I thought. I took the medicines, tucking them into my purse. Truth was, I was scared. Sarinka had convinced me just how close I came to permanent damage this time. The scars didn't bother me so much, but the beating I took—and the joy the men had taken in it—left me somber. Lyon hadn't been joking around, though why he hadn't let them finish me off, I wasn't sure. Maybe he *had* told them to kill me, but something interfered. I couldn't remember.

Turning to Hans, I slid my arms through the heavy jacket he held for me. Jason had brought me my long leather duster. The coat would help keep the chill off my legs. My regular jacket had been torn up during the fight. Jason also remembered to bring me clean underwear, a clean pair of leather shorts, and a button-up sweater that would keep my arms and chest warm, but that wasn't too hard to get into.

I slid Xan in her scabbard. "I'm taking her anyway. I may not be able to use her very effectively, but I feel naked without her." Except this time, I slung the scabbard over my right shoulder.

"Let me carry her for you," Hans offered. His weapon of choice was a battle-hammer that hung from his belt.

"Are you sure?"

"I offered, Fury." With a smile belying his size and fierceness, he took the sword from me and slid it over his back. While I missed having easy access to her, the truth was that any lightening of my load was a relief at this point.

Jason handed us each a tiny bag of charms. "I don't know if these will do any good, but they're to ward off madness."

"I have a bad feeling we're going to need it," Hans said, draping his over his neck.

I followed suit. "We'd better get moving if we're going to stop in UnderBarrow."

I dreaded facing Tam's people and telling them what happened. It hadn't been my fault, but being the messenger was never easy. No matter how little you had to do with a situation, bearing bad news always left the messenger with a taint around them. They were forever connected with the misfortune.

"Let's go. Queet around?" Jason asked. He handed Hans a bag. "I brought some of your things from the store, too. We need to book it. Tam has been out on the Tremble for around two days now." He didn't say it, but we all knew how short of a time it took to drive someone over the line.

I'm here. Queet swirled around me.

"Then I guess, we start out." As I thanked Sarinka and said good-bye, I hoped we'd see her again. And I prayed that, in trying to rescue Tam, we wouldn't need rescuing ourselves.

An hour later, we were at the edge of the Sandspit. Readerboards warned against going in, especially pregnant women. Patches of rogue magic were hiding all over the Sandspit, and passing through one could be deadly.

Marlene had been pregnant with me when she crossed through the Sandspit, too tired to go around it. The result? My DNA shifted and boom—one minor goddess coming up. There were rumors of women being paid to wander around there until they came to a patch. Some idiots wanted to adopt a god or goddess for a child for their own ego. Even darker, some slave traders were looking to pay for children with "talent," as they called it. And of course, the Conglomerate looked the other way if the payoffs were big names in the business world.

"How far to UnderBarrow?" Hans asked as we stared over the unending dunes.

"We cross to the center, to the World Tree," I said, stepping through the open gates after a long breath. I'd been here more than once since Tam and I had become an item, but every time it made me nervous, and every time I was sure something bad would happen.

UnderBarrow was located at the base of the World Tree. Once a thriving industrial area of Seattle before the World Shift, the Sandspit was a two-hundred-acre wasteland. To the north lay Darktown. To the west—the Bogs, and to the east—the Metalworks. Gaia had struck home with her lightning, and as the great rails and trains had melted, the sand became infused with her anger and rogue magic. Chaos reigned here, and the Seattle World Tree had risen out of the ground, dimensions opening through its branches. The sand glowed, though you mostly saw it during the night as a pale blue light among the shifting dunes that continually moved in the ever-constant winds.

I braced against the biting wind as we wound our way through the meandering course that would take us to the center. Dusk had already fallen, and the snow froze on the sand, making the stinging grains hurt even more as they pelted my face, mingling with the thick of the storm that was blanketing the city. More snow seemed on the way and if this kept up, we'd be in for a long, cold winter. My sore eye ached, though the cold actually seemed to help. We trudged along, diving to the side occasionally as snow-lightning crackled, rolling low to the ground like a neon snake through the rising mist.

"Boy, they weren't kidding when they warned against going into the Sandspit," Hans said, watching as a brilliant blue bolt thundered by. "What the hell? How can lightning be so low? There's no thunder."

"Ground lightning. Another delight that seems prevalent here." I adjusted my bag on my shoulder, wincing against the stiffness in my side. "I'm not sure what causes it, but it's not the same as lightning from the sky."

"It's inherent within the magic here, feeding off all the impurities mixed into the sand. I'm not clear on how it all works, but I remember hearing something about it in our geology class when I was in school." Jason covered his face with his jacket, trying to shade his eyes from the onslaught.

Jason is right. Queet spoke loud enough for everyone to hear. *The ground lightning has a sentience of its own, though nothing like human thought. It can be vicious.*

Some twenty minutes later, we had wound our way through the labyrinth of dunes, obstacles, and storm to reach the center of the Sandspit.

There, rising up from deep within the crater, was the World Tree. At the bottom of a pit well over one hundred feet deep, the massive oak spread its branches every which way, a tangle of limbs that webbed out. Along the trunk, at the base of the thicker limbs, were portals to other realms. An incandescent and eerie green glow shone from the heart of the tree, lighting the chasm all the way down.

There were a number of World Trees, spread across the globe, each with their own portals that crossed into other realms. In Seattle, the World Tree was oak, but in other areas, the trees were native to their area.

All the trees were linked, though nobody had ever quite figured out how. Though it was possible to travel from tree to tree, the governments had learned early on *not* to send their soldiers through to attack neighboring lands. The battalions vanished forever. Any gear they been carrying had melted, falling as slag at the base of the roots.

Gaia was in charge of the World Trees, and she made no bones about reminding people that she would do as she saw fit.

At the edge of the crater, near a massive pile of scrap metal, a staircase remained hidden from sight. The first time we had entered the pit, Tam had guided us. Now, I knew it by heart.

The stair was steep and dangerous, and the sand slick. I led the way, as beat up as I was. Jason had only been here a couple of times. Hans, never. But I'd visited Tam in UnderBarrow weekly. As I stepped over the side, I gingerly reached down to feel with my foot. There it was! My foot landed on the stair. As I sucked in a deep breath, the muscles in my side twinged, reminding me just how unhappy my ribs were. I slowly let out my breath and, one step at a time, began my descent.

I focused on the steps in front of me. Looking back to see how Jason and Hans were doing could easily cost a misstep and send me over the edge to a long, nasty tumble. They'd have to fend for themselves. The light of the World Tree provided enough illumination to see by, the portals glimmering, vortices of glistening light that opened into other realms, other worlds.

I wonder where they all go. At times the impulse to take a chance and pop through were strong, but I always managed to corral myself. The Abominations came from Pandoriam, a monstrous realm of chaos and anger. What if there were other, more iniquitous realms waiting out there? The thought of facing creatures worse than the Aboms always put a crimp in my hunger to go gallivanting through space.

Time began to blur. Watches and phones and all things electronic ceased to work when we neared the Sandspit, and they sure as hell didn't work *in* the Sandspit. Or UnderBarrow, for that matter. In fact, time did whatever the hell it wanted to. Slowed, quickened, stopped outright. It was easy to lose track of the outside world in here. I shouldered on, testing each step as I descended into the crater, trying to ignore my face, which was stinging like crazy. As soon as we got to UnderBarrow, I was putting more salve on it.

The next moment, I glanced over at the tree and realized that I was almost to the bottom. The World Tree was like that. You'd go down, down, down and then, without warning, you'd be at the bottom. I stepped off into the sand and waited for Hans and Jason. A moment later, Jason jumped lightly off the stair to join me, and after him, Hans.

Hans looked down at the tangle of knotted roots that had forced their way aboveground, rising like gnarled fingers from the compacted sand below. The roots were knee-high in some areas, extending out from the tree like bony tendrils, and they glowed, pulsing with a deep, slow rhythm.

"They mirror Gaia's heartbeat," Jason said, reverently kneeling by one.

"That's what Tam told me. I wonder if any of the Greenlings have ever been down here." The Greenlings were sentient plant beings—Gaia's henchmen, so to speak. They had waged war during the World Shift, striding before her as she brought humanity to its knees. They would do so again in a heartbeat, if need be.

"I imagine the roots of the World Trees were where they were born," Hans said. "What better place to spawn them?"

It made sense to me. "All right, now to UnderBarrow."

Around the base of the World Tree, with a quarter turn, I ducked into the mouth of a cavern that was hidden in shadow. *Duck* being the operative word, given the opening was barely five feet high. Jason and Hans followed, and Queet ghosted around me.

The entrance led to a massive cavern with walls that shimmered from the magic compacted into the sand. The ceiling was a good twenty feet high, inlaid with crystals set into a star-shape pattern. Their light brilliant blue and green lights radiated off the walls. It was the sign of the Tuatha de Dannan, the Bonny Fae. And Tam was their leader, the Prince of the Northwest Clan, the Lord of UnderBarrow.

An opening at the back of the cave led to a long, narrow passage. There were no guards here. Tam's people knew we were here. I led the way again, traipsing through the tunnel until we came out into another chamber much like the first, and a throne sat in the middle of the room. The throne was empty, and the Fae milling through the room turned as we entered. Damh Varias, one of Tam's advisors, approached.

"Lord Tam is not here, milady. We have not seen him in a couple of days." He sounded worried. While Tam was often gone for a day or two at a time, I had a feeling they sensed something was up.

"Can we speak privately? My friends and I have news you should hear." I had some semblance of standing in the Court of UnderBarrow. Everybody knew that I was Tam's girlfriend, although here they called me his consort.

Damh Varias held my gaze for a moment, then motioned for us to follow him into another hallway. We entered yet another chamber—one I hadn't seen before—with a table and benches in the center. He gestured to the serving woman.

"Bring us chacolia." The Fae loved chocolate, and they had made it a passion to develop new drinks. Chacolia was a spicy, sweet cacao-cinnamon chocolate drink that packed the punch of highly caffeinated coffee. In fact, a couple mugs of it set you good to go for hours. I welcomed the thought. Not only did it provide energy through the caffeine, but the drink acted like a sustained, time-released lunch. After the girl set the tray on the table and served us, she exited the room, curtseying to both Damh Varias and to me.

As soon as she shut the door behind her, I turned to the advisor.

"Tam's been captured by the Devani." As he paled, I explained what had happened.

"Two days then, he's been out on the Tremble." Damh Varias paced the length of the room. "The Fae are not immune to the energy there. This could be bad. Very bad. He hasn't been in contact with us, and if he could, he would have let us know what was happening."

"We're heading there now to spring him. If we can find him," I added slowly, not wanting to think about the possibility but realizing it had to be voiced.

"You put yourselves in jeopardy, you know." Damh Varias turned to me. "You already look like you've been pummeled well and good, milady."

"The Order of the Black Mist is responsible. Tam told you about the Thunderstrike? Apparently they're out for a little revenge. Lyon sent his men after me."

"They make a deadly mistake, then. You are the consort of our prince. The Bonny Fae claim you as their own until, unless, Lord Tam should part from you. Even then, we likely would watch over you as a friend to the realm." Damh Varias was a tall, thin man, showing gray at the temples, which meant he was old. *Very* old. Older than Tam, who had seen the Weather Wars in person.

"I'm grateful for that. They roughed me up pretty badly. I'm not going to be running any races soon. But we have to get up to the Tremble and do our best to find Tam before the energy begins to warp his mind. We can't leave him out there." My chin trembled as I realized how afraid I was that we'd be too late. I hated to admit vulnerability, but there it was: I was in love with Tam and now I was terrified that I was going to lose him.

"The Tremble isn't far, but we need to keep clear of the trains and their stations," Jason said. "I spotted a few Devani around the Monotrain platform at the Trips, near Sarinka's place. I called a friend in Darktown and he confirmed they're hanging around the Monotrain platforms there, too."

"I hope to hell they aren't looking for me." I paused. Could Tam have been forced to tell them about me? Or were they just on guard? But the soldiers of light had never before been all too particular about public transportation, so the thought that they might be looking for someone specific was a credible one.

"I doubt it, but we can't take chances. We have to get to the Tremble unnoticed." Hans wiped his mouth with his hand, shaking his head. "We can do that until we hit Croix, but then it's going to be more difficult. We'll stand out."

Damh Varias cleared his throat. "That you make an attempt to rescue our prince does not go unnoticed. Or unrewarded. I will send someone with you to help. She's skilled with both regular bow and an expert mark with the bariclore."

I blinked. Bariclores were illegal to possess

in the city proper, though there wasn't much the government could do to stop people who lived out in the wild from owning them. They were projectile weapons, a lot like a bow and arrow, but they were as small as a stunner, and they propelled darts that could be rigged to tranquilize an enemy. Possession of a bariclore within city limits could cost twenty years in the work mills.

"We'd appreciate all the help we can get," Jason said. "I have no idea of how we're going to find Tam."

"Elan will be able to help you. Wait, and I will summon her." Damh Varias exited the room, shutting the door behind him.

"Are you sure it's wise, letting someone tag along we've never met?" Hans frowned. "What if she's a spy?"

"A spy for who? My boyfriend's—*your friend's*—people? They already know everything he does about us. Jason is right, we need the help. The Tremble scares the hell out of me."

Hans shrugged. "Okay. Good by me. I just wanted to make certain we know who we're traveling with."

"She's not likely to be a spy for the Devani." Jason fell silent as the door opened and Damh Varias entered, followed by a tall, willowy woman. Her hair was the color of sand, and her eyes sea-foam green. But she had a regal, piercing look to her, and her jaw was rigid.

"May I present Elan. She is one of Lord Tam's bodyguards when he chooses to utilize them, and she's an expert markswoman. Elan, you know who Fury is. These are her friends, as well as Lord Tam's friends. May I present Jason and Hans. And the misty one is Queet."

Queet laughed. *Thought you hadn't noticed me, Lord Varias.*

"Not a chance, ghostly one."

Elan stiffly clicked her heels together. She wore gray jeans and a pale blue tunic, and her boots were leather with steel-toes. Her hair draped down in a long braid that set off the angular nature of her face and nose.

I started to say hello but Jason beat me to it. "Elan, thank you for your gracious offer. We're so grateful for your help. I'm Jason Aerie." He took her hand. Instead of shaking it, he brought it to his lips where he gently placed a kiss on the top of it.

I glanced over at Hans, who repressed a snort.

"Well met, Jason Aerie, hawk-shifter." She gently retrieved her hand and turned to me, inclining her head. "Lady Fury, daughter of Hecate. I humbly offer my services." Then, with another quarter turn, she faced Hans. "Hans of Temple Valhalla, well met to you, brother in arms."

Hans grinned at her. "You know all the right things to say. But well met to you, and thank you for your help. So you—"

"You carry a bariclore?" Jason interrupted. His eyes were bright and as I studied him for a moment, a light clicked. Jason was preening. He had been bowled over by Elan.

I scanned her quickly, but long enough to realize that she actually looked a lot like Eileen, Jason's fiancée who had been murdered. Tall and thin, with angular features, Elan could have been a kissing cousin of the late hawk-shifter. Even her name was similar.

"Yes, I'm an expert mark with both the bow and the bariclore. I usually don't use the tranquilizing darts in city limits, but seeing that we're headed out on the Tremble, I'll bring a few. I can carry it beneath my cloak."

The handheld crossbows were also illegal. The law permitted us to carry knives and daggers and even swords, but distance weapons were prohibited for private use. The government was more afraid of assassination than it was of people gutting their neighbors. Though it made no sense. Magic more than made up for the mayhem caused by distance weapons.

Another thought occurred to me.

"Is Tommy-Tee still here?" I hadn't seen the street musician for a while.

Tommy was one of the Broken, addicted to Opish and too fragile to watch after himself. But he always tried to do what was right in his addled brain. Tam had brought Tommy with us to UnderBarrow after the quake had left the singer homeless, and there was some hope that they might be able to bring his mind back from wherever it had wandered. Tommy lived in a perpetual Tremble of his own, and it occurred to me that he might be able to steer us through the district better than we could steer ourselves.

"Tommy is with us still, yes. And I know what you're thinking but he cannot go with you. While he would be the best suited to navigate the Tremble, it would undo all the progress we've made. Tommy-Tee will never be fully mended. But he can function better on his own with some help. Taking him into the Tremble would unweave our magic."

"Was he telling the truth? Did he really live through the Weather Wars?" No human had a life span that long.

But Damh Varias nodded. "Yes, he was telling

you the truth. There's so much there that he's seen. He was here, where the Sandspit is, the night the World Shift went down and the World Tree was born. That's what broke him, and that's also what extended his life. As far as we know, he's one of a kind."

I thought about what he said. That would make Tommy-Tee the oldest human alive, it seemed. But then, was he still human, after all this time?

"All right. We need to get on the road," I said. "Damh Varias, do you by any chance know a safer route than if we go through Uptown and North Shore? Even if we went around the Edge and took a ferry back over, we'd still have to go through North Shore. I can't chance being stopped along the way, and my kind are always viewed as suspect in the upper districts, especially at night." While I couldn't live in Uptown or North Shore there, it wasn't technically illegal for me to be in the streets, but at night the Devani would be out in full force patrolling and they never needed a reason to stop anybody. Given the circumstances, I didn't want anything to muck up our rescue.

"We can get you to the lower border of the NW Quarters without being noticed, though it will be by boat. The waters surrounding the Tremble are dangerous and turbulent, and unless it's an absolute emergency, we don't attempt landing there. The Locks are deadly." He shrugged. "It's the best we can do."

I nodded. "Your help is welcome. Where do we find the boat?"

"Elan will lead you. We have tunnels that you can take out to the edge where the Trips meet Pacific Sound. Our boatman will be waiting." With that, he ushered us to the door. "Bring him back, if you can. He's the heart and soul of UnderBarrow. While others can lead, and his brother would willingly step in, Lord Tam is our prince."

I nodded, tears springing to my eyes. "I'll do what I can. I want him back, too."

"I know, Fury. I know." Damh Varias reached out to me, pulling me in for a long hug. Before I realized what he was doing, some of the shock and soreness began to drain away, replaced by a golden glow as he siphoned the pain from me. When he stood back, he held his finger to his lips and waved us out.

Chapter 10

Elan led us through a tunnel that Tam had never mentioned. The passage was old, that much I could tell by how smooth the walls were. The floor was compacted dirt, almost as hard as the stone of the walls themselves.

I slipped ahead to walk with Elan. She didn't *feel* Bonny Fae to me, though she looked the part. "How long have you lived in UnderBarrow?"

She smiled coolly. "Ask what you like. You needn't cloak your questions beneath pleasantries. I'm new to UnderBarrow, in from the Wild Wood east of Bend."

Appreciating her bluntness, I nodded. "I wondered. You seem too outdoorsy to live in a Barrow for long. There are Woodland Fae out in the Wild Wood, aren't there? Cousins of the Bonny Fae?"

"You're correct. I'm one of the Woodland Fae. I'm an otter-shifter, to be precise. Woodland Fae are often animal shifters, while the Bonny Fae aren't."

That explained the different energy I felt coming off of her. She reminded me more of Jason than Tam, when I thought about it. The shifter nature would account for it. I wondered if Jason sensed it too. A glance over my shoulder showed him talking to Hans, but he glanced up, meeting my eyes before his gaze flickered over to Elan and once again, I saw the flicker of interest. Yeah, I wasn't imagining it. He had crushed and crushed hard.

I returned to my conversation. "I didn't know any of the Fae could shift. Of course, I'm only familiar with the Bonny Fae, so my experience is limited." I winced as one of my ribs twinged. This was going to be an uncomfortable trip. "Why did you come to UnderBarrow? Or is that too personal? I'm not prying, just curious."

Elan shrugged. "Tam asked me to come. Well, he asked both my brother and me. We're twins. I'm an ambassador. We're discussing setting up an exchange program between our two nations— the Bonny Fae Nation and the Woodland Fae Kingdom."

That was news to me. I still wasn't clear on the nature of how the Fae worked. Tam didn't like discussing politics when we were together.

"I didn't know the Fae considered themselves sovereign nations."

"We do, regardless of what the Americex Corporatocracy chooses to portray to the people of this country. They like to think they're in control, and they are—in the urban areas. But we have our treaties and if they try to push in on our territories, they know they can't win. Once humans get out in the Wild, they stand at a distinct disadvantage.

If you want to know the truth, and don't think the Conglomerate doesn't know this, the Devani wouldn't last ten minutes if they tried to enter the deep forest."

She sounded so certain that I had to ask. "How do you know?"

"Because they've already tried, and they've already failed. News of this sort seldom leaks out to the public, but those of us who were there know, and we remember just how vulnerable they can be to the *right kind of attack*." A look of dark triumph crossed her face, the kind that warned, *Better to be my friend than my enemy.*

I stopped pressing. She had already convinced me it was in our best interests to take her with us. My thoughts returned to Tam. I was trying unsuccessfully not to worry. Worry clouded the mind and slowed the reflexes. But I kept coming back to the fact that he was out there on the Tremble. Jason slowly inched by to join Elan, patting me on the shoulder as he passed. I fell back beside Hans. He gave a subtle nod ahead at the pair.

"You sense what I sense?"

"Yeah," I said, keeping my voice low.

As I watched them walk together, speaking in low tones, it dawned on me that they looked like old friends, comfortable together in a way that usually took years to achieve. Maybe they'd been together in a different lifetime. Or maybe, there *was* such a thing as love at first sight. Maybe the concept wasn't a myth.

"How are you and Greta doing?" I hadn't had a chance to catch up with Hans for a while. He wasn't merely the muscle at Dream Wardens, he was also Jason's assistant. And when he was hanging around the shop, I always seemed to be busy with a client.

"All right. She's nearing the end of her training period. Her flying-up ceremony is scheduled to happen near mid-winter. Once that's done, we can get married." He beamed. They had been engaged for several years, but until Greta finished her training, she wasn't allowed to marry. He added, "She's hoping you won't be offended if she doesn't ask you to be a bridesmaid. Her Temple Sisters expect her to ask them. And there are a lot of them."

I laughed and shook my head. "Not at all. In fact, I'm more than happy to sit in the audience and watch you two stroll down the aisle. But I get extra cake."

Over the years, laws and regulations had changed, as had traditions, but marriage was still an option a number of people chose. I was more than happy to cheer on Hans and Greta, but to be honest, I was relieved I didn't have to take part. It was one less thing to worry about.

"Extra cake it is, then." He paused, then asked, "How's it going with you and Tam? I have to tell you, Jason and I were both caught by surprise."

"I know you were. I wasn't sure about Jason. He's a hard read at times. So, Tam and me? We're good. I never expected this to happen." I paused, cocking my head as we approached a faint light. "We're coming to the end of the tunnel, I think."

Ahead, the flicker of illumination appeared to be coming from an opening. We weren't anywhere near sunrise, so it had to be either an energy field of some sort, or a light source.

Sure enough, Elan turned, motioning for Hans and me to catch up. She jerked her head toward the light. "Energy veil. From the other side, unless you know what it is, the portal actually looks like a big nasty thorn bush. Few people ever come out this far on the edge of the Trips. Five hundred yards to the right is the outer edge of the Peninsula of the Gods. We're about ten yards from the edge of the Pacific Sound. The boat should be waiting for us."

"Whose boat is it?" Jason asked.

Elan let out a soft laugh. "Mine. No more talking. I doubt there's anybody near, but we don't want to take any chances." And with that, she moved ahead, then pushed through the veil of energy.

The boat was waiting straight ahead, a small cruiser, agroline-driven but with the ability to windsail as well. It was difficult to see it in the darkness, save for the dim light emanating from the central cabin.

Fury, I can go on the boat, but I can't venture out to the Tremble. The distortions there wreak havoc with spirits. Queet gusted around me, a fine vapor of mist in the falling snow.

My heart sank, but I had wondered about the viability of having him there, especially since he had been on shaky ground lately. *Then you should stay here. Check in with Hecate and let her know what we're doing.*

I wish I could go. I'm sorry. I really am.

That's okay, Queet, we all have our limitations. Go now. We'll be back before you know it. But even as I whispered the words, I felt the doubt creeping in my heart. Queet silently vanished, but I thought I heard him call out *Good luck, my friend* before he left.

We followed Elan aboard to see a man who looked remarkably like her manning the wheel.

"This is my brother, Laren. He's my twin." She grinned as he clapped her on the shoulder and motioned to the wheel.

"Do you want to drive?"

Elan shook her head. "No, you take the helm, but mind you, keep to the shadows and watch for any of the shaygra's boats. The last thing we need is for the golden boys to stop us. I'll conceal our guests below deck." She paused. "You know where we're heading?"

"Yes, and I can't say it makes me very happy, but we do as we must. I've set course for the outer edge of the Tremble, off the NW Quarters. I've recharged the guns should we need them." He glanced over at the rest of us. "We carry weapons. This ship *cannot* be confiscated. You should know that we will not allow the shaygra to board us. We will go down fighting and self-destruct if worse comes to worst."

" 'Shaygra'?" Hans asked.

"The 'Golden Men.' The Devani. They and their masters are always seeking information on our people, precisely because they can't control us. We won't give them any opportunity to learn more about us than they already know." Elan motioned for us to follow her. We crossed the boat to the port side, where she stopped by what looked like a built-in banquette. But she reached beneath the lip of the seat and with a soft *click*, smoothly opened a lid.

"The Devani expect to find holds like this. But they seldom look below." She leaned in, then motioned for me to step forward.

As I looked into the chest, I found myself staring at an open bottom that led into a dark space below. "Is that the hold?"

"Not exactly." Laren winked at me. He seemed a lot less serious than his sister. "*That* is an interdimensional space that we've set up. It's activated by thumbprint and can't be discovered physically or magically without the right print unless you have the passkey code. And only Elan and I know that code."

"Then, essentially we're heading down into something like a private little reality."

He nodded. "You may find yourself getting confused while you're in there, but it won't be for too long. But for everyone's safety, we have to ask you to hide."

I glanced at Jason. We'd be at their mercy, and we didn't really know who these two were. At least, not beyond what we'd been told. But we didn't have any other choice, and if Damh Varias trusted them, then I would trust them too.

"Of course." I glanced over the side. "How far of a drop? Is there a ladder?"

Laren shook his head. "No, just sit on the side and slip in. The drop is difficult to describe but you won't be hurt. Getting out will be just as easy."

Hans and Jason still looked leery, so I decided to be the guinea pig. I gingerly stepped into the banquette and sat down, then slid my feet through the square hole in the floor. Immediately, my feet felt a floor below. Curious. My legs were tingling all over but not in a bad way, and I decided to go for it.

I stood, and suddenly found myself in a gray room, dimly lit, with five chairs along the wall. A table stood in the center of the small room, and on the table were a loaf of bread, some fruit, and a round of cheese. I looked up to tell Jason and Hans that everything was okay, but no longer could see them. All I saw when I looked up was the ceiling. The next moment, Hans appeared in the room beside me, and then Jason. They looked as surprised as I felt.

"Well, it looks like they were prepared. I wonder how often they smuggle passengers around." Jason let out a soft laugh before sobering again. "I asked Elan how long the trip would take and she said an hour or so. It would be quicker but they travel in stealth mode, and that requires more time."

"We might as well sit down and eat." Hans picked up an apple and bit into it. "We don't know how long it will be until our next meal. If we're lucky, we'll find Tam right away, but it's been two days and who knows where he is."

"The Tremble isn't that big." But even as I started to say it, I stopped. The Tremble might not occupy more than five or six miles, but even so, with the warps in reality it would take us two or three days to travel through on foot. *At least.*

Without another word, I sliced off some bread and cheese and dropped into a chair. Even though I had slept all day, my bruises ached. The walk through the tunnel had jarred me more than I wanted to admit.

As I bit into the bread and cheese I was pleasantly surprised to find it moist and sweet, with a creamy texture. I leaned back, surprised when the chair turned out to be a recliner with a foot rest that popped up.

I closed my eyes. "I'm going to nap. Wake me

when we get there."

And with that, I finished my food and drifted off to sleep.

"Kae? Kae? Time to wake up." Jason was the only one who still called me by my birth name. At times it endeared me to him, while at times it irked me. "Time to get up. We're here."

I fought my way awake, my sore eye sticking shut until I wiped away the goo clinging to my eyelashes.

"What the? Oh." I pulled out the salve and swiped another layer on. I wanted to slather another dose of All-Heal onto my ribs too, but Sarinka had warned me not to. I wasn't sure what could happen but I decided to stick to the expert's opinion for once. Groaning and more than a little stiff, I eased my way out of the chair and lightly stretched, trying to keep from overstraining. I glanced up.

"It looks like just a ceiling."

"They're waiting for us. See that faint red dot?" Hans pointed at a flickering light. It was so faint I hadn't noticed it. "We just go through there."

"How do we reach it? The ceiling seems a ways off."

"Easy-pie. Watch." The burly Theosian walked over to beneath the red dot, reached up, and the ceiling seemed to lower itself to meet his arms. He hoisted himself, holding onto something I couldn't see, and vanished, his feet giving one final kick.

"You next." Jason led me to below the dot. "Just reach up."

I did, and found hands grabbing hold of my

fingers, guiding them to a solid surface. It had to
be the edge of the hole in the banquette. I groaned,
the pain in my side searing as I lifted myself
through the swirling ceiling. My head popped
through, and I saw Hans watching me.

"Help me up. My side is burning like hell."

He caught hold of my wrists and I groaned
again as he began to lift me up, but then, someone
was bracing my legs, helping push me through so
the majority of weight wasn't resting on my sides
and arms. The next moment, I was through and
back up on deck. Jason came popping out right
behind me.

"We're nearing the shore," Elan said. She
pointed and in the distance, the faint silhouette
of a dark shoreline rose out of the water. I
shivered, folding my arms. The NW Quarters was
as frightening as the Tremble, though in very
different ways. The NW Quarters might technically
be part of Seattle, but it was run by the Grungees,
a gang of bogeys who had banded together to form
a tribe that was part militia, part wildmen. Human
and proud of it, the Grungees hated Theosians. In
fact, they weren't all that fond of Otherkin of *any*
kind. They also despised government authority
and considered themselves anarchists.

"Be careful. None of you will be particularly
welcome in the Quarters. But you shouldn't have
more than a couple hours' walk to the border of
the Tremble." Laren eased the boat toward the
shore, the craft sliding silently through the water.
"I'll wait a little ways out in the harbor for your
signal, Elan. If I don't hear from you in three days,
I'll return to UnderBarrow and we'll decide what
to do next. Go, and may the Queen of the Forest
watch over you."

She gave him a gentle kiss on the cheek. "And Mielikki watch over you too, my brother." Turning to us, she said, "It's too cold and too deep to wade through the water. We'll take the rubber raft. It's tied to the stern. Jason, Hans, please wrestle it in." She gathered her weapons. "Anything sharp needs to be sheathed or covered. We don't want to puncture our raft."

Within five minutes, the men had managed to reel in the rubber raft from where it drifted behind the boat. Elan got in first, smoothly lowering herself on the rope ladder attached to the side of the boat until she was able to step into the raft. She moved to the center to keep it balanced while the rest of us joined her.

Hans went next, and then I lowered myself down the ladder. Even though my feet were bearing most of my weight, my ribs and shoulders still ached. Hans cautiously reached up to balance me as I stepped into the raft. He guided me to sit by Elan, then moved to the front. When Jason joined us, he took the back. Laren untied the knot connecting the raft to the boat. Jason and Hans manned the oars, slowly paddling toward shore, taking care to make as little noise as possible.

As we glided toward the shore, the mist rose off the sound, rolling in like a thick tide, cresting over the rocks on the shore that led up to the embankment. The giant river stones were big enough to sit on. Some were big enough to lie on. They had been brought down by the glaciers so long ago that even the Fae couldn't remember. The ice sheets had stretched across the Canadian Empire and the Americex Corporatocracy. During the Weather Wars, we had been headed into a global catastrophe of human making, but Gaia had dialed the planet's warming back, swinging the pendulum the other way. Now we faced long winters and cool, shorter summers.

The oars softly broke the surface of the glassy water, but the only other sounds we could hear were the lapping of the waves and the sound of snow falling. Pacific Sound stretched out toward the Olympic Peninsula, a thin strip of land dividing the Pacific Ocean from the sound. Once, the peninsula had been twice its size, but erosion and quakes had widened the sound, and eaten into the shore. The forest wild had taken over, the mountains and woodlands driving out most of the populace. It was said that the trees were as wide as a house there and one day I wanted to visit. But the ghosts were also thick, and creatures who had long inhabited the darkened forests.

We bumped up against the rocks and Hans grabbed hold of the roots of a tree that had almost been swallowed up by the sound. He gave one big heave, pulling us in. I crawled out of the boat, cautiously climbing the rock incline that led to the embankment. Jason followed and then Hans. Elan tied the boat to the tree root, then joined us. Chances were it wouldn't be here when we got back, but we had to take the risk. Once we were on the rocks, Elan and Jason led the way while I followed, with Hans coming behind me, and we headed up into the land of the Grungees and the NW Quarters.

Chapter 11

The NW Quadrant was so rough-and-tumble that the area almost made the Junk Yard look tame. Situated between the upscale North Shore—which was walled off by a gated barricade—and the Tremble, the NW Quarters was a small, rough division. A road leading across the Locks to Briarwood ran alongside the inner gate of North Shore to keep the two districts separated. If anybody living in the NW Quarters wanted to get out for the day, they had to first travel along the narrow strip of land bordering Edlewood Inlet into Uptown and Portside. Or they had to catch one of the express Monotrains that bypassed the high-and-mighty North Shore community that catered to the elite among the human community. Namely: those who wanted to live segregated from Otherkin.

The NW Quarters had never recovered from the World Shift. While Darktown had a lot of ruins and rubble, the NW Quarters was a labyrinth of dust and stone ruins. The few buildings remaining were shells, used by the Grungee gangs that ran the district. They were basically fallout shelters from the storms and from each other. But there was always news filtering out of the NW Quarters of buildings that had collapsed, trapping and killing occupants. But nobody in the city went into rescue mode. Seattle grudgingly accepted that it couldn't clean up the district, so it put it on permanent ignore.

As we scrambled up the embankment and over the bent guardrail, the snow began to fall harder. I shivered, my breath coming in puffs. The road leading toward the northwest boundary line dividing the NW Quarters from the Tremble was on a grade so steep that my legs ached at the very thought of the hike. The asphalt was cracked from years of neglect. The rumble boys liked to tear it up on back roads like this, and their studded tires and spiked slow-down prongs weren't kind to roadwork. Street races were illegal within the city limits but nobody was about to come up here and challenge the Grungees over a piece of torn-up asphalt.

"We've got perhaps a quarter mile before we reach the plateau that turns off to the Tremble," Elan said, her voice sounding as enthusiastic as I felt.

"In other words, suck it up and get moving." I sucked in a breath of cold air.

She followed suit. "My thoughts exactly. But have weapons prepared. We're close enough to the border that we *may* make it to the Tremble without meeting anybody who lives here, but I'm not going to bet on it."

I gently slapped my hand against my thigh

and my whip took form in my palm. Distancing myself from the others, I gave it a tentative crack. My entire side quivered, a flurry of spasms racing up and down my body, but I managed to keep it together.

"How do you feel?" Jason asked.

"Not great, but it's doable. But I think if we get into a tussle, I'll let you guys go first and I'll take up the rear."

"Do what you can, but don't hurt yourself any more than you have to," Elan said. "We'll do our best to keep out of any clashes." She set out, leading the way. I came next, with Jason beside me, and then Hans behind us.

We silently made our way up the steeply graded street, keeping to the far outer edge. The road curved from northwest to north, and to our left, the water below gave way to a deep ravine. The thicket was heavily wooded and I could smell the snow falling on cedar and fir as the wind picked up. The white noise of the snow rustling against the brambles and foliage, the constant swirl of the winds, lulled me into a wary but comfortable silence. The air was chill enough to pierce the lungs and nose, so I wrapped a scarf around my face, noticing the others were doing the same. We moved on, our footsteps muffled by the snow that covered the road.

We were near the top when a sudden roar of a gunning motor roared from the darkness above. Instinctively, we edged to the very side of the ravine as a blur of headlights came raging around the bend that led to the top of the plateau. The rumble car screeched around the bend, flashing out of the snowfall. Beside it, in the opposite lane, was its opponent. Both cars took the bend too wide, and not ten yards beyond us, the car in the wrong lane hit a patch of black ice and skidded to the side, the sound of metal screeching against metal breaking through the night. The vehicles were locked together, the impact sending them into a spin.

Out of control and unable to stop, the cars hit the guard railing about fifty yards down the road from where we had first climbed up the embankment. The rails were old and the rusted metal gave way as both cars careened through the bent metal, locked in battle as they poised for a single second teetering on the edge. Then, with another shriek, they toppled over the side to the rocks and water below.

"The rumble boys should have stayed home tonight," Elan said quietly.

"Should we try to help?" Even as he asked the question, Jason added, "Never mind. I know the answer already."

"They won't survive the icy water. There's no place on the rocks for their cars to land. Look if you like, but by now they're on their way to the bottom of the sound. I doubt if they could get out of their vehicles, as tangled up as they were." Elan turned back to the road. "Let's get moving in case any other fools decide to play chicken with their lives tonight."

I glanced over my shoulder one more time, but Elan was right. The rock embankment below wasn't wide enough to support one car, let alone two. The drivers were dead men the minute they hit that guardrail. We returned to our hike, and within a few minutes, we were standing on the plateau. Ahead, to the left, was a large stone wall, twenty feet high and as long as I could see. Along the face of the wall, a gate allowed entrance and exit, but even from here, I knew that nobody who went in there came out. At least, not without help. There were no guards because none were needed. The Tremble swallowed up people, absorbing them into the landscape. The few who managed to get out again were folk heroes.

To the right, a series of rubble-worn buildings and roads stretched into the fog and snow. Lights shone through the night from the NW Quarters, but they weren't beckoning and I knew they weren't there to guide strangers. *Lure* strangers, maybe, but guide? No.

"Shall we do it? We might as well head for the nearest entrance." Elan moved toward the nearest gate. Without anything else to add, the rest of us followed.

We were crossing the street when a car screeched around a corner, blocking our path. At first I thought it might be more of the rumble boys, looking for easy marks, but then another car eased in behind it, again appearing out of the fog. As the back doors opened and several burly boys appeared, I caught my breath. Their eyes shone in the darkness, crimson, sparkling in the night. One gave us a slow smile. Beneath the glow of the streetlight, I could see the tips of his fangs.

Oh freaking hell. As we began to back away, one step at a time, they surrounded us.

"Put down your weapons. You know you don't have the tools to kill us."

I slowly slapped the whip back on my leg. They were right. Even Elan's darts would only be able to hit one of them before the others swarmed. As we slowly raised our hands, I realized what a dangerous situation we were in. We were trapped in the NW Quarters without any hope of help, facing a nest of vampires.

Five vampires versus the four of us promised dismal odds. At least for us. For them? Not so bad. Vampires weren't often found outside of the Junk Yard or the Tremble or other dark shadowy places, and they certainly weren't welcome in most districts. Originally created by a magician during the skirmishes that became the Weather Wars, they'd been meant to be a super-race of warriors, but the government soon found out that their elite guardians weren't having much in the authority department and boom, so much for mageogenetics. They were rare, or at least *running into one* was rare. They had kept to their own until the past hundred years or so, but now they could be found crawling out of the woodwork, no longer skulking in the shadows.

The vamps were dressed in black suits, and even though it was night, two of them were wearing sunglasses. Most likely it was fashion, because light other than sunlight or UV lamps didn't faze them. I wasn't sure what a raging fire or a lightning bolt might do, but with the snow falling, I doubted we'd be having any good jolts driving down from the heavens tonight.

"What do you want?" Somebody had to speak first, so it might as well be me.

"You look mighty tasty. Fresh fare," the vamp on the left said. He looked like a typical Suit, except for the crimson glow of his eyes.

Fuck. We were *takeout*? I paused, glancing at the others. Elan gave me a cautious shake of the head, as did Jason. Hans just looked pissed.

"I'm sorry, but we don't have time for this. We're in a hurry. I'm on assignment for Hecate and I'm sure she would appreciate it if my friends and I weren't detained. Or hurt."

It wasn't strictly true, but she wouldn't berate me for namedropping to get out of serving as a blood bank for a hungry vampire. Besides, vamps tended to like Hecate, given her affinity for the night and the underworld. But I had to choose my wording carefully and hope that I didn't offend them. I was aching and in a bad mood, but even I knew that diplomacy was a keen necessity. Luckily, vamps weren't just top-of-the-chain predators. They had brains. They were originally created for intelligence and strength. Even with their ability to destroy, they were cunning enough to know when it was better to reason.

The leader hesitated.

"I'm a Theosian." This could backfire really easily, but the NW Quarters Grungees didn't like the vampires any more than they liked my kind, so maybe we'd get an "enemy of my enemy is my friend" vibe going.

"What are you doing here?" he finally said.

I glanced over at Jason, who was standing frozen. Vamps didn't mesh well with Otherkin, either. In fact, vampires pretty much didn't like anybody but themselves. Elan was silent as well. Hans, however, gave me an encouraging nod.

"We're headed out on the Tremble to rescue someone. The Devani exiled him there the other day. He was a pawn in their games. We want him back." I also happened to know just how little love anybody in the NW Quarters had for the Devani.

Another moment, and Head-Vamp motioned to

the car. "Get in. If your story checks out, we'll drive you back to the gate. But first, our sire's going to want to meet you. Let's get back to HQ, boys." And without further ado, they pushed and prodded us into their long black cars and we were whisked off through the rowdy streets of the NW Quarters.

Headquarters was apparently a bombed-out mess of rubble, though it was still along the edge of the Tremble. But the rubble was just a cover. As we approached, a hidden door opened, leading into a scrap heap of twisted stone and metal. The asphalt turned into concrete, sloping down. We were headed into an underground bunker, which made sense. Vampires could be struck down by sunlight, an unfortunate side effect that mirrored the legends for which they were named.

The vamps had divided us up. Elan and Jason were in the other car, Hans and I were together. Nervous, I glanced at the burly bodyguard. Hans must have sensed my worry because he took my hand and gave it such a gentle squeeze that I couldn't help but wonder. He could break hands if he squeezed hard enough.

It will be okay, he said in whisper-speak.

One of the vamps turned around and arched his eyebrows as he stared at us. "Worried, then?"

So vamps had exceptional hearing, too. That was news that might just come in handy later. I cleared my throat. "Not really, but I'm worried about our friend who's stuck out on the Tremble. I hope this doesn't take much time because Hecate's not going to be happy if I'm detained."

I wanted to text her. Surely Hecate wouldn't

leave me to the mercy of vampires. But if I made a move toward my phone, they'd probably get themselves in a lather. And Queet wasn't around to run back to tell her. So we were on our own for now.

"We'll get you to where you're going, *if* you're for real." He turned back around, and I motioned to Hans to keep quiet. We didn't need them eavesdropping on us.

I found myself holding my breath. I didn't trust the roof to hold up over our heads. After all, most of the buildings left in the NW Quarters were damaged, and none could possibly meet any structural codes required now.

Another moment and we parked beneath a decaying sign that had at one time been readable, but now was a rusted vision of its former self. The vamps got out and motioned for us to follow. The garage was small and in all likelihood hadn't started out as a garage but as the bottom floor of some building. Yellow lights illuminated the path toward the exit, and another series of bare yellow bulbs lit the way toward a door that looked to be heavy steel. There had been some retrofitting going on.

"This way." The vamp wasn't exactly rude, but he wasn't expending any effort to be polite, either. He started to give me a little shove, but I turned to glare at him and he paused, then pulled his hand back. So Hecate's name wielded some clout here after all.

The walls were dirty concrete but it was hard to tell what color they had been painted due to the yellow hue of the lights. I suspected they were either a light gray or a pale yellow. They also had large cracks running along them, which made me nervous. The last thing we needed was to be buried under tons of dust and concrete. I whispered a quick prayer that Gaia wouldn't set off another quake while we were down here.

We joined up with Elan, Jason, and the vamps from the other car and headed toward the metal door. It had a keypad entrance, and one of the vamps shielded it from our view as he tapped in the code. But I had excellent hearing, and whisper-speak wasn't limited to voices. I tried to home in on the tone of the buttons he pressed. I could hear the notes, and the four keys went in a descending order, high pitch, lower, lower still, and lowest. The door clicked and he pushed it open.

As we followed him into a corridor, it was a stark contrast to the soft yellow lights of the garage. The flickering fluorescents cast a bluish shadow over everything, and made the pale skin of the vamps even more grayish.

While vampires of mythology could mesmerize and all seemed so very beautiful, these boys seemed to have missed the boat on that. History said that vampires could hypnotize with a stare, but I had my doubts looking at the vamps who surrounded us. I wasn't sensing any magnetic charm so either the mageogenetics hadn't held true, or something was off base here.

I strained to remember my history lessons. Lore said that the techno-mages had missed the boat with vamps on the charm thing, but they *had* managed to buck the natural scheme of life. All vampires after that first failed attempt were, indeed, undead.

The original batch of genetically engineered soldiers had been bred to feed off blood, and their saliva contained a virus that both killed and resurrected their enemies. The idea had been to turn opponents into zombie-like warriors, under the control of their sires. But it hadn't worked out that way. The resulting fallout proved deadly as the newly turned vampires retained their free will and reasoning. They weren't mindless zombies and they didn't obey their masters. In fact, history said they bolted as soon as they came back to life.

The entire genetics plan had been scrapped, but not before damage was done. All vamps were infected with the virus, but only humans were resurrected into vampire-hood with it. The infection just killed Otherkin. Theosians were an unknown factor. There were too few of us to know what exactly happened. No matter which way you sliced it, vamps weren't buddies to anybody but themselves, and even *that* was suspect.

Jason, who had been silent up until now, suddenly paled and let out a gasp. He glanced over at me, alarm filling his eyes. Something must have occurred to him, but if he tried to tell me in whisper-speak, chances were the vampires would hear him. He twitched, and his breath was coming in short, shallow gulps.

We came to the end of the corridor, where another door and lock-pad waited. This time, the lock was thumbprint oriented. The vamp in charge pressed his thumb to it and the door clicked softly and swung open. As we followed him inside, the decor shifted so abruptly that for a moment it was hard for me to take in the difference.

We were still in a hallway, with doors to either side, but gone were the sterile tones of the fluorescent lights. Here, lush hues of red and black colored the walls. Great drapes hung from the ceiling. The tapestries looked vaguely Orieasian in design. The floor shifted from concrete to a sparkling tile, a diamond pattern in ivory, red, and black.

A distinct, spicy jasmine scent hung heavy in the air. I recognized the fragrance from Aliana the Spice Goddess, one of the Market vendors in Darktown. I bought my perfume from her and this scent was one of her signature blends. Which meant that Aliana had a connection with the vampires. *Just lovely*, but good info to have.

The corridor appeared to open out into a large room. As we approached, our guide turned around and gave us a fangy smile. "Listen well. I will tell you this once, and once only. Be polite, state your business when spoken to, and if your story checks out, our master may let you go. Lie and we'll find out quickly enough and ensure you never do again."

"What should we call him? Your master?" As I spoke, Jason stiffened again, his attention focused on the vamp.

He let out a gruff laugh. "I doubt you've heard of him, *yet*, though soon the entire city of Seattle will know his name. Kython's becoming quite popular, so when I take you in, I suggest you do your best to ingratiate yourself."

Kython—he was the vampire Shevron was worried about. Len was too interested in him. By the look in Jason's eye, I realized he had already figured this out. No wonder he was so on edge. But before I could say a word, our guide escorted us through the archway.

Chapter 12

The room was opulent. That was the only
word for it. Opulent and frighteningly expensive.
Silk and satin tapestries draped the walls, and
the furniture looked straight out of some art
museum, crafted in velvet and leather and
metallic embroidery. Everywhere, surfaces were
covered with bric-a-brac and art. Even I was
able to recognize them as original pieces, rather
than off some counterfeiting press. Everywhere I
looked, the room was a jungle of wealth, a show of
supremacy.

At the center, on a showpiece of a chair that
could easily pass as a throne, sat Kython. It was
easy to tell he was the heart of this place. I found
myself drawn to him and realized suddenly that he
was incredibly gorgeous. He was mesmerizing in a
way that his minions weren't.

With skin so pale, and eyes that burned a
brilliant crimson, it almost hurt to look at him.
Kython was the epitome of the vampires of legend,

rather than the vamps the history books talked about. For a moment I questioned all I had been taught about vamps. Were we just indoctrinated to believe we had created the creatures? Did they really have a supernatural background that went beyond mageogenetics? Because Kython in no way resembled what I expected.

He sprawled in the chair, one leg hanging over the arm. Dressed in black and white striped pants that made him look taller than he probably was, Kython wore a crimson shirt slid open to his navel. Silver suspenders glittered against the silken shirt. His long, dark hair fell to his waist, brushed smooth as silk, and he wore a black top hat banded with silver. His skin was white as porcelain, his lips as black as jet. He was an unliving statue in red, white, and black, so exquisite to look at that I couldn't tear my gaze away. He held reflective sunglasses in one hand, and in the other, he held a riding crop, which he lightly tapped against the arm of his chair.

"Well, well. So we have guests." His voice was smooth and rich.

I still couldn't look away. There was something special about Kython, all right. A shiver ran down my spine as I stared at him. He was dangerous and deadly, but it was so easy to see how he drew acolytes to his feet. I bet the women were lining up to offer themselves as bloodwhores in his service.

Beside me, Jason tensed. I reached out slowly, placing a hand on his arm. He stiffened, then relaxed just enough to tell me he wasn't about to go on the attack.

"I take it you're Kython?" I stepped forward, straightening my shoulders. My ribs protested but I had to put on the show of being in charge. Thank gods for my corset. Without it, I'd be two fucks away from losing it due to the pain.

"I am." He looked me up and down, his gaze lingering over my whip tattoo. "And you are?"

"They call me Fury. I'm a Theosian, bound to serve the Great Mother Hecate. I'm on a mission. I have to enter the Tremble. I'm charged with finding someone who was exiled there, thanks to the Devani. I need to find him before the Tremble takes its toll on him." I looked him straight in the eye. "Will you please allow us to go on our way?"

Kython tapped his crop against the back of the chair, staring at me for a moment. "That depends. Possibly. You serve Hecate, you say? What do you do for her?"

I exposed the tattoo on my neck. "I wear her mark," I said, shifting so he could see the triskelion of three snakes entwining. At the gleam in his eye, I quickly shook out my hair again, covering my neck. No use laying too much temptation in from of him. "I hunt down Abominations that come off the World Tree."

"But not vampires?"

I shook my head. "No. Not vampires."

"Tell me about this person you are out to save." He was toying with me. I could hear it in his voice. He wanted to prove his power, which pissed me off.

But I managed to remain civil. Diplomacy was king here, and I couldn't let him see that I was afraid of him. Respect was a good thing. Fear? Not so much.

"His name is Tam O'Reilly. He's—"

"*The Prince of UnderBarrow*?" This time, Kython straightened up, his feet hitting the floor. He let out a snort. "The Devani actually had the nerve to exile the Prince of UnderBarrow out on the Tremble? I'm surprised there hasn't been an outcry from Briarwood."

"That might not be too far from coming. We're hoping to avoid an incident." If Kython knew who Tam was, then perhaps we had more leverage. But his next question took me by surprise.

"What is this prince to you? There has to be more to this story." The vampire was staring directly at me and I knew I couldn't play dumb. He was able to read reactions better than I wanted to give him credit for.

I let out a slow breath and glanced at Jason, then Hans, both of whom nodded me on. "Tam is my lover. I'm his consort. He was dragged away the other night when we inadvertently got caught in a riot. He stepped between the Devani and me. He told me to leave before the Devani could get their hands on me."

"Because, they do so *love* collecting Theosians." His words held a hint of amusement mingled with irony. "Do you know how I know this?"

I slowly met his gaze again, not wanting to get caught up in his web. But instead of trying to mesmerize me, he was staring at me frankly. And right then, I knew. *Kython was a Theosian.* Somehow, he had been turned into a vampire.

"So we *aren't* immune to the effects?"

He let out a low chuckle. "Then, you understand me? Oh Fury, dear Hecate's avenger. Do you really believe everything you learned about vampires? Remember that the victors write the history books. Everything is always colored by the nature of the winner."

"True enough." I let out a long breath. "So the whole story about mageogenetics?"

"Vampires are no more engineered than is the sunset or the beauty of the stars." He leaned forward, resting his elbows on his knees as he held my gaze with those brilliant crimson eyes.

"Then how were you created, if the government didn't have a hand in engineering you?" Hans spoke up, shifting from one foot to the other. "I've heard the rumors before that it was a lie but thought they might just be conspiracy theories."

Kython turned his attention to Hans. After a moment, he said, "Another Theosian, if I'm not mistaken. And who are you bound to?"

"Thor." Hans was a man of few words.

"The Thunderer. Well then, you know the story of how we were created. But the reality is that the government discovered a nest of vampires and captured them. They did attempt to mimic the process of turning in order to create their super-soldiers, but it failed dismally. The creatures they created are neither vampire nor human, but a sub-race of dangerous mutants. But they are *not* vampires. Neither do they have our abilities. They drink blood, but also eat flesh and cannot turn others. We've been killing off the ones we find, but unfortunately, they breed."

"You mean, they have children?" The thought was so ugly that it made me cringe.

"If you can call them children. Their whelps are just as feral and dangerous as the parents, at least what young they don't eat. Like vampires, they're nocturnal. They live in caves, mostly, though a few inhabit the subterranean areas of cities. None of them can be reasoned with."

"What are they called?"

"We—the vampire community—call them ghouls. It's the most befitting name."

"So Theosians can be turned?"

Kython nodded. "Yes, we can. It's a horribly painful process, however, unlike with humans."

"Who were you bound to?" Hans asked.

Kython bared his fangs, smiling as he laughed. "Oh, that is a fitting question. But *were* is not the appropriate word. I was bound to Coyote, and I'm *still* bound to him even though I was turned into an actual vampire."

That fit. And Coyote wouldn't be likely to turn away one of his servants for being a vamp. "That doesn't surprise me," I said, then realized I'd spoken aloud.

But Kython just laughed as he leaned back against his chair. "True that. But I don't wish the process on any of my fellow Theosians. Humans can handle it, and they often end up happier than before. It's a harsh world for their kind. But with Theosians, not only is it painful but it leaves you feeling split. Coyote won't free me, so I must still answer to him, even though my nature pulls me otherwise."

I thought over what he said, and when I probed his energy, I could feel the pull he talked about. In that one moment, I felt a little bit sorry for him. He hadn't had a choice, either way, and he was caught between the lure of blood and the call of the gods. But perhaps that would be a plus for us. He knew what it was like to serve the Elder Gods. Maybe that would stir whatever empathy he had left.

"Then, will you please let us go? Every minute we stand here is another moment that Tam is in danger." I took a step forward, holding out my hands. Kython's guards immediately moved in, gently pushing me back away from the vampire.

Kython bit his lip, one of his fangs piercing the

skin. He didn't seem to notice. After a moment, he shrugged. "Very well. I'll let you go. But you owe me a favor. I'll collect later, and it won't be anything that would go against your grain. But remember, all of you, that I am letting you go free. You are *all* in my debt."

Before we could speak, he motioned us away. Jason opened his mouth but I grabbed his arm, shaking my head. We couldn't afford a showdown here.

Jason glared at me, but pressed his lips together in a thin, white line. Elan touched his arm lightly. He shook his head, but deflated. Kython proceeded to ignore us as his guards motioned for us to follow them. We returned to the cars, then without further word they drove us to the border of the Tremble. The walls were high, but narrow arches offered entry every five hundred yards or so, unfettered by gates or fences.

As we stepped out of the cars, the dark vehicles silently backed away and vanished down the street. We stared at the arch. It stood open, with no visible means to keep people in or out. The sky gleamed with the silvery wash that came with midnight snow and we could see the faint outline of landscape through the entry.

"I guess we go in?" There really wasn't much to say about Kython. Right now, our focus needed to be on the Tremble, and on Tam. We would have time enough later to dissect everything that just happened.

"Right. Then, let's get moving." Elan took the front, motioning Jason to her side. With Hans and me following, we stepped through the gates, into the Tremble.

The Tremble was like one of the Broken, only in the form of land.

We quickly discovered that the arches leading into it were actual power vortexes. As we crossed through, there was a definite shift, as though we stepped from one world into another. Once inside, the Tremble took over and everything that made sense went away.

The landscape took on a surreal edge, as though someone had taken the NW Quarters with its bombed-out buildings and heaps of rubble and painted it over everything with a watercolor wash before folding up the edges and giving the landscape a couple of twists.

Nothing settled right. Look at a pile of rubble and suddenly, it would shift, turning upside down. Stare at the shell of a building long enough and you'd realize that it folded in half somewhere in the middle, and was leaning to the left at a torturous angle. Stairs led up to the sides of walls, off-center from doors. The streets had reverted to dirt and grass, and snow covered everything with a cloak of brilliant white that was too crisp and too clean. Angles were too harsh, curves too smooth, and nothing jived right. It was enough to give a person vertigo.

Every once in a while someone would wander by, almost always one of the Broken. They paid no attention to us, just slowly moved along on their way. Live in the land of the surreal too long, and the mind bends to fit the landscape. But the human mind wasn't meant to view more than three dimensions—at least not visually—and the

struggle led to breakdowns. And breakdowns led
to the Broken.

My stomach twisted, a knot forming as I tried
to find something that made sense. Even the air
seemed off. Oh, I could breathe, but nothing felt
tangible. And yet, everything was *too* vivid, *too*
graphic, *too* edgy.

"Holy fuck," Hans whispered under his breath.
"What is this place? How are we going to find Tam
before the Tremble drives *us* over the edge?"

"I thought I could track him, and if things
weren't so twisted, I could." Elan looked around,
a hopeless tone creeping into her voice. "I'm not
sure where to start. *How* to start."

Jason glanced at the sky. "I'll take wing and see
if I can spot him from above. I think flying over the
Tremble might be easier than walking through it.
The disorientation might not hit me so hard from
up there, and I can scan for Tam faster."

"Are you sure?" Elan frowned at the clouds
that had socked in. "I have a feeling this storm has
barely started, and the energy of the Tremble must
extend upward as well. We just don't know how
far."

It was snowing hard now, and even with the
silver sheen reflecting between surface and clouds,
the night felt close around us. I shivered again, my
muscles aching, and the pain in my side increasing
with the chill.

"Before we go much farther, I need to apply
another layer of the All-Heal Sarinka gave me. The
movement is getting to me." I didn't care about
side effects, at least not at this moment. I needed
to be clearly focused and not distracted by the
throbbing in my side. It was as though somebody
was using a rounded baton to jab me over and

over.

"Then we'll stop here for a rest. You apply your ointment while I fly up to see what I can see. Here's a good place to sit." Jason motioned toward a nearby boulder that looked more convoluted than it should, but as I cautiously touched it, the rock felt solid beneath my fingers.

I sat down, then opened my bag as Hans set it beside me. Digging out the salve, I without further ado unhooked my corset, wincing as a muscle decided to spasm because of the movement.

Elan took the jar of salve from me and knelt beside me. "Here," she said softly. "Let me do this. You just breathe and relax."

"That's harder than it sounds," I said, smiling through the ache. Truth was, the corset helped me keep it together. Without it, the bone-weary throbbing set in. But as Elan spread the salve over my bruised skin, the deep pulse began to lighten and my breath came easier. Finally, she finished. Shivering, I let her help me fasten myself back into the corset, then slid my jacket back over the top. The pain was still present but the salve was a wonderful topical and I leaned back, wishing I could take a nap.

I closed my eyes, but images of Tam floated through my mind and though I tried to push the worry away, it refused to budge. I knew full well that I wouldn't be able to sleep until we found him, not without the aid of Sleep-Eze.

"Here. You need this." Hans held out a chocolate bar.

I took it, glancing at the brand. I was wrong. It wasn't a chocolate bar, it was one of the meal rations they handed out to factory workers in the Metalworks. The bars kept them at it for long hours when the production lines were in full steam.

The Corp-Rats had managed to push through laws eliminating required breaks for shift workers, although companies were expected to give a nominal twenty-minute lunch. Fifteen minutes twice a day doesn't seem like much, but when you took it away, production went up, but standards went down. The meal bars were super-charged with drugs to clear the mind and boost performance, and they were standard freebies at a lot of the factories now. The Metalworks was littered with wrappers during the busier seasons of the year.

I stared at it, wrinkling my nose. They weren't particularly tasty, but they worked. I tore open the wrapper and bit into it, chewing away.

Jason stood back. "I'm ready. I won't go too far."

"Please don't. We don't want to have to come looking for you, too." Elan gave him a nod, taking his gear from him.

"Believe me, I don't want to get lost out here anymore than you want me to." With that, Jason shimmered, and out of the flash of smoke, a great hawk appeared. Without a word, he flew up, spiraling into the sky.

I watched him go, silently eating the meal bar. As I swallowed the last bite, I had to admit, bland or not, the food packed a punch. I was already feeling stronger.

"I wouldn't want a steady diet of these, but I have to say, that does the trick."

Hans nodded. "I use them when I'm out tracking a case, or when Thor wants me to take on some hare-brained scheme. He's like that, you know. He doesn't always think before acting. Or ordering *me* to act." But he was grinning as he said it, and I had the feeling Hans and Thor had managed some pretty interesting shenanigans in their time.

Elan was watching Jason as he flew away. She shaded her eyes from the falling snow, turning as he finally flew out of sight. "I hope he's cautious. We really don't know how the Tremble might affect him in hawk-shifter form. I'd hate to see him get vertigo and go tumbling to the ground."

"I hadn't even thought of that, so thank you for that visual." I glanced at her, but she just gave me a faint smile.

"You're welcome. I wouldn't worry about it much, but the truth is, none of us know much about the Tremble so we should watch every step we take here."

"Well, I don't even want to think about the possibility of him taking a nosedive out of the air." I wiped my hands on my shorts, then pushed myself to my feet. "Should we stay here? Do you think he can find us if we continue to search?"

"I'd advise against wandering off. But I think—" Elan paused, holding a finger to her lips. "Do you hear that?" she mouthed.

I closed my eyes and listened. There. In the distance, a faint noise. A whine, like a motor revving at a high speed, but without much power behind it. I stood, poised with Hans and Elan, waiting. The noise grew louder as a whirl of snow funneled up from the ground, swirling to create a thick white mist. Combined with the falling flakes, it created a whiteout in the immediate vicinity. The inability to see what was coming knotted my stomach and I ducked behind the boulder on which I'd been sitting. Elan and Hans joined me.

Then, high beams pierced the veil of misting white, and an odd vehicle skidded to a stop near us. It was an aereocar, a combination mini-car and drone, with a giant propeller atop the roof. I frowned as the door opened and out popped some *thing*.

Not human, the creature wasn't an animal either. Like the landscape around us, she seemed oddly familiar and yet oddly out of sync. Bipedal, covered with a light sheen of fur, her face was mildly cat-shaped, the eyes distinctly feline, but the nose and the lips were human, and the body shape was long and lithe, but humanoid. By the shape of the breasts, I figured the creature was female, but everything else was lost in the flurry of the storm. She appeared to be wearing a loose jumpsuit of some sort.

I stiffened, hand on thigh ready to awaken my whip. I didn't want to make a move that could be seen as threatening, but I wasn't about to face down someone who could be dangerous without a weapon in my hand. Elan slowly eased her bow up but did not aim yet, and Hans straightened his shoulders, hammer ready.

"There's no need to prepare your weapons," the creature said. Her words echoed, reverberating before I could understand them.

"Who are you?" I eased my hand away from my thigh, but remained cautious.

"My name is Rasheya. I'm here to rescue you. The storm's rising. You can't be out here when the Starklings arrive. They'll devour you down to the bone, and they come at night, when the storms appear." She glanced at the sky. "They'll be here soon."

"Wait, they come by air? Our friend's up there!" Something about her told me she was speaking the truth. "He's a hawk-shifter."

"Head northwest as fast as you can. Follow my tracks while they're still visible. There's an underground bunker near here. Go, and I will take to the air and find your friend." She turned, and in one swift jump, leaped back into her vehicle. The propeller started and, even in the storm, she lifted off.

I blinked. If the government knew about her aereocar, she'd be in deep shit.

But Hans clapped my shoulder, nodding to the tracks. "Let's get moving. I believe her. I don't know why, but I do."

"She speaks the truth. I can tell. Whoever— *whatever* these Starklings are, they're dangerous. I heard the fear in her voice." And with that, Elan forged ahead, plowing through the rapidly accumulating snow.

I swung in behind her, and Hans behind me. As much as I wanted to stick around and wait for Jason, the urgency in Rasheya's voice touched tinder to spark and I had no desire to be here when the Starklings descended. But I prayed to Hecate that the cat-woman found Jason before anything else did.

Chapter 13

What we had thought was a storm was actually just a precursor. The real storm hit as we followed Rasheya's tracks. The snow began to fall in thick, heavy flakes that obscured our sight. I was actually relieved. It was easier to focus when my mind wasn't trying to make heads or tails of what I was seeing. The surreal landscape slipped into a dreamlike one, and we trekked on, trudging through the endless blanket of white. I blinked, realizing I had no clue of how long we had been moving. I felt swathed in layer after layer of gauze.

How long have we been walking? I can't remember. When did we enter the Tremble? Was it today? Yesterday?

I struggled to remember, but my memories were vague, shifting with the blowing snow. Every time I thought I had an answer, it suddenly vanished, jarred out of place by another thought and then, suddenly, I couldn't remember the question and panicked.

"Hans? Hans?" I glanced around, looking for him and Elan. For a moment they seemed to have disappeared, but then I saw them, moving between the flakes, eyes wide. "Hans, I'm scared."

Elan hurried over to my side and took my hands. "Breathe. Close your eyes and count to ten, and breathe slowly."

I obeyed. Again, time seemed to vanish, but there was a point where I suddenly felt like I was back in my body. I slowly opened my eyes.

"What?"

"The Tremble. This is a dangerous space for sanity, Fury. Which is why we have to find Tam and get out of here." She squeezed my fingers, the warmth of her skin flowing through me like a potion as it revived me and washed away the fear. I gazed into her eyes, wondering if she shared Tam's magic.

Hans exhaled, then sucked in another long breath before opening his eyes. He looked shaken. "I hate this place," he said. "I hate it and I'm never coming back once we get the fuck out of here." He scanned the skies, blinking as the flakes coated his lashes. "I wonder if Jason's all right."

"I don't know. I hope so." I glanced around. I suddenly remembered Rasheya's warning. "We need to move. Whatever the Starklings are, she said they come in on the storms. I'd rather not find out the hard way just how dangerous they are."

We trudged forward again. It was getting difficult to follow Rasheya's tracks, the snow was filling them up so fast, but we could still see the faint lines created by her aereocar through the blanket of white covering the Tremble.

I glanced at Elan and Hans. "I suggest we walk three abreast. The energy of the Tremble is beginning to affect all of us and we don't want to lose track of one another."

My legs were burning with the cold, but the pain took my mind off my sides and arms. I moved to the center to give Elan better latitude with her bariclore. We plunged forward into the storm. We had been walking for a while longer when there was a flutter nearby. I froze, my skin crawling with the same feeling I got when I was near an Abomination.

"Something's near and it's bad. So bad." I wanted to turn and run—I had never felt quite so overwhelmed, but the sounds were coming from all sides now. I slapped my thigh and my whip came off in my hand. Elan raised her crossbow, and Hans his hammer as we turned to stand, back to back, to form a triangle of protection.

A flicker here. A flutter there. A whisper of sound all around. They're here. They're here and they're hungry.

The whispers echoed in my mind as I raised my whip, the light of it glowing with a comforting fire. I unsheathed my dagger with my left hand, poised and ready, all thoughts of the pain gone as adrenaline fueled my body.

And then, they came, swarming in. Birds with razor-sharp beaks, but twisted in ways no bird should be. Their wings beat so fast they were surrounded by a blur of movement, and their brilliant eyes shone, a gaudy candy-colored pink. They were black, like crows, but their heads and eyes were oversized and as they darted toward us, I realized they were trying to peck our faces. Elan shouted as one dove to the side and stabbed her wrist. As the blood began to flow, the swarm of Starklings went into a frenzy, creating a massive flurry that mingled with the snow to blot out everything else.

I raised my whip, pulling away from Hans and Elan so I wouldn't hit them, and brought it down through the center of the swarm with a massive crack. The fire blazing off the thong met the moisture in the snow and set up a web of sparks that raced through the nearest Starklings. They shrieked as the lightning crackled along their wings, frying them. I let out a battle scream, stabbing one with my dagger that was near enough to reach. As my blade pierced the body, the Starkling exploded, spraying my hand and dagger with a viscous blue liquid that burned like liquid nitrogen.

My first instinct was to drop to the ground. I plunged my hand in the snow, but the cold only made the pain worse. Without thinking, I thrust my hand in the air, pulling every drop of heat I could to me. The faint glow of fire began to surround my fingers, soothing the ache, and as the relief grew, so did the flames. I grew the ball of flame surrounding my hand. As the fireball increased, I turned to the swarm of Starklings. They were attacking Hans and Elan, who were doing their best to shield their eyes while fighting the monstrous birds.

With a sudden fury, I straightened my shoulders and raised my whip, the fire racing from my fingertips through my chest and into my other arm.

I channeled the flame into the whip until it was a blaze of light. Raising it, I began to swirl it around my head, faster and faster. Flames roared off of the lash. And then, I struck toward the swarm, aiming for the central Starkling who seemed bigger than the others.

As the tip of my whip hit the bird I shouted, "Drop and cover your face!"

Elan and Hans obeyed without question. The resulting explosion covered us with the frozen fire. I had crouched to protect my legs as well, and while a few drops hit my skin, I managed to mostly keep clear.

I glanced up to see a fair-sized hole in the swarm, but we were still vastly outnumbered. I wasn't sure how long we could keep this up. Eventually, they'd break through our defenses and we'd be so much bird food. As fresh recruits started filling in the hole, it struck me that we might not make it out of this.

Hans let out a roar and the clouds echoed him back with thunder, momentarily stunning the birds, but within a few seconds they recovered before we could escape from them.

"Elan, have you got anything to help?" I could summon more fire but the creatures kept coming and I knew I didn't have enough reserves to take them all on.

She shook her head, shooting another bird that was far enough away that its deadly blood didn't spray all over us. Hans clobbered another, and yet another, and I pushed to my feet again, aiming for one at the edge of my whip's reach.

One of the Starklings dove in and pecked my forehead. I shrieked, stabbing at it with my dagger but came dangerously close to stabbing myself. Hans managed to grab the bird and wrestle it away from my forehead, tossing it to the ground where he smashed it with his hammer. The spray of blood hit us full force and I clenched my teeth, trying to ignore the sudden onslaught of pain. We went in swinging, Elan switching to a thin, long dagger when she ran out of bolts.

Then, as the swarm rose up as one, ready to swoop down on us, a *whoop whoop whoop* sliced through, adding to the cacophony of storm and swarm. *Rasheya, in her aereocar*. She dove straight through the swarm, scattering the Starklings who apparently decided they'd rather find prey that wasn't airborne. As the birds circled, then headed back in the direction from which they'd come, I dropped to my knees, feeling totally wiped.

Rasheya jumped out, and I saw that there was a large hawk on the seat beside her. *Jason*. Thank gods she had found him.

"We need to get undercover before they come back with reinforcements. You're about two hundred yards from the entrance. Head directly that way." She pointed to the north. "You'll find a large pile of rubble under the snow. Look for a trap-door handle. I'll be right behind you. I'm going to keep watch and make certain you aren't attacked from behind."

She jumped back in her aereocar and slowly began driving behind us as we headed toward sanctuary. And hopefully, safety.

The trap door was easy to find with Rasheya's directions, and by the time we opened it, she had vacated her aereocar. With Jason in tow, who was now back in his human form, she joined us. Up on the Tremble, her appearance had vacillated, but here, she was definitely female, though I still wasn't sure if she was a shifter of some sort.

The door led to a tunnel that was about twenty feet deep. The ladder down was an easy climb, ending at the start of a corridor. As I looked down the dimly lit passage, it wasn't hard to tell that whatever this place was, it had been here a long time and probably pre-existed Rasheya and whoever she lived with. The energy was different too, as though the chaos of the Tremble couldn't penetrate through the layers of earth over our heads.

"Thank you." Elan was studying the passage as we moved through the ancient brick. "We were almost out of luck."

"Not a problem. I happened to be on patrol and saw you wandering past. It's obvious you don't belong here, so I decided to check you out." Rasheya's voice had a cheerful note about it, though it was hard for me to understand how anybody could be cheerful out here.

"Where are we?" Hans asked, looking around. He was covering our back as Rasheya led the way. Elan and Jason were in front of me.

"Welcome to Asylum. This is one of the few safe places on the Tremble. My grandparents discovered the passages. When they realized that the energy can't penetrate down here, they and their kin turned it into a safe haven. You don't want to be out in the open during storms. The Starklings wait for them, both rain and snow. They're quiet in summer so we take advantage of their absence to find and store food." She glanced back at me. I was getting used to her cat-like appearance, although she still seemed a disturbing blend.

"Are you a shifter?" I decided to be blunt. This wasn't the moment for subtlety, given the race against time to find Tam.

Rasheya laughed. "No. I'm not. Nor am I Theosian. I'm one of the Mudarani. I don't think there's much written about us. We don't change form."

As we hurriedly made our way through the winding passage, I wracked my brain for any memory of anything about the Mudarani, but came up empty. And it would have been rude to ask the others if they knew anything about her kind, at least in front of her.

Another few twists and turns through the brick passage and we came to a T-junction, with a door to the right, a door to the left, and a door straight ahead. She turned left and we followed her through into another passage, then stopped in front of the first door we came to.

"Here we are. I've brought you to the visitors' center where we keep all those seeking asylum. I'm one of the intake specialists, so I'll be taking your story and figuring out where we can place you."

It was then that I realized she thought we had been exiled here. We entered the room, which contained a large table surrounded by chairs, a sideboard with a water pitcher, a bowl of apples, and a tray with crackers and cheese on it. A large monitor hung on the wall. I gratefully dropped into a chair, groaning slightly as my side let out a twinge.

"Are you injured? I can call a medic." Rasheya seemed so open that I felt like shaking her. I knew they were probably cautious, and she most likely had somehow pinpointed us as friendly sorts, at least to her. But I wanted to warn her not to be so open and helpful.

"Thanks, I have salve for my injuries. I'm just

sore and likely to be that way for a while."

"Why did the Devani exile you here? What crime did you commit against the Conglomerate?" She pulled out a tablet, surprising me.

"Does that work here? I thought electronics didn't work out on the Tremble."

"We're below the Tremble now. The magic that permeates the space only saturates the ground to a depth of about five feet. That's why Asylum is underground. We're actually out of range of the magical effects that distort reality aboveground, and down here, tablets and phones work, though we have them all routed through an intranet rather than linked to the outside. All news is brought in via a server that's proxied to hell and back. We have to avoid the authorities tracing any feeds back to us. We need the Corporatocracy to remain oblivious to us or they might try to come in and shut us down. At this point, they believe we're all a scattered bunch of the Broken."

I glanced at Jason, then let out a soft sigh. "We're not exiles. We're actually here on a rescue mission. We're looking for a friend of ours who was caught in a raid. The Devani sentenced him to a year's exile and dumped him here. We had no clue what to expect once we crossed the borders. None of us had ever heard of the Starklings, let alone the Mudarani."

Rasheya paused, her assessing stare sliding over us. After a moment she nodded. "You're telling the truth. Now and then the Devani sends in a warlock to infiltrate."

"I'm no oath breaker," Jason said. "I'm a magician, but I'm no oath breaker."

"I know. I hold my position as an intake officer because I can sense lies. And I sense nothing but truth from the four of you." Rasheya pushed aside her tablet. "Tell me who you're looking for. He might have come through here."

"Tam O'Reilly, the Prince of UnderBarrow." I told her what had happened, and how Hecate had discovered what the Devani did with him.

She smiled softly. "He's your mate, isn't he? I can tell."

I blinked. "Yes, we are lovers. And I'm worried sick about him. We all are."

"Let me go through the files to see if anybody reported him coming through here. Meanwhile, I can't invite you into the heart of Asylum unless you join us, but you are free to stay here and rest and eat. The door there leads to the bathroom," she said, pointing to one of two side doors. "I'll be back in a little while. You can't go looking for him while the storm is raging, anyway. The Starklings are thick during winter, and they always come with the storms. In fact, I think they're created out of the energy."

As she left the room, I rubbed my head, once again trying to figure out how long we had been out here on the Tremble. Time ran differently, much like in UnderBarrow. I leaned my head down on my arms and closed my eyes, wanting nothing more than to take a nap.

"How long have we been searching?" Hans asked, sounding as weary-worn as I felt.

"Hours, I guess. It was near midnight when Kython found us in the NW Quarters. I have no clue how long it's been since then," Jason said. "I can't read time right here. Usually, I'm a pretty good judge, but the moment we crossed the border, all that went out the window. The distortion that permeates the area also plays havoc with our senses."

Rasheya appeared again. "I think we found your friend. We have him here. I should warn you, he was injured by the Starklings and he's still pretty out of it. But come, see if you can identify him."

My heart thudded in my ears as I jumped to my feet, my weariness forgotten. "How injured?"

"Follow me." She wouldn't say any more as she led us through the other side door. We hurried along yet another brick corridor almost indistinguishable from the one through which we had entered Asylum. I noticed numbers were located near the ceiling every ten yards or so. They were four-digits, and in descending order. We were under 2832.

"Locations?" I pointed to the numbers.

She nodded. "We have to keep track, given there are miles of tunnels in Asylum. We keep to belowground mostly. When you get out on the Tremble itself, reality starts bending rapidly, and it's easy to get lost. Those of us on the Recon-Team have trained for years to be able to handle it. But down here, it's easy to get lost just because of the labyrinth of tunnels. So, we have a detailed location system."

"How long have you been here?" I noticed a lot more doors and side tunnels branching off from this corridor. There were actually people wandering the hallways here. They gave us cursory glances, but no one stopped to say anything.

Rasheya shrugged. "I was born here. The Mudarani are born from the side effects of the Tremble, much like you Theosians emerge from the Sandspit's magical interactions with your mothers' DNA. When they started using the

Tremble as a place to keep the unwanted, the Corp-Rats engendered far more than a holding colony. And they never came out here to find out what's really going on, though we always keep watch." She paused, then shook her head and stopped talking. "Through here, please."

She led us through a door at location 1143, and we found ourselves in a medical wing. The main hall was reminiscent of a hospital, though the equipment we passed was out of date. But outdated or not, the machines appeared to be working, even if it wasn't the latest technology. Nurses crossed the hall, reading charts, talking with one another, carrying trays with meds on them. I had a feeling that the medical unit saw a lot of cases.

"This is our hospital. As you can guess, there's more danger than we know how to deal with. Another thing to be aware of, besides the Starklings and the Packravagers and the carnivorous plants, is that the Tremble shifts and changes. You can be walking along one moment and a crack in the earth will open up without warning. Or you might be entering a building and then the door vanishes and you find yourself trapped inside a wall. Of course, the latter is an instant death warrant. Nobody can survive that."

The thought of being caught inside a materializing wall was petrifying. "Does the reverse hold true? Has someone been caught when some place they're in dematerializes?"

She hung her head, nodding. "Yeah, actually. One of my comrades—one of the Recon-Team members—was in an aereocar when it vanished out from beneath her. She was flying too low, and got caught in the energy field of the Tremble. She fell to her death." The tone of her voice told me that her friend had been more than just a work partner.

Jason was frowning. I doubted he'd noticed the inflection in her voice. "So, the way it seems is that the energy surrounding the Tremble extends a certain distance above- and belowground?"

Rasheya gave him a nod. "It does. And it varies depending on where you're at. We've never found it extending into Asylum, but there's always the chance. So we keep a close eye out and make regular sweeps. Here we are."

She stopped in front of a windowed door. "You wouldn't believe how long it took our ancestors to turn these tunnels into viable living spaces. But, they managed. My grandparents were part of the original Recon-Team after Asylum was set up."

After we found Tam, I really wanted to sit down with Rasheya and have a long talk with her about the nature of Asylum and her life here.

Hans must have been thinking the same thing, because he said, "Question. Why do you stay here? If you can build Asylum and keep it going, then why do you all stay?"

A veiled shadow crossed her face. She brushed her hand over her eyes. "Because when you are born on the Tremble, or when you stay here too long, you can't leave. Those who try get sick and die if they don't return. If you can escape before you've been here too long, you'll be all right, but stay longer than a couple weeks and it changes you. I was born here. I can never leave."

Before we could say anything, she opened the door and we followed her into the room. There, unconscious and lying beneath a heavy cover, was Tam.

Chapter 14

He was under a heavy green blanket, his eyes closed, his hands folded on his chest. For the briefest of seconds I thought he might be dead, but then I heard the faint hiss of breath as his chest rose ever so slowly. I rushed forward, pushing past Rasheya to stand by his side. As I cautiously lifted his hand in mine, the warmth of his body flooded through me and I could feel the life inherent in his heart. He would live. That much I knew.

Rasheya joined me, standing on the other side as Jason, Hans, and Elan gathered around the foot of the bed. "I found him on a recon-mission yesterday. He had fainted. Starklings were moving in to devour him—they don't wait till you're dead. I chased them off and brought him back. We had no clue who he was. He's woken a couple of times, but seems withdrawn."

"I can tell you why," Elan said. "When one of the Fae are wounded, especially the Bonny Fae, they go inward to heal. He's in a deep healing coma and will wake when he's well enough to stand. By the looks of him, I'd say it won't be long."

I leaned close. Coma or not, I had to speak to him. "Tam. Tam? It's me, Fury. We found you, love. We came to rescue you and we're going to take you home."

"You should stay through the night. The storm is only getting worse and you can't take him till he wakes, anyway. Rest and eat, then we'll help you find your way out."

I looked around for something resembling a clock. "What time is it? We've lost all sense of time while in here."

"It's seven a.m., outer time."

That meant we had been going all night. "It would be best if we slept till night. If we head out during the day, there's a better chance the Devani will notice us once we leave the Tremble. That's the last thing we want. We need to get back to Darktown in one piece, and take Tam to UnderBarrow so their healers can look after him." I glanced around. "Can we rest in here with him? I don't like the idea of being split up again."

Rasheya nodded, a somber look on her face. "I'll have pallets brought in for you. We can offer you food and warm blankets. We'll do our best to escort you back to the border of the Tremble, but I'm afraid that's as far as we can go."

"We have a boat waiting for us. I hope Laren's still there," Elan said. "My brother will sail us back to the Peninsula of the Gods. But going through the NW Quarters isn't wise. Neither would be crossing through North Shore or Uptown. Even Croix, at this point, is suspect."

"The Devani are moving." Rasheya turned at the door. "Don't be surprised if the Corp-Rats are making a play for more power. They forget the

World Shift and all that happened. It seems long past to them. They assume that Gaia won't move against them again. It's a dangerous world and growing more so."

I thought of the Order of the Black Mist. With Lyon and his group on one side, and the Corp-Rats on the other, it was inevitable there would be a clash at some point. The question was, would we be ready for it, and able to survive? Then, a thought struck me cold.

"Can you imagine what would happen if Lyon and the Order of the Black Mist decided to unleash the power of the Tremble and blanket the land with it? Could they even do so? If you want to talk about chaos, that would do it."

Rasheya gave me a blank look. "Lyon? The Order of the Black Mist?"

"Nothing. Never mind." I shook my head. "I hope I'm just coming up with random horrors. Go. We'll wait here."

As she withdrew from the room, I slumped in the chair nearest Tam's bed. I wanted him to wake up. I wanted to press my lips against his, to feel him warm in my arms. But I was afraid of hurting him, or disturbing the healing sleep he was immersed in. I restrained myself, simply holding his hand to my cheek and resting my head on the side of his bed as I sat there.

Rasheya returned with several men who looked to be Mudarani as well, all carrying pallets and blankets for us. As they arranged them around the room, I joined her as she arranged trays filled with cheese and fruit. Two other women joined us, a younger one carrying bread and an older one who brought in a tureen of soup. Both women looked a lot like Rasheya.

Rasheya noticed my look. She smiled. "May I present my sisters. Taya is the eldest, and Feranya is my younger sister. They work here in the hospital."

I held out my hand but Taya ignored it, giving me a friendly yet aloof nod. Feranya dipped into a quick curtsey before shyly stepping back. She looked to be pre-teen, and she tucked one finger in the side of her mouth, chewing on her nail. The faint sheen of light fur stood out on her face. It was then that I also noticed pale whiskers emerging from the sides of their noses. They were more cat-like than I first thought.

"So the Mudarani aren't shifters. Or Weres, I assume. But you resemble cats. You said that the energy of the Tremble is responsible for your race, but do you think there might be any connections between you and the Jagulins?" It seemed there might be some connection. But the Jagulins were shifters, come to think of it.

Rasheya shook her head. "No, we're very different. I don't suppose the Mudarani will ever fully know how our species began and I suppose it doesn't really matter. I have no idea if we have any relatives in other countries, but we're pretty much clustered in small areas throughout the Americex Corporatocracy that are similar to the Tremble. We keep to ourselves, and if the government knows of our existence, they haven't said anything yet."

I thought about my chip and how afraid it had made me when I was young. And how now, with it altered, I was forever trying to stay several steps away from the authorities. "Are you afraid they'll find out?"

Rasheya glanced at her sister Feranya, who shivered, shaking her head slightly. "We try not to dwell on that. For one thing, coming out on the Tremble to find us? Not easy, even for them. But there are things about our race of which we do not speak. Not to strangers, even ones who understand our need for secrecy." She held my gaze. "I know your kind are prized by the government, and watched. And I know your chip has been altered. Your Bonny Prince talks in his sleep. You'd best tell him watch his tongue when he wakes, lest he talk around unfriendly sorts."

I caught my breath. What if he had talked where the Devani could hear him? Would they be looking for me even now? I turned to Jason. "Do you think I should worry?"

He didn't flinch. "We can't be sure yet. But when we get back, I suggest you hide out in UnderBarrow for a few days until we know for sure. There's a good chance they would find out about your connection with Dream Wardens and we don't want them trapping you there." *They might be there even now* was what he wasn't saying.

Rasheya pointed to the food. "Eat. You should eat."

"How will we get Tam back?" I settled in at the table and picked up a roll, tearing the soft yeasty bread in half. I layered cheese and meat in the bun as Hans, Jason, and Elan joined me.

Elan shrugged. "If he's still unconscious, we will carry him. My brother can contact Damh Varias for help once the boat nears the Peninsula of the Gods. We have a short-distance encrypted communications relay." She carved off a slice of cheese and neatly swallowed it. "Good food. Thank you. I imagine you don't have much extra out here."

Rasheya shrugged. "We share what we have. Some seasons are lean, others are flush. We've learned how to store food for the former, and enjoy the latter without going overboard. We can grow a few crops, though there's no telling what the Tremble's going to do to them. One year our tomatoes were as large as bowling balls. We made a lot of sauce that year. Another year, we barely saw them the size of marbles."

I thought of what she had said—that those adapted to the Tremble couldn't leave it. "Then, you're stuck here. So you have to make the best of what you have."

"That we do."

"Once we make it out, I'd like to repay you by sending supplies. What can you most use?" I didn't have much, but I was determined to hit up Hecate in order to repay them. Rasheya had saved our lives. She had saved Tam.

Feranya, as shy as she was, spoke up. "We can use bandages. We're running low and have nobody on the outside at this point to send them in. We also need baby supplies. Staples. I guess. Anything helps." As the girl trailed off, Rasheya pulled Feranya to lean against her, holding her gently by the shoulders.

"She's right. We can use just about anything you care to smuggle in."

Elan finished her sandwich. "My brother and I run the boats. We'll manage it. The problem is finding a way to get the supplies into the Tremble to you. Do you have a way of keeping time with the outside world? Maybe we can set up a meet."

"Down here, yes. If we set up a time we can probably manage it. There are tunnels to the cliffs beneath the Tremble. We could lower a ladder to a boat snuggled up against the coast. The problem is, we can't go down to get the supplies, so we'd need to rig a method of bringing them up." But even as she spoke, a ray of hope filled the Mudarani's eyes.

"We can do this. It will be our thanks for your efforts. We will bring everything we can, because we may not get another chance for a while."
Elan sat back, pursing her lips. "Can we leave through the same route? It occurs to me that the journey back the way we came will be even more dangerous."

"Yes. We can manage it. But you should rest now," Taya said. "The trip through the tunnels to the cliff entrance should be safe, but there are creatures who manage to break through our outer labyrinth, as we call it. If we are cautious, we should pass through without a problem. Especially with a larger party."

"Starklings?" It occurred to me that the Starklings had put me off birds forever.

"No, but just as bad. A few lycanthropes, and other creatures. But as Taya said, we may not see hide nor hair of any of them if we take enough people with us." Rasheya stood, glancing at the pallets on the floor. "Get some sleep. Tonight, we'll lead you through the tunnels. Your boat may not be there, but you will be able to use your phones if someone eases out on the ledge over the water. You can call the boat then."

And with that, she and the others took their leave.

I curled up on the floor beside Tam's bed. Soon, the sound of steady breathing came from the others. They had fallen asleep and I wished I could. I was on the edge of dozing when a hand dropped over the side of the bed to stroke my hair.

"Fury?" His voice was raw, but Tam was awake.

I scrambled to my feet, holding my fingers to his lips as I settled in beside him on the side of the bed. "Are you all right, love?" I whispered.

He nodded, then blinked, looking around as he took in his surroundings. "Where am I?"

"Below the Tremble, in a place called Asylum. They rescued you from the surface. We've come to take you home." I leaned down, pressing my lips to his forehead. "I've been so worried. *We've* been so worried."

"I'm sorry. I'm so sorry." He struggled to sit up and I helped brace him as he pushed his way to a sitting position. "I tried to get free from the Devani but they caught me. If you had stayed, they would have caught you too." He paused, pressing his lips together. "I couldn't let them catch you. Your chip. They would have never let you go." Suddenly he paused, staring at my face. "What the hell happened to you? You're hurt."

I didn't want to worry him but he'd find out sooner or later. "Lyon's men jumped me when I was chasing an Abom, which Lyon may have somehow summoned. They beat the crap out of me, bruised a few of my ribs. I'm not fully up to speed, I'll tell you that."

Tam wrapped his arms around me but stopped as I groaned. Gently, he drew me into his embrace. "My love, I thought I was protecting you. I'm so sorry. I wasn't there."

"You couldn't have stopped them. There were three. They were all tough, and they were waiting for me. But it pretty much guaranteed my fears that the Order of the Black Mist is after me."

I leaned against his chest, melting into his arms. The scent of his body, the feel of him holding me, reassured me in a way that nothing else could. I hadn't realized how much I longed for someone to be with until I had Tam. Now, I harbored the secret fear that he would vanish, swept away by the violent tides that surrounded my life.

"Fury, when the Devani were heading toward us, the only thing I could think about was making certain they didn't get to you. I couldn't bear it if they caught you," he murmured, then pressed his lips to the top of my head.

I wanted to crawl into bed with him, to make love with him no matter how much it made my ribs hurt, but we couldn't. Not here, not with the others watching. I settled for holding him close. As he tightened his grip, I gasped again as my ribs protested. He immediately let go and I shifted so that I was lying with my head on his shoulder. Three words were poised on my tongue, but I couldn't say them yet. I was afraid to say them. But the moment I knew we found him, I also knew that he had won my heart.

"I'm not going to say what I'm thinking right now," I said. "I don't want to jinx things. I don't want to say a word until we get back to UnderBarrow. But I think you know what I'm feeling."

"Four-letter words raise the ante. But we're not playing games. We'll talk when we get home." And this time, his lips met my own and he kissed me, deep as the ocean, his tongue sliding against my own. And he tasted like honey wine.

We rested in silence, me propped against his shoulder, until he finally let out a long breath. "I suppose we need to talk about what we're going to do when we get back."

"About that. I have to ask you something."

Reluctantly, I told him about him talking in his sleep. "Is there a chance you talked in your sleep around the Devani? That you mentioned me and my chips?"

He thought for a moment, then shook his head. "No, I didn't sleep while I was in custody. That I guarantee you. They exiled me to the Tremble the next day. So you should be safe. But I won't be. If they find out that I escaped from the Tremble, they'll send the Devani for me, though I doubt they'd dare enter UnderBarrow, and if they do try, they'll find a resistance they never dreamed possible. Even though the chances of them discovering my absence are pretty nil if I avoid the sky-eyes, I'll have to stay out of sight. Maybe I should head to Briarwood for a while. They have no jurisdiction there. Briarwood and the Wild Wood are sovereign nations within the Americex Corporatocracy. They can't follow me into the woods."

I froze. "You'd really leave?"

"Just for a while, love. I have to figure out what to do." He suddenly paused. "You will come with me, won't you?"

"How can I? Hecate holds my leash." Tears sprang to my eyes. I was too tired and too achy for this conversation. "We'll talk about it when we're back at UnderBarrow. For now, let's just enjoy being together."

I closed my eyes, drifting into a light slumber. The next thing I knew, I woke up to find Tam up and dressed, and the covers tucked gently under my chin. The others were already awake and eating. I pushed myself up, stretching. The moment my arms were over my head, I regretted the move, letting out a loud yelp. Tam jumped to his feet, but Elan was faster, carrying my salve over to me. As I eased off the corset, Tam's eyes glittered and he hung his head when he saw the black bruises covering my side. Elan began soothing the All-Heal across my skin as I spread a layer of AntiBruise around my eye.

Rasheya walked through the door. She stared at the bruises, shaking her head. "I don't know who you got in a fight with, but I hope the other guy lost."

"I wish." I yelped again as Elan hit a particularly sore spot.

"I've got a group of Recons waiting out in the hallway. It's around sixish, off the Tremble. I figured if you leave now, you might make it home before midnight."

Elan and Tam helped fasten me back in the corset and we gathered our things. Rasheya patiently waited for us, then—when we were ready—we headed out, following her group into the intricate tunnels that made up the outer labyrinth of Asylum.

For once we lucked out. With a group of almost fifteen, nothing dared come near us, although throughout the twisting maze we could hear grunts and groans, and garbled voices speaking in odd cadences that made it impossible to catch what they were saying. I thought about Queet. He would have never managed it out here. The energy was too convoluted.

"I imagine you don't have many ghosts out here on the Tremble."

Rasheya glanced at me. "We have our spirits,

but they're just as Broken as those who wander the twisted plains above. I feel sorry for them, actually."

"You'll remember our meet-up?" Elan asked.

Apparently they had made plans out of my earshot.

"Yes, we'll expect your ship in ten nights. I've got it marked on my calendar. We'll meet you at the entrance—where we're going right now—at midnight your time. Don't be alarmed if we are a little late. The oddest energies can muck up the works. But we'll do our best to be there. And thank you. We've been dreading the winter because two of our usual suppliers have just vanished. They usually come through every few months and take orders. But the past three months, nothing. No word. And I have a very bad feeling that something put a stop to their business. I don't know if they supply any other groups, but..."

"Do you want to give us their names and we can look into it for you?" I wasn't terribly enthusiastic about looking into the whereabouts of smugglers, but the Mudarani were a good people, from what I could tell, and without their racketeers, they'd be lost.

"I'll have to ask the Elders. If they agree, I'll have their names for you when you bring the supplies. We have to protect our sources, you understand." Rasheya stopped at a metal door with EX-2 printed over the top. "Here we are."

She unlocked it, standing back as the wind off the Pacific Sound came whistling through the exit. I peeked outside and up. We were about fifty feet from the top of the cliff. There was a narrow ledge. About four feet in width and twelve feet in length, it overhung the choppy water below. The outside of the door matched the stone face of the wall, and I realized that from any distance, it would blend in with the cliff side with no problem.

Elan stepped out onto the ledge and pulled out her phone. "I got a signal." She sat down, cross-legged, and called her brother Laren.

I turned back to Rasheya. "Thank you for all your help. You saved all of us. We'll do whatever we can to return the favor."

"It was my pleasure. And making friendly contacts is never a waste. Outside of the Tremble, or inside." With a soft smile, she pulled back. "We'll wait in here until your boat arrives, but I'm going to close the door for now. So you can either sit on the ledge or in here with us. You have only to tap on the door and we'll open it."

I glanced at Elan. "Anything?"

She held a finger to her lips, then went back to speaking. After a moment, she put away her phone. "Laren's almost here. He found an out of the way place to shelter, and he's been waiting to hear from us. He was about to head back home in a couple of hours. He's been here every night since he dropped us off. I don't know how time works out on the Tremble, but it's been two nights since we entered its borders." She tapped on the door and when Rasheya appeared, said, "My brother will be here in a few minutes. Is there a chance that your people could lower us to the boat when he arrives?"

Rasheya motioned to one of the men by her side. He had a long coil of rope looped over his shoulders. "We can do that."

We waited in silence until Laren appeared. Without a word the Mudarani uncoiled the rope and then, one by one, they began to lower us to the boat. When the five of us were onboard, Rasheya gave us one last wave and shut the door, and the cliff once again looked merely like a cliff. Laren and Elan stashed Hans, Tam, Jason, and me below deck once again, where we sprawled on blankets, resting, as we made our way back to the Peninsula of the Gods. I thought about putting in a call to Hecate but decided it could wait until later. Weary and sore, I curled up beside Tam and closed my eyes, once again tumbling into an uneasy slumber.

Chapter 15

Elan led us back through the tunnels leading to UnderBarrow. Now that I knew about them, it seemed a far safer way to travel than using a shortcut near the Junk Yard. The question was, would the Bonny Fae get bent out of shape if I asked to use it all the time. I might be Tam's consort, but I wasn't part of their world and I knew and accepted that. I also attracted too much attention. I didn't want to give away their secrets by accident.

Damh Varias hurried down the corridor to meet us. "They let me know you were coming in through the tunnels." He stopped, dropping to one knee. "Lord Tam, thank Danu you're safe." As his gaze flickered up toward Tam, the love and affection he felt for his prince washed over his face, along with relief. He turned to me. "Lady Fury, you've brought our prince back to us. We owe you a debt that we can never repay."

"It wasn't just me. Elan, Jason, and Hans... we *all* brought him back. And Laren and his boat as well." Wearily, I dropped into a chair. As much as I'd slept the past twenty-four hours, I still felt wiped out.

Damh Various must have sensed my fatigue, because he motioned to a servant. "Take Lady Fury to her room, if you will." Turning to Jason and Hans, he asked, "Will you rest and allow us to feed you?"

As Jason shook his head, I said, "I can't stay. I have to check in with Hecate. But if Tam's correct, then I don't have to worry about the Devani showing up at my apartment or at Dream Wardens, which is a huge relief."

"Rest assured. I wasn't asleep during the time the Devani incarcerated me. They won't be after you." Tam still looked a little shell-shocked. He reached for my hand. "Are you sure you need to leave right now?"

The longing in his voice reverberated through me, setting off a shock wave of desire as he pulled me to him. The Bonny Fae had a natural charm, and I had given into it fully.

"I want to stay." I snuggled in his arms. "But I really do have to check in with Hecate. She's waiting for my call."

He nuzzled my hair. Reaching up to stroke my face, his fingers gently pushed back my hair, then trailed down to cup my chin. "Fury, go to your goddess. Then return to me." His command was simple. Tam had an authoritative way about him that never seemed imperious or demeaning.

I touched his nose with my own, then pressed my lips to his cheek. "I will. I just need to check in with her."

"I'm assigning two of my men to go with you. I won't chance you being attacked again."

I paused. That was going to be a problem. "Lord Tam, I'm sorry, but no." In front of his people, I gave him his due. "That simply won't work. I can't have bodyguards trailing behind me all over the city."

"Even if I insist?" Again, the cajoling voice. But as melodic and teasing as it was, I sensed an undercurrent of irritation. Tam was used to being obeyed in UnderBarrow.

"Even if you insist. I'll be cautious."

"I have to go over to the Peninsula of the Gods to see Thor. I'll go with her," Hans said, clearing his throat.

Tam's gaze flickered to the burly Theosian. Then he let out a soft snort. "Well, with one of Thor's chosen beside you, I suppose you'll be safe enough. But promise me you'll keep alert? You won't let down your guard? And you'll come back when you're done?"

"I will. And the sooner we go, the sooner I'll be able to return. Meanwhile, *you* be cautious and make certain nobody outside knows you've returned. If word gets around that you were exiled to the Tremble and then escaped, there will be rewards on your head. You're AwOL now, and the Devani aren't happy campers when their prisoners run off."

"She's right," Jason said. "Don't come to work until we talk about what needs to be done. As much as I'd like to see the new software system up and running, it will have to wait."

Tam nodded. "I know. As much as I'd like to argue, I know you're both right. I'll have the healers check me over to make certain I didn't sustain any long-term damage from being out on the Tremble." The pretense suddenly dropped away and his voice took on a deadly edge. "They think they can treat the Prince of UnderBarrow like a common prisoner. There *will* be ramifications and I do not promise they will be peaceful."

I stared at him. Just how far could— *and* would—the Bonny Fae go in paying the government back? They were a sovereign nation, bordered within the confines of another nation. But I had a feeling the Fae could raise serious havoc when they wanted to.

The corner of Damh Varias's lip turned up and he cocked his head. "Yes, milord. Do you want me to convene the Comh ná Shanair?"

I glanced over at Tam. I had no clue what they were talking about, but the hushed emphasis that Damh Varias had put on the words meant that whatever it was, the Comh ná Shanair was important.

Tam gave him an abrupt nod. "Yes, schedule it for two weeks from now to give them travel time." Then, without missing a beat, he turned to me, grabbed me by the shoulders and met my lips with his. The surge of his anger underscored his passion and I had to restrain myself from letting out a moan as my body responded, my pulse quickening as the kiss went on and on. He fisted my hair, pressing his lips against my neck. In a daze, I pulled back, letting out a soft murmur as we parted.

"I'll be back." I could barely tear my gaze away from his. Tam's warrior side had come to the surface and I wasn't used to it. My own blood quickened, like recognizing like, and I leaned in for another kiss before turning to join Hans, who was patiently waiting.

"Go, and be safe. All of you. Thank you, for all you have done. I must rest for a while now." And then, without a blink, Tam turned, striding toward a corridor leading to the Healer's Hall.

Damh Varias blinked. "The Devani have stumbled into a minefield. They have no idea what dread retaliation they have set off. The Bonny Fae make wondrous friends. And deadly enemies. And Prince Tam is well known for making his enemies pay."

I stared at him, realizing how little I really knew my love. "Tam isn't going to let this go, is he?"

With a shake of the head, Damh Varias turned to go. "Milady Fury, the Bonny Fae have long memories, and they hold their grudges even longer. When you are in Lord Tam's favor, life is good. But cross the line and his good nature ends. There's a reason he was known as the 'Blood Prince' back in Eire."

When I started to ask what he meant, he merely held up his hand.

"No more. Not now. We can talk again later. I will entrust Elan to see you out. Lady Fury, I will, no doubt, see you soon." And with that, he headed back the way he had come. I took my sword from Hans, aching as I strapped Xan over my back. It felt good to have her there again, even though I knew I wasn't up to using her yet.

Elan let out a soft breath. "Lord Tam has as good as declared war on the government. And all the Fae will back him up."

My stomach lurched. "The Conglomerate won't take kindly to that."

"You do not know the full power of our people." She smiled, then, but her teeth were clenched and she looked like a snake ready to strike. "Come, I'll see you out to the Sandspit."

As we followed her to the entrance, Jason hung back for a moment. "Elan, may I speak with you?"

"Of course." She waved as Hans and I headed out the exit, into the depths of the chasm housing the World Tree. What they had to say to one another, I did not hear.

As soon as we were out of the Sandspit, my phone immediately began dinging with text messages. Five from Hecate, three from potential clients, and two from numbers I didn't recognize.

I checked Hecate's texts first as Hans and I caught the nearest Monotrain to the Peninsula of the Gods. I glanced around the car, making sure that there wasn't anybody who looked suspicious, but the only people out this late were a few kids who were already drunk and heading to yet another party. One of the boys wore a shirt that read "Orphex" printed over a ten-pointed star. A popular group, I found their music strangely disjointed and too electronic, but then again, I grew up on bands like Viscous and Mausoleum. Dark, moody music, the kind you listen to when the world seems darker than a starless night. The kid glanced over at Hans and me, and his eyes widened.

For a moment, I felt a quiver of fear. Being recognized right now was the last thing I wanted. Even though Tam had assured me that he hadn't given away my secret, I was running on adrenaline, primed for paranoia.

Actually, I thought, *paranoia is only a*

problem when they aren't *out to get you. The Devani would snatch me up in a second if they knew about my altered chip.*

But as the boy approached us, he offered a tentative smile. In a subdued voice, he asked, "Are you Theosians?"

Hans and I glanced at each other. Hans nodded. "We are at that."

"I thought so." He seemed to want to ask another question, but then, with a shrug of frustration, turned to go back to his friends.

"Wait. Was there something else?" I was tired. Hans was tired. I was sore. I didn't need any more entanglements right now. But the kid looked so grateful that I couldn't resist.

"Yeah, there is. I know you can't become a Theosian if you aren't born one, but...You both serve the gods, right?"

I nodded. "As far as I know, every Theosian is bound to one of the Elder Gods or Goddesses. Why?"

"Because I want to join a temple and my parents say that only Theosians can. They want me to apprentice in the Metalworks. But I don't want a life in the factories. I feel like I'm supposed to be working for one of the gods." He stammered out the last, staring down at his feet. I recognized that stance. It was common in people whose dreams were constantly being crushed.

"Listen to me, the gods don't turn away people just because they're human. Theosians aren't clergy. We're different. We're direct servants of the gods. But the priests and priestesses? And the receptionists and clerks and janitors and everybody else who help keep the temples running? They're human or a shifter or perhaps

Fae. Your parents probably don't know that."

Actually, his parents probably wanted him to get a job down in the Metalworks so that they could siphon off his paycheck, but I wasn't going to plant that idea in his head. I might be wrong, and it wouldn't do any good to make him angry at them.

"Yeah, I thought so." He let out a sigh, his shoulders relaxing. "Thanks. I finish school in two months. I really don't want to spend my life in a factory." With a wave of thanks, he returned to his friends.

Hans leaned over and, in whisper-speak, said, *You know you just set up the blowup of the century. That kid's going to join any temple that will take him and his parents will go ballistic.*

I snorted. *Not my fault. He doesn't want to spend his life grinding away in the Metalworks, and I don't blame him. At least in the temple he'll have a sense of purpose more than he will with the endless shift-work of the factories.*

With a shrug, Hans went back to looking out the window.

We arrived at the Peninsula of the Gods and, as we ducked out of the Monotrain, the snow was falling so fast that it was hard to see my hand in front of my face. The flakes clung to our hair and shoulders, and by now, we were walking through an ankle-deep blanket on the sidewalk. The walkways had obviously been shoveled earlier. The snow banks to the side were deep and mounded.

"Winter's going to be a rough one this year," I mused. "Gaia is coming down hard on us with the cold weather."

"She's taking us back into an ice age. The climatologists agree. With all the changes we've made since the World Shift, and the changes Gaia brought about, we're headed toward the deep-freeze end of the spectrum." Hans glanced up. "Sky-eyes are out tonight. They usually don't run around here much. I wonder what's going down."

I caught sight of a drone passing by. "I hate those things. But that one's too far away to make out who we are."

As we came to the Temple Valhalla, Hans waved and peeled off to go talk to Thor. I hurried to a jog, still nervous that Lyon might have his cronies out looking for me, but before I realized it, I was at Naós ton Theón. Ten minutes later, I was through the scanners and in the waiting room, listening to the soft hush of the central heating system as Coralie let Hecate know I was there. She called me back immediately.

As I entered her office, a hush fell around me and I felt protected and safe. Hecate was sitting behind her desk, with a sympathetic look on her face. She motioned to the sofa.

"Sit down. You look like hell."

That's because she's been through it, Queet said, appearing out of the side wall.

"Queet! I'm so glad to see you. It's a good thing you didn't go to the Tremble with us. It's not safe there for anybody, spirits included." The words spilled out then as I launched into telling them what happened. "So, Tam swears he didn't fall asleep while he was in custody. I wish I could be certain."

"We can find out." Hecate picked up her phone. "Coralie, would you ask one of Pythia's priestesses to come in?" To me, she said, "We'll have her do a reading to find out if he could have been brainwashed into believing that he didn't say anything. Usually the Fae are exceptionally resistant to such treatment, but we need to make certain."

"Thank you," I said. "By the way, has Captain Varga said anything? Did we clear his boat?"

"He did, and you did. He's left you a bonus, by the way. But Fury, a serious problem's come up and we have to address it. We will as soon as—"

A tap on the door interrupted her. As the priestess of the Oracle entered, Hecate motioned to a side desk. "Lay out your reading there, please. We need to know if Lord Tam accidentally divulged Fury's secrets to the Devani."

The girl nodded. She was dressed in a diaphanous powder-blue shift that floated around her body, barely touching her breasts and hips. We could see everything through the transparent material, but even though the girl was curvy, with rounded breasts and full hips, there was something mystical about her rather than sexual.

She slid into the chair and opened a small pouch, spilling the contents on the desktop. Bones scattered out. I recognized them as snake vertebrae. Examining the pattern, she began to read.

"There is a dark cloud around the agents you fear. They are driven by secrets and agendas hidden so deep that their masters have no clue of what they plan. Expect changes. Drastic changes that will not serve the greater good. But the one you fear spoke out of turn, his memory is intact in that regard. He stilled his tongue during captivity. He kept his silence. But there was something he no longer remembers. He angered his captors. They sense a threat within him." She looked up, her eyes glazed over. "He's a marked man, an enemy of the government. If they encounter him again, they will kill him."

Crap. Tam had a bounty on his head. The Devani would be free to kill first and ask questions later. Which meant he had to avoid the sky-eyes at all costs.

"One more thing. He bears a chip. They implanted it during the struggle when he was exiled. If they pick up on it, they will track him and hunt him down."

A tracker chip. Tracker chips were used to electronically monitor criminals who were released back into the public. They might already know he was no longer out on the Tremble. And while they couldn't enter UnderBarrow, Tam couldn't leave it without being caught. If he showed up in Darktown or any other part of the land within the confines of the Americex Corporatocracy, Tam was as good as dead.

I leaned back, breathing deeply. "He kept my secret, but he doesn't know about the chip they planted in him. The Tremble scrambles your brain. If he knew about the chip when he was dumped over the border, the memory got lost along the way."

Which meant, I had to get back to him. Had to let him know.

Hecate spoke up. "Queet, will you please warn Tam? Then return immediately. We have a bigger problem brewing and Fury's going to have to address it." Hecate gave me a sorrowful look. "I hate to burden you with this so soon, but there's no other choice."

I bit my lip. The last thing I needed was another problem, but Theosians weren't allowed to beg off from their duties. We were bound to the gods, and when they called, we answered.

I'll be back in a flash. Tam gave me leave to enter UnderBarrow without an escort when he and Fury started dating.

Before I could say a word, Queet vanished.

I stared helplessly at Hecate. "Things feel like they're spiraling out of control."

"Haven't they always been out of control? Think about it, Fury. Even the Elder Gods are in charge of very little in this world. The government thinks it retains mastery over the people, but in actuality, it controls far less than it thinks it does. Even if you combine all the leaders of the world together along with their armies, they could not stand against Gaia." She paused, an odd look on her face.

"What?" I asked. I knew that look. It usually meant that she was debating whether to fill me in on some secret to which she was party.

After a moment, Hecate motioned for the priestess to gather her things and leave. "Thank you, and thank Pythia for me, would you?"

The girl swept the snake bones into the bag, then curtseyed. "Of course," she said, closing the door behind her.

Hecate crossed to the door and cracked it open, peeking out. Satisfied, she closed it again and turned around, pressing her back against it. She gazed at me for a long moment. "I am going to tell you something and you may not tell anyone. Not even Tam or Jason. Do you understand?"

I held my hand over my heart. "I promise on my oath."

She nodded, then slowly let out a long breath. "There are stirrings among the Convocation of the Gods. Worries that the governments of this world have forgotten just what powers Gaia wields. In their grasp for control, they edge ever further into dangerous territory. We know that the World Regency Corporation was hiding the Thunderstrike when it was stolen. They have been punished for not turning it over for destruction immediately, but it brings to question just how many other artifacts, spells, and machinations the various governments are hiding."

"You think there are more?"

"Almost certainly. If they think they can go up against Gaia and win, they're pathetically mistaken. They do not realize just how powerful the Elder Gods are. We've played down our influence here. And truly, there *are* boundaries beyond which we cannot act. But they aren't quite so firm as we've led humans to believe. If push comes to shove, we will take up arms, and we *will* win, though blood would stain the streets red."

I shivered. This was not the pep talk I was hoping for. After a moment, I hugged myself. "So what's going on now that you needed to talk to me about?"

"I've had spies doing their best to find out everything they can about the Order of the Black Mist. The graveyard that you chased the Abom into? It was defiled. Bones were taken. I'm thinking that Lyon is dabbling in necromancy—" The phone on Hecate's desk rang and she glanced at the ID. "Crap. What now?" She grabbed the receiver. "I have to take this."

She turned and I did my best to avoid eavesdropping. But after a moment, she let loose with a rash of curse words and slammed down the phone, turning back to me.

The edge in her eyes brought me to attention.

"What's going on?"

Hecate licked her lips. "I was right. The Order is messing around with death magic. A new portal has just opened on the World Tree, and it leads into the realm of Tartarus. That was Hermes. One of his Theosians just reported in that the dead are pouring through the portal, into the streets. We have to close that vortex."

I stared at her. "What do you mean when you say 'the dead'?"

She let out a low growl. "*Dead*, as in re-animated bodies. Zombies. They're swarming out of the Sandspit into the streets of Darktown. I'm afraid we have to call out all hands on this one. I need you to go in and see what you can do, but you'll have to be careful, because it looks like the Devani will be sweeping into the area."

"What? Shades of old horror movies."

"It's far worse than that, Fury. Not only that, but apparently this is happening right now in several other countries on several other World Trees. As you know, the Order is worldwide, and they are making a major play right now."

I leaned back. Great. Just great. "It was bad enough when they found the Thunderstrike. That alone could have shifted things on a worldwide basis. Now, it seems they have decided to launch concurrent attacks to make it harder to shut them down."

"They mean business. This could lead to a worldwide epidemic. You have to shut down the portal. And then, we have to figure out how to take out the Order."

I exhaled sharply. "Just how am I supposed to close a portal?"

"I don't know. I'll research while you head out

there. But I need you there. Temple Valhalla is sending warrior priests into the streets to fight against the dead, and so will Naós ton Theón. The phone tree is on the move, gathering more volunteers. You won't be going alone, though."

"Thank gods. I can't imagine trying to take this on by myself." The last thing in the world I wanted to do was head out in the middle of the night and take on an army of zombies, but the panic in her voice filtered through and I realized this was a full-scale emergency. "I want Hans, if you're talking to Temple Valhalla."

She picked up the phone. "I'll call and they should send him right over." A few moments later, she headed for the door. "He's on his way. Follow me."

As we swept out the door, Queet suddenly reappeared. I paused.

Queet, go tell Jason I'm going to need him. I'll pick him up at the shop. Tell him lock the door and make sure the shutters are set. I'll call when we get near. Then hurry to UnderBarrow. Tell Tam— or Damh Varias if you can't find Tam—to make certain his people stay inside. If anyone tries to exit the Barrow at this time, they're going to be in a world of hurt. You'll understand when you get there. Hurry. We don't have a moment to waste.

Queet didn't question. He just vanished, on his way. I caught up to Hecate as she turned the corner at the end of the hall, dreading the coming battle.

Chapter 16

The moment we entered the training room, I caught sight of someone I knew and a wave of relief washed through me.

"Tymbur, you're going with me?" If he was, then it suddenly brightened our odds.

Tymbur was pledged to the Elder God Hades—the god of the Underworld. And if we were going to fight zombies, then he was my choice for a sidekick. Tall and lean, he was a handsome man with dark skin, dark eyes, and a shock of brilliant blond hair.

"Yes, and pleased to serve beside you." His voice was soft, belying the power he had over the dead. Tymbur had been a servant of Hades for far longer than I had been alive. He looked to be a little older than I was, but I knew that he had been born three hundred years before. Theosians aged normally till their prime, and then the aging process slowed dramatically. I would begin to see the effects of that soon myself.

"Then you know what we're up against?"

"Zombies, yes, brought about by the Order of the Black Mist. We'll also be taking a friend of mine. He's a priest of Hades who can do some serious damage on the creatures. He'll help protect us while we inspect the portal."

Just then, Hans burst in the room, his hammer firmly planted on his shoulder. "I'm here."

"I told Jason to wait for us at Dream Wardens. He's gathering together as many scrolls as he can. This is Tymbur. He's bound to Hades."

Hans gave him a quick nod. "Has anybody ever shut down a portal before? Besides Gaia?"

Hecate shrugged. "I don't really know. There's so much about the World Tree that even the Elder Gods don't know. I wish I could give you concrete instructions on how to handle this. I'm going to get someone working on figuring out how the Order of the Black Mist opened it in the first place."

"Well, it sounds like they did a good job."

"The Convocation of Gods has an emergency meeting scheduled for a few minutes from now. We won't take long, but we have to agree on a course of action before any of the Elder Gods actually does anything. Pythia is going to try to contact Gaia. After our meeting, I'll join you at the World Tree." Hecate fell silent as we stared at her. Gaia seldom talked to anyone, even the Elder Gods.

Tymbur gave her a quick bow. He was an odd mix of courtliness and off-the-wall crazypants. But he was always up for a good scuffle, especially when it concerned anything in the dead zone.

"Always at your service, Hecate."

"You should get moving," Hecate said. "But be cautious. The zombies are attacking on sight and many people have already been hurt. Some have killed. Also, we don't have a clue what the magic of the Sandspit might do to them. I wish it would dispel them, but we don't seem to be that lucky. Plan to engage."

"How *do* we put a stop to them? We can't exactly kill them, since they're already dead," Han asked. "I'm going to call Greta in on this. She's back at Temple Valhalla right now."

Tymbur shook his head. "Zombies are difficult. They'll keep going until you destroy their bodies. It's a gruesome task, I admit, and not one for the squeamish. You have to blow them to bits, tear their limbs off, cut off their heads, smash their brains. If you can't do this, then stay behind because if they catch you, they *will* bite. They'll try to eat you alive. And if they manage to bite you, once you die the infection will manifest. A magical infection, yes, but an infection all the same. And then, we'll have to put you down the same way. It's messy and it's terrifying."

He rattled off the facts like he might be talking about attending a seminar. Hans grimaced, but stood his ground. "I'm bound to a god of battle. Thor would kick my ass if I let fear stand in the way. No worries, I can handle myself. And if I go down in battle, then I'm on my way to Valhalla."

"Tymbur's right. Think twice. This isn't a go-round in a street brawl. We're talking serious hack-and-slash, beat-their-brains-out stuff. And if we run into Lyon, it's going to be a lot worse." My stomach lurched at the thought, but I had no choice. I had to handle whatever was waiting.

Hans shrugged. "Fury, I've handled worse. You've got my back, I've got yours. Trust me."

I placed my hand on his arm. "Thanks. Truly. Thank you."

"Then we're set," Tymbur said.

"Go now. I will be there as soon as I can." Hecate motioned to a man who was waiting by the door. He was wearing body armor. "He'll drive you."

At that moment, Tymbur led a young man over to us. He couldn't be more than twenty-five, and he was human. "Meet Montran. He's the priest of Hades I told you would join us. Don't let his age throw you. He's one of our most powerful foils against the undead of any sort."

Montran inclined his head ever so slightly. Cloaked in black, with a silver sigil around his neck, it was difficult to see any of his features, but from what I could see of his eyes, he looked so serious that it threw me. Then again, the situation *was* dire, and the priests of Hades were always more somber than others.

"I'll do whatever I can to help." His voice was a startling mix, high pitched yet gravelly.

"Fury," Hecate warned. "You need to hurry."

We scrambled for the door and headed out. Greta joined us as the driver led us up the tiers until we reached the parking lot where a limo was waiting. Within minutes, we were headed through the snowstorm, back to the Sandspit.

Hans tapped me on the knee. "You know that if the Devani are around, you'll have to make yourself scarce."

"I can't run away from this, Hans. No matter what, I've got to see this through. Besides, the Devani aren't likely to be going near the base of the World Tree." I stared out the tinted window into the silent streets as Hans filled Greta in on what we needed to do. She had a massive sword with her that made Xan look like a toothpick, but somehow,

I didn't think she'd have any trouble wielding it.

We were nearing the Junk Yard when a sudden influx of cars stalled traffic. I frowned, pressing my nose against the window.

"What's going on?" I asked the driver.

The man glanced over his shoulder. "I don't know. I'm trying to find out. It's like everybody decided to descend on this intersection at once."

My inner alarm was clanging loud and clear. Something was up and it wasn't good. As the driver pulled up the traffic app on his view-screen, I called Hecate. She answered on the second ring.

"We're stuck in traffic and it looks like it's getting worse. The driver is trying to find out what's going on."

"Are you near the Junk Yard?" Her voice sounded hollow, as though she was walking through a tunnel.

"Right."

"Then tell your driver to turn around if he can possibly do it. If not, get out of the car and *get out of there now*. Tell him to abandon ship, too. A massive riot has started on the border between Darktown and the Junk Yard. The Devani are there. Rioters who think the Devani shouldn't be there are there. And the zombies have started to swarm the area. It's one mega clusterfuck and there's no way you can get through. Take an alternative route, get to that portal and do what you can to shut it down. The Convocation has just ended and I've got one task to do before I head down there to meet you."

I recognized the *do-not-disobey-me* tone in her voice.

"We're on it." As I disconnected, I turned to Tymbur. "We have to get out of here. Driver,

Hecate just told me that if you can turn around, do. If not, we *all* get out and take off on foot. It looks like Lyon and the Order are getting what they hoped for. The whole situation has descended into chaos. The Devani are roughing up the locals, the locals are fighting back, and the zombies are crashing the party. All in all, a really bad guest list."

The driver shook his head. "I can't turn around now. We're stuck in the middle of an automotive pile-on. The only way I could drive out of here would be if I had an aereocar." He thumbed toward the door. "Everybody out. I'll make my way back to the temple."

"Should we lock up?" I started to ask, but then I realized that it didn't matter whether or not we locked the doors. If looters wanted to tear the car apart, they would. We were out of the car with our gear in under a minute.

As the driver set off toward the Peninsula of the Gods, I glanced around to get my bearings. We were at the southern-most tip of Edlewood Inlet, at a juncture in the road that would take us either toward Croix, toward the Junk Yard, or toward Darktown. Unfortunately, to get to the Sandspit, we'd have to pass through the crowds ahead.

"Which way should we go? We don't want to get caught by the Devani." Actually, getting embroiled in any sort of riot sounded like a bad idea. "We need to get to the Sandspit as soon as possible."

"Damn, Jason's waiting for us." I motioned for everybody to move off the road. We took cover beneath the awning of a food market, where I pulled out my phone to call him. "Listen, there's a riot. Yes, that's the one, all right. We're heading on foot to the Sandspit. We'll have to go by the burrow-lanes because the streets are dangerous. Do you think you can make it safely?" I paused while he talked. Then, "Are you sure? All right, we'll meet you there. But try to get into UnderBarrow until we get there. The zombies are bad news."

As I tucked my phone away, my side twinged. I hadn't put on any All-Heal in a while and was feeling it. "Let's head for UnderBarrow. If we're lucky, the zombies won't be paying attention to the hidden stair. But the Sandspit's going to be a bitch with them wandering through it. Obviously, the rogue magic isn't killing them because they've found their way into the streets."

Hans pointed to the sky. "Sky-eyes. There are a lot of them up there tonight. But they're focused on the riots, I think. We better get moving. The storm's getting worse."

He was right. The snow was coming down so fast and hard it was difficult to see. My legs were icy cold, but I pulled my duster tighter, trying to stave off the chill. I caught sight of a burrow-lane behind a mini-mall.

"That way." As I led them into the narrow lane, the sounds and shouts behind us became muffled.

"I know several shortcuts that can get us to the Sandspit quicker. But we have to go through the Tunnels." Montran's voice cut softly through the chill.

I caught my breath. The Tunnels were dangerous. Lyon and his group were headquartered down in the underground labyrinth that had been part of underground Seattle in the distant past. I shifted, easing the stitch in my side.

"There's one problem with that. The only

entrance I know that leads to the Tunnels is at the corner where the Bogs meet the Sandspit. We're headed toward the Sandspit, so how would going through the Tunnels get us there?"

Montran gave a little shrug. "There's more than one entrance, you know. I happen to know of a hidden entrance about one block away. We can get there by going through the burrow-lanes and be there in less than five minutes."

I felt like an idiot. *Of course* the Tunnels would have more than one entrance. It made a lot more sense than thinking the only entrance was a hidden one tucked away in the Bogs.

"Well, that works" was all I said. Then another thought crossed my mind. Jason's old mentor was hiding out down in the tunnels. Terrance, or Bodie as he called himself, was a spy for the Crystal Guardians, a watchdog group run by the Greenlings. He had deserted the Cast, faked his own death, and gone underground in the Tunnels to keep an eye on the Order of the Black Mist. It occurred to me that he might be able to help us. But then I realized how much time it would take to find him. And once the zombies started attacking people, they would multiply. A lot of innocent victims could die in the time we took to go hunting down Terrance.

"Let's go. Montran, please lead the way."

He nodded, turning to jog down the burrow-lane. We followed, and with our numbers, none of the Broken or bogeys bothered us as we silently raced by as the first hints of dawn streaked past the clouds.

The Tunnels were a scary place at best. While they weren't frightening in the same way a haunted house was, or fighting an Abom was, their spookiness was born of the history surrounding them. And there *were* monsters down here. My first time down was so bad that I had hoped to avoid a repeat.

Montran led us through the burrow-lanes, toward the walls enclosing the Junk Yard. He turned off onto a dead-end lane, and we jogged along to the very back. There, a grate covered a manhole from years gone by. As we watched, Montran reached down. A small *click* broke the silence as the grate slowly swung upward. The manhole cover opened like an iris aperture in one of the UnderSubs that dove into the watery depths of the ocean.

"See the ladder? That leads down to a passage that leads to a major thoroughfare in the Tunnels. Thrill seekers use this entrance when they want to chance danger or some equally stupid pastime. A lot of university students are hazed by being required to journey from here to another entrance about ten blocks north. I'm surprised you didn't know about it," Montran said, shining his wrist light down into the hole. The rungs were solid steel and led down into the darkness.

"I never had much to do with the Tunnels. Aboms don't know about them. At least I've never encountered one who did. I prefer to spend my spare time relaxing rather than seeking out any more danger than I already have in my life."

I glanced at the sky. It was still snowing. It hadn't stopped for hours, and the silvery light that hinted we were near dawn was clouded by the frozen flakes. I was cold and wet, and I needed a hot shower. I really, *really* needed a shower. Behind us, as the sounds of rioting echoed in the distance, shouts and screams grew louder, filtering through from blocks away.

"Do you think Jason's okay?" I turned to Hans, trying to ignore the ever-present pain in my side.

He pressed his lips together, thinking. After a moment, he said, "Well, the riots aren't near the center of Darktown yet. He should be all right."

I nodded. There wasn't much we could do about Dream Wardens anyway. Or Jason. "I guess we just have to hope for the best."

Montran motioned for us to line up. "I'll go down first. Hans, you go second. Then Fury, Tymbur, and Greta. All right?"

I glanced over my shoulder. "It looks clear. No bogeys around. My guess is that they heard about the rumble going on and decided to see if there's any easy pickings to be had." I glanced at my phone as I brought up the GPS. The sounds of the crowd were echoing louder. The riots appeared to be moving toward both the Trips and the Junk Yard and we were near enough to get caught in the tangle if we waited much longer.

The thought of the Devani marching into the Trips turned my stomach. Hundreds of line workers and factory lifers would be caught on their way to work during shift-change, which was coming up in less than an hour. The riots would spill into neighborhoods filled with kids, and the golden soldiers wouldn't think twice about taking out their aggression on children.

The Devani didn't give a damn about age or ability. A seven-year-old was as viable a target to them as a twenty-year-old. And I had seen them treat the elderly with the same violence as they attacked burly-boys.

"Damn it." I eyed the manhole, wrinkling my nose. "How do we always seem to end up underground? Lately I've spent more time under the earth than on it."

"Well, hang on for another round," Montran said, lowering himself onto the ladder. "You're about to go again. Hurry up. Don't dawdle."

"Hold on one second."

I shaded my eyes. In the silver pre-dawn light, I could see smoke rising from a couple blocks over, but there was no way of knowing what was going down. I wanted to call Tam but electronics and UnderBarrow didn't mix. Nothing worked within the confines of the Sandspit.

Deciding that I had to do something, I texted him and "I MISS YOU, STAY SAFE" as we headed down into the Tunnels. I wasn't sure when I'd see him again. I tried not to think *if* but the word lingered in my thoughts. With a deep breath, I pushed away the fear and glanced up at the sky. It seemed like a million miles till dawn. With a prayer that we wouldn't meet Lyon along the way, I swung over the edge.

Chapter 17

As we descended through the narrow passage, I tried not to think about Lyon. The truth was, he scared the hell out of me. I had thwarted his plans in a big way and I shouldn't have been surprised by the attack, but somehow, it hadn't crossed my mind that he might come after me. But now that we were headed right into his home turf, my stomach knotted with the thought that next time, I probably wouldn't come out alive. Not if his thugs caught me while I was alone.

I scrambled down the ladder and jumped off to the side. As I glanced around, I realized that the passage here looked very little like Tunnel Pike, where Lyon kept court. Instead of a tidy brick passage stretching fifteen feet overhead and wide as a city street, we were in a tunnel that was about ten feet high, with one side raw, compacted dirt and protruding tree roots.

The pungent scent of mold filled my nose, sour and tangy. I grimaced, trying to keep from swallowing the scent, which was so thick it filled my throat.

The brick walls here were weathered, looking like they could easily crumble away, and the lighting here was even dimmer than it had been in the other entrance. But at least we didn't have to go through an abandoned sewer entrance first, let alone a vortex that acted as an alarm system.

"I thought you said this was a major thoroughfare in the Tunnels. It looks more like a back-end burrow-lane." I scratched my head, trying to puzzle just how far we were from the Sandspit.

Montran snorted. "I said this passage *leads* to a major thoroughfare. We're not taking that route."

"Of course we aren't." I realized I was stepping in a puddle of slime and eased to the side, trying to scrape off the sole of my boot on the wall.

"So which way do we go?" Greta asked as we came to a juncture that split off in three different directions. She didn't speak much, but when she did, her voice was steady. I felt surprisingly comforted knowing she was with us. A Valkyrie had to be able to kick serious butt and be able to hold her own in rocky situations.

Montran paused, eyeing each passage for a moment. "To the left. This runs directly beneath the Junk Yard and will take us into the Sandspit. There's an exit shortly after you cross the borders that leads to the southeast corner, beneath Malloy Avenue. The exit comes out through one of the sewer grates there. We'll have to duck into the sewer tube near the end, but it shouldn't be too bad. I hope."

He didn't sound all that convincing, but nobody argued with him as he turned into the left passage.

The passage narrowed and debris began to litter the floor. The tunnel here was crumbling, and as we continued along, the piles of bricks became more frequent, leaving gaping holes in the walls. As we skirted the mounds of broken brick and rubble, I pulled up my Trace screen. The last thing we wanted was to be surprised by any Aboms that might take a notion to join the fray. It also occurred to me that if Lyon had summoned the Abom I'd been chasing, he might be hiding a few more around the area. But the screen was clear.

As the tunnel curved, bending to the right ever slightly, a large heap of rubble blocked our way a few yards ahead. We would have to go over it, rather than skirt around. The walls were compacted dirt from where the brick had given way, and on one side, there appeared to be rounded holes carved through the dirt, large enough for someone, or *something*, to crawl through.

I tapped Montran on the shoulder and nodded to the openings. "Look."

He motioned for us to stop, and sniffed the air. "Something's been through here. It smells like decay."

"Zombies, by any chance?" Hans asked.

Tymbur moved to one side and began a low incantation. Hans and Greta took up positions near the openings, watching for anything that might come through. Montran held up the ankh that was hanging around his neck, studying it. Another moment and he dropped the chain.

Montran shook his head. "No. No ghosts or zombies. Some sort of insect, I think."

I stared at the holes. They were a good four feet in diameter. With a shudder, I said, "I really don't want to meet the bug that created those passages. Let's get moving."

He frowned, studying the holes in the dirt. "I'd say some form of cockle-roach. Giant ones. They're meat-eaters as well as scavengers, so be cautious. The last thing we need is a standoff with one of those."

Cockle-roaches had evolved from their ancient kin the cockroach—which we still had plenty of. But cockle-roaches, thanks to the magic running rampant after the World Shift, had evolved a spine. Oh, they still had their exoskeletons, but they now had bones inside their bodies too, supporting their enlarged structures. They were tougher and meaner, but still had no real intelligence. But like most insects, they worked together via a hive-mind.

Greta and Hans approached the pile of debris first, with me coming next and Montran and Tymbur bringing up the rear. Cockle-roaches were meat-eaters, and they were most certainly alive. If we encountered them, better those who were adept at fighting be in front.

The lowest point on the heap of bricks and stone was about chest high, at least for someone Han's height. For me, it was almost neck high. Hans cautiously picked his way to the top, peering over, with his hammer ready.

"Oh crap!"

The debris pile exploded with him on it as three cockle-roaches shook off the bricks from where they'd burrowed beneath it. I slapped my hand against my hip, bringing my whip to bear. Greta had her sword ready and without hesitation, she dove into the pile of bugs.

They swarmed at her as Hans rolled to his

feet. He came in from behind as I scanned for the cockle-roach farthest from either of them. I raised my whip and brought it solidly down on the back of the gigantic bug. Normal whips wouldn't touch the hard shell of the creature, but my whip was far from normal and it split the exoskeleton just enough for me to see the mealy white flesh beneath. The cockle-roach turned as I hit it again, focusing on amping up the flames that were shooting off the lash. This time, the whip bit deep, splitting the shell fully in two and cleaving the cockle-roach in half. A stream of steaming guts poured out, stinking up the passage as its legs scrambled for a few seconds before they stopped twitching and it lay, dead.

I turned to see how Greta and Hans were faring. Greta had been bitten by one, but she had skewered it with her sword, pinning it to the floor. The cockle-roach was still attempting to skitter away but it was only damaging itself further. I motioned for her to stand back. I brought the whip down over its head, severing it from the body. As Greta retrieved her sword, Hans managed to stun the remaining bug with his hammer, and Greta moved in, finishing it.

We stood there, panting, while Montran and Tymbur kept watch for any more that might be in the area. My side was burning, but I was more concerned about the deep puncture the cockle-roach had left on Greta's hand. As I examined it, Hans once again crawled up the debris pile and warily peeked over the edge.

"They're all gone, I think." He dropped to the other side, gingerly poking into the rubble with his hammer. Nothing else emerged.

"Greta was bitten. Cockle-roaches carry germs.

I don't have anything on me for infections, just for bruises." I glanced over at Tymbur. "You have anything?"

He shook his head. "No, but Montran, don't you?"

"I have a few simple healing spells. It might stanch any infection she may have brewing in there. Give me a moment here and I'll cast it on her." He shifted through his pack, coming out with a small silver caduceus.

"I didn't know priests of Hades were versed in healing." It seemed odd to me, given he was in the service of a god of the Underworld.

"A witch who cannot hex, cannot heal. And one who cannot heal, cannot hex. The same with the priesthood of all gods of healing and death. We must balance the energy on both sides. They are two faces of the same coin." He took hold of Greta's arm and placed the caduceus on the bite, murmuring soft words. *"To cleanse, to mend, to bind, to heal. By the power of Hades I command thee."*

A faint golden light flowed from his fingers into the caduceus, and melted into her skin like butter on a hot sidewalk. She caught her breath, her eyes widening, before she relaxed.

"How does it feel?" Montran asked.

"Not as hot. It feels like it might actually be healing up." She let him bind it up with a bit of cloth from his pack, then Hans motioned for us to join him.

Once we were all on the other side of the rubble, we could see where the cockle-roaches had been hiding, burrowed deep under the debris pile. I saw something glistening inside the hole left when they dislodged the pile and cautiously moved closer.

"Cripes. Look." I used my dagger to shift around a pile of dried fecal matter to show an oothecae—an egg sac. About the size of a handbag, it was a dark reddish-brown.

"Let me take care of it." Hans readied his hammer, but I stopped him.

"Not so fast. What's beneath it?" There was something shiny and it wasn't the cockle-roaches' egg sac. I gently levered the oothecae aside with the tip of my dagger, then tried to catch whatever it was with my blade. I really didn't want to climb in there. Who knew what germs filled the air in that fetid hole.

As I drew the object back to me, I realized it was a necklace of some sort, surrounding the vertebra of someone's neck. I guessed it was a woman, but we wouldn't ever know for sure and I had no inclination to tell the authorities about what we found. Gingerly, I slipped the necklace away from the bones and tucked it in my pocket. We could examine it later. Maybe there would be an inscription and we could take it back to whoever the dead woman's relatives might have been. But given we were down in the Tunnels, chances were she was a runaway or loner.

"Okay, do your best." I stood back.

Hans took aim and with one blow, smashed the egg sac into mush. "There's a host of the critters prevented." Sounding satisfied, he shouldered his hammer and we took off again.

I was wearing Xan over my left shoulder, and I realized how much the weight was dragging on me. But I felt naked without her, and frankly, bruised or not, I had already decided that I'd rather use her and break a rib than be unarmed.

Montran moved to the front again and we took off, following him. Along the way, we heard a number of muffled noises and grunts, but apparently we appeared threatening enough that nobody else came out to play other than the cockle-roaches we had encountered. Twenty minutes later, we were at a square hole in the wall, which led into the sewer tube that Montran had mentioned. It was obviously well used, because it stank to high heaven in there.

I wrinkled my nose, hoping that the smell would be the worst thing we'd encounter.

Montran stepped through the hole after peeking through, motioning for us to follow. As we came out into the sewer tube, I almost gagged. In the center of the tube, a deep channel cut through the floor, and a current of wastewater, brown and stinking, flowed by. Either side of the channel, the walkway was wet from splash-overs, and I tried to push the thought of germs and sewage to the back of my mind. The cockle-roaches had been bad enough.

Montran pointed toward the back wall, where the channel flowed into an underground passage. At the end of the wall was a grimy ladder laden with years of mold and gunk that led up to the surface.

"I told you it wasn't far," he said.

"Let's just get this over with." I motioned to the ladder. "I need out of this place soon."

He led the way and, when we got to the ladder, he cautioned us not to touch the rungs with bare hands. "If you have gloves, wear them. If you don't, then use a cloth or something to put some sort of barrier between you and that mold. I have no idea whether it's sentient or not."

Along with Wandering Ivy and the other sentient plants, a group of molds had evolved a sort of hive-mind intelligence, and they worked to bring down victims. They were toxic, and when their victim succumbed to their poison, they would cover the body and dissolve the flesh and grow from the nourishment.

I found a thick handkerchief in my pocket and tore it in two, using my dagger to start the rip. Then, wrapping a piece around each hand, I volunteered to take the ladder first. I really wanted fresh air and I didn't care whether it was ten below and snowing like a son of a bitch. I was to the top before Hans was even on the first rung. I eased the grate open, peeking up. We were in a deserted lane. At first I thought it was a burrow-lane but then realized it was a back street. There was nobody in sight. As I eased out of the manhole, trying to keep my footing on the layer of snow and ice that had built up on the road, I could see, about two blocks down, the entrance to the Sandspit. We had made it.

"We'll have to be very cautious. No screaming, no loud noises. Zombies are highly attuned to noise and follow it like a beacon," Montran warned us. "Tymbur and I will spread out to the left. We don't want to go single file because if they come at us, we need a clear vantage to work our magic."

"Speaking of your magic, will it affect us if we're engaged in fighting them?" I didn't know much about death magic. While Hecate used it at times, I wasn't geared toward its nature and so I had never learned much about it.

Tymbur cleared his throat. "Probably not. Most of Montran's spells affect the dead only, except for healing. My spells are more volatile, but I'll be cautious about what spells I'm throwing around."

I pulled out my phone. "Call Jason." The dial tone turned to a beep-beep as my phone dialed Jason's number. A few rings later he came on the line.

"Where are you? Queet said you'd be waiting by the Sandspit for me. Well, I'm outside of it, hiding in a tree on the other side of the street. I'm trapped in the maple. There are zombies at the base and I'm stuck. I tried calling but got no answer."

"It took us longer than I thought. We're on the way." I glanced around, trying to pinpoint how close we were. "I think we're less than two blocks away, on Malloy Avenue. We took the Tunnels to get here and you know cell service doesn't always work down there. We're on the way. How many of them are there?"

A pause. Then, "Five below my tree. But the area is crawling with them. I tried one of my Turn-Back scrolls on them but it only worked on one. Why don't you wait there. I didn't know where to go so I decided this was as safe a place as any until you contacted me, but I can shift into my hawk form and meet you at the end of Malloy Avenue and Whip Street. You know, near Beggar's Barn."

Beggar's Barn was a fast-food joint that served questionable meals for a very low price. I never ate there and neither did Jason, but a lot of bogeys and the Broken did, considering that was all they could afford.

"Be careful. We'll head over there now." As I hung up and told the others where he was and where we were going to meet, a blinding flash filled the air and nearby apartment buildings and businesses went black. "What the hell? Come on, let's go get Jason before anything else happens."

I broke into a quick jog, the others hot on my heels. As we traversed the distance between us and Beggar's Barn, which was directly across from one set of gates into the Sandspit, I tensed. The cockle-roaches had been bad. The Tunnels nerve-wracking. But now we were headed into the middle of it, into the fray. I had never had to face a zombie, and the only analogous thing I could think of was facing an Abom wearing a human vehicle. But the Abom could only eat your life force and body. It couldn't turn you into one.

As we rounded the corner, I spied a hawk flying through the snow. Jason was having a rough time trying to keep from getting bounced around by the winds, which were howling now. The perfect backdrop to a zombie fight, I thought. Howling winds, snow and ice, and a messy battle ahead.

Jason reached the Beggar's Barn the same time we did. He touched down and, in one of his shimmering flashes, turned back into himself. "I'm so glad to see you. You don't know how glad I am to see you. Those freaking zombies scared the piss out of me. I swear, I about peed my pants when I was up there in the tree because I didn't know if they could climb."

"They generally can't," Montran said.

I quickly introduced Jason to Montran and Tymbur, and then we headed across the street to the Sandspit. "We can't lose track of each other. I suggest we chain-link. Anybody got a long-enough rope that we can all hold onto?"

Hans rummaged through his pack and came out with one. It was thin, very strong, and I recognized it as being Fae-made. Fae rope was incredibly light and hard to sever. It also held knots extremely well.

We lined up, this time deciding single file would have to work, given that we were headed into the Sandspit, visibility was almost nil, and we needed to keep close contact.

"At least it's not as bad as the Tremble," I said, taking my place behind Hans and Greta.

"You can say that again," Hans said. "That place gave me the fucking creeps."

"You were out on the Tremble?" Tymbur gave me a long look. "When we have time, I'd like to ask you about it. But for now, let's go try to do something about that portal."

We were in marching order—Hans, Greta, me, Tymbur, Montran, and Jason. Hans glanced back at me and I gave him a nod. In silence, we stepped into the Sandspit and headed for the World Tree.

Chapter 18

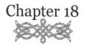

I was getting to know my way around the Sandspit far better than I ever hoped to. At some point, I'd have to try crossing through to the World Tree with my eyes closed, but tonight was not that night. I tried to shield my face against the pelting sting of the snowflakes. The wind was whipping them around so hard that they felt like bullets of ice, driving into my skin. My legs were, thankfully, partially covered by my duster, but that didn't stop the cold from seeping through every bone in my body.

The Sandspit was big enough that I hoped we'd make it to the World Tree without encountering any zombies. Usually, the only creatures I ever encountered in here were Aboms. Speaking of...I pulled up my Trace screen again to check, but there weren't any in the area. Relieved for small favors, I caught my breath and let it out in a slow stream, watching as it coalesced into white puffs in front of my face.

A gust whirled past, railing against us. My head began to spin as I realized that the blast was also filled with rogue magic. It spun around us, a vortex of wind and sand and snow and sparkling magic. I tried to hold my breath to avoid inhaling. Some magic worked via air transmission through inhalation, much like a potion needed to be drunk to be effective. But the sudden jolt as the magic glommed onto me sent me gasping as I stumbled away, trying to escape the million little sparks that raced over my body, like bees stinging me.

Jason took a step toward me, then stopped as

his eyes went wide and he shifted into hawk form. Hans let out a grunt as snow took the rough form of a very large, burly man and promptly sucker-punched Hans in the gut, doubling him over.

Montran shouted something to Tymbur, who was scrambling, trying to get out of the way. The next moment, a loud thunderclap filled the area and the cloud of snow and sand vanished. The sparks disappeared, Jason shifted in midair, landing in the snow with a thud, and Hans leaned over, trying to catch his breath.

"Come." A familiar voice echoed through the storm.

"Tam!" I raced forward, heedless of any danger, as he slipped out from behind a pile of twisted metal. He opened his arms as I slammed into his embrace, almost knocking him over.

"Love, relax. It's all right. Queet told us what's happening. He's waiting back in UnderBarrow." But his voice said that it was anything but all right. "Hurry up. You're close to the World Tree, but there are—"

"Zombies. We know."

"Yes, they've tried to infiltrate UnderBarrow but we shut down the main entrance. We'll go in through the secret one near here."

I hadn't known there was a secret entrance to UnderBarrow, but then again, there was a lot I didn't know about the Fae sanctuary.

"How did you stop the magic?" I had never encountered anybody who could circumnavigate the rogue powers of the Sandspit.

"I didn't. Hecate did. She's waiting by the World Tree for you."

"Hecate? She's here, too? She was supposed to meet us, but I wasn't sure when she'd make it. I really didn't look forward to tackling this without her guidance. For one thing, I have no idea what to do."

As Tam led us toward a rusted heap of scrap metal, I told him what had happened along the way.

"I wasn't sure what opened the portal, but I knew one had opened," he said. "Several of my people had run-ins with zombies as they were returning to UnderBarrow. Then, about twenty minutes ago, Hecate showed up. She told me what we are facing." He stopped abruptly, leaning in to kiss me again. "I missed you. I miss you when we're apart. You know that, don't you?"

"I miss you too. I never knew I could get so used to having someone around. To *wanting* them to be around." Admitting the last was hard. As much as I cared about my friends, the thought of being vulnerable made me queasy.

"Come," he said again, hurrying around the scrap heap to the other side. He stopped by the sagging door of a rusted-out car. Leaning inside, he popped open a trap door buried beneath what looked to be a thin layer of sand, but as I leaned closer I saw that it was actually sand solidified into a tile that was glued over the top of the trap door. "Hurry."

He vanished down the ladder inside the surprisingly well-lit hole and I followed, the others behind me. We landed at the bottom of yet another tunnel, but Tam confidently led us through the passage, which broadened out to become a hallway. I recognized the symbols on the wall as belonging to the Bonny Fae. We were back in UnderBarrow.

As we entered the throne room, Hecate was waiting beside the throne. She was dressed for battle in her long indigo robes, carrying her staff and her snakes. Vipers, *viper xanthina* to be specific, the three snakes wrapped around her, their brown and gray scaled bodies embracing her arms and neck as their heads bobbed gently, watchful eyes gazing over the crowd that surrounded the goddess.

She was seven feet tall today. The Elder Gods could change their height as they wished. As she shook out her hair, it flowed down her back. Her eyes blazed. She was a terrifying sight, both beautiful and dangerous. The rush of power washing off of her was so strong that instinct took over and I immediately went down on one knee. A wave of love—the purest, most unadulterated kind—ran through me as I knelt by her feet. Sometimes, when she was *standing in her power*, as she called it, the warmth that echoed toward me made everything else fade. The only thing that existed was the two of us, goddess and most willing servant. Most Theosians experienced this with their gods at one time or another.

"Rise, Fury." Her voice reverberated through the chamber, and as it echoed from wall to wall, Tam's people shifted. The Elder Gods still held a place of power among human, shifter, and Fae alike.

Shaking, I stood, grounding myself as much as possible. The fact that she was surrounded by a hundred awestruck Fae played into the energy that roiled around the room. And coming in off the past few days, I was hypersensitive, so I wasn't surprised that I had automatically dropped into worship-mode.

"I'm glad you arrived safely." She glanced around the room, playing to the audience. Then, with a little smile, she cupped my chin and leaned down to kiss my forehead. "Most beloved of my Theosians, may you walk forever by my side."

To everybody else, it was a ritual, more than an honor. But although I knew Hecate was fond of me, this was one hell of a show. I wasn't sure what she was up to, but then she leaned closer and whispered at a level so low that only I could hear her, "This should cement your place here." And then, she stepped back.

As the crowd murmured, I restrained a smile as I ducked my head, curtseying for effect. Might as well play it up, if she was going to.

Tam swung in by my side, taking me by surprise when he said, "Gracious Hecate, please allow me to make my official welcome. I would ask for your blessings on my relationship with your Theosian, Fury."

I blinked, but Hecate reached out and lightly placed her hands on both his head and mine with her hands. "I approve and claim alliance with the Lord of UnderBarrow. But now, we must retire to conference, if you would, Lord Tam."

"Of course, Lady Hecate. Please, follow me." He turned, nodded to the crowd as he took my hand, and led us out of the throne room. The others followed, and the crowd watched as we left. As soon as we were privately ensconced in a conference room, Tam pulled me to him, kissing me so deep that it felt like I was melting into his arms, becoming one as the kiss swept me out of the present and into a glowing light where there was only the two of us. A brilliant rain of colors showered around me, and a stray thought swept past. *So this is what it means to be in love with one of the Bonny Fae.*

Tam gently disengaged, then stroked back my hair. "I know. This may not be the time for what I have to say, but how can I let you head into danger without telling you how I feel? Without a kiss that speaks my heart?" He glanced at the others who were studiously ignoring us, then moved aside to one corner, pulling me along with him.

I ignored the stitch in my side, realizing how much I just wanted to stay here, with him, safe. I wasn't sure I liked the feeling. My sharp edges felt like they were eroding away just a little, leaving me more vulnerable and less alert.

"Tam, let's talk after I come back."

He shook his head. "No. We talk now. Or at least, I talk now. Fury, I've loved before, I'm sure you have figured that out. I've been alive a lot longer than you have. But it's been centuries since my heart has sung like it does in your presence. I want...never mind what I want. Leave it at this: I love you. I've loved you for a few years now. Yes, I watched you grow from a teenager into an adult. I never thought of you as anything but a willful, brave soul then. Just a young woman struggling to survive in a world that had already left its harsh and indelible mark on you."

"But that changed," I said softly.

"Yes, it changed. Around five years ago, something began to change. I began to see you as a woman. And I waited, patiently, for the right time when I thought you might be willing to listen to my feelings. But make no mistake. I love you, and now that we're together, those feelings have grown in leaps and bounds." He stopped, breathless. His eyes sparkled with a light that underscored his words. I had no doubt he was telling me the truth. He was laying out his feelings on a silver platter and offering them up to me.

I almost choked. The words had already run through my own head and heart, but when it came to saying them aloud. Well, saying something out loud made it so very real. But one more look in his eyes as he ran his hand gently down my cheek, and I knew I had to see this through, to wherever it led.

"I love you, Tam. I do. I don't know what that means for us, but know that I love you." And then, I was in his arms again, kissing him, burying myself deep in the warmth of his arms.

"I appreciate your desire to reassure one another, but we have to get moving." Hecate's voice was almost droll, but there was no sarcasm in her words. She cleared her throat as we parted. "Queet, did you tell Tam about the chip?"

No, Hecate. I thought I would leave that up to Fury. Queet suddenly rushed around me, his misty form billowing like smoke. He seemed to be quite chipper, given the circumstances.

You feeling better?

Yes, Fury, thank you for asking. I seem to have regained my strength, thanks to Hecate and the cleansings she did for me.

"Chip? What chip is this?" Tam slowly let go of me, returning to the table where he offered Hecate the main seat. She politely declined, allowing the Lord of UnderBarrow to keep his usual place.

I bit my lip. This was not a conversation I wanted to have at this moment. "You need to stay in UnderBarrow, Tam. Unless you can smuggle yourself over to Briarwood or the Wild Wood. A priestess of Pythia did a reading for us back in Hecate's office. She said that while the Devani had hold of you, they implanted you with a chip. You're a marked man. They'll kill you if you show up off the Tremble. At least, if you aren't in your sovereign land. You're lucky they don't monitor the Sandspit all that much. Or maybe they do, and are out there now, looking for you."

He paled even further than his so-very-pale skin. His long curls of dark hair swaddled him like a dark shroud against a ghost and his angular features took on an even more pinched look. "How is it that I don't remember this?"

"The oracle said that being out on the Tremble scrambled your memory about that. You didn't spill the beans about me, no worries there, but your memory of being chipped vanished."

"Then..." He paused. "Never mind about that now. As long as I stay here, I'll be safe from the shaygra and their stunners. I wish I could go with you." He paused, looking torn.

"You are needed here. Don't put yourself in danger. We need you alive, and so do your people. *I* need you alive." I reached out, lightly touching him on the arm. "Live to be a hero another day."

With a final nod, he took his place at the table. "Then, if I cannot go with you, what can I do to help? I understand you are looking to shut down a portal on the World Tree?"

"Lyon opened it, we think." I shrugged. "I know that spells are hard to undo if another magician casts them, but does the fact that the portal is on the World Tree make a difference? Hecate, what happened at the meeting of the Elder Gods?"

She glanced at the others. Besides Hans, Jason,

Greta, Tymbur, Montran, and myself, Tam was present, along with Damh Varias, and Elan.

"Usually, temple business would be just that. Temple business. But you are all involved in this, and since Fury would tell you anyway, I'll go ahead and break protocol this once. The Convocation of Gods met. They appointed Hades, Thor, and me to be the main contacts, since our Theosians are directly involved. Since I already told you I would come to help however I could, Thor and Hades decided to let me be the liaison."

"Somehow, I cannot see Hades choosing to walk down the city streets," Tymbur said softly.

"Somehow, I think you are right. So I came." Hecate spread her hand over the table and an image of the World Tree appeared, spots glowing brightly all over it. "Here, you see the World Tree and the portals that Gaia forged on it. Others have come and gone, but only hers remain steady. But see this? The red one?" She pointed to a crimson splash on a second-tier branch. "This is the portal through which the dead are marching. Lyon did, indeed, open it. I cannot close it myself, but I have here a charm that can. I got it from Athena, who gave it to me. She rules over order and law, and can counter the chaos they inflicted. But the charm must be activated and thrown through the portal."

I heard the hesitation in her voice. "You cannot do it, can you?" I guessed. "You're not allowed to take such a direct path."

She lowered her head. "Correct. The Convocation of Gods cannot take action on this. Not directly. I can advise, guide, and provide auxiliary support. There are reasons we can't step in, but those I cannot go into. Not yet."

"Then somebody has to work their way through

the zombies up on the World Tree, activate the charm, and throw it through." I let out a long, slow breath. "I'll do it. But I'll need help."

Hecate caught my gaze. "I was hoping you would volunteer. But I won't order you to do so. This won't be easy, Fury. This won't be easy at all."

I had the feeling there was more she wanted to say about it, but wasn't. I glanced around. "I need backup. I can't fend off the zombies if I'm focusing on closing the portal. Like Hecate, I'm not going to ask anyone in particular to go."

Tymbur stood. "I'm here to help, and so is Montran. We will go."

Hans and Greta jumped to their feet.

Greta thrust her sword into the air. "We'll help you or die trying. Better to die in battle than whimpering on the sidelines."

"You know I'll do what I can. I can fly up into the tree and do my best to take care of some of them as they come through the portal." Jason stood, taking his place by the others.

"I will come, too." Elan stepped forward, raising her bariclore.

A thought crossed my mind. "Just how many are we talking about? Zombies, that is. Are they coming through in a continuous stream?"

Hecate shook her head. "No, but rapidly enough to be a problem. I hate to say it, but in the time it took all of us to get here, there are probably enough loose in the streets that it's going to cause an ongoing problem. We must shut down the portal, but that won't stop the scourge. And since zombieism spreads, the infection will already be contaminating the city. I'm afraid that Seattle has more problems than just fighting off the undead."

Tam's expression darkened. "I would call the

city leaders and tell them, but considering my status right now, that's not possible. However, I can call the leaders of the Were communities, the shifters, and ask them to carry the news."

"You can't call them, though. In fact, you should get out of UnderBarrow now, while the chaos is diverting their attention." My gaze fastened on Laren. "Laren will take you. He can carry you in the ship. He can transport you through the Locks, over to the Wild Wood past Wild Wave Inlet." Tam opened his mouth and I knew he was going to protest. "*Please* don't refuse. This is the best opportunity for you to get out of here. Damh Varias is trustworthy, he can keep UnderBarrow going for now. Tam," I said, feeling tears well up. "You have to escape until we figure out how to fix this mess with the Devani. I keep thinking there has to be a reason they targeted you. It can't be just random."

Damh Varias took my side, to my surprise. "The Lady Fury speaks with wisdom. Now would be the easiest time to smuggle you out. You must not allow yourself to be trapped here, and you know that our *other* methods of transportation are out of kilter right now."

"She's right, man. Go. Get out of here." Jason shook his head. "We didn't rescue you from the Tremble just to see you trapped in this place. We'll take care of Fury, I promise. We'll send her to you as soon as we can."

"Then I'd best be off with haste." Tam let out a long sigh. "I will go to the Lord of the Cascadia Fae. We have an alliance."

As I watched him, I suddenly saw the years weigh in on him—it was no more than a shadow, but for a moment, he looked ancient as the hills, ancient as the ocean. Ancient and tired and angry. The power behind the façade he wore on a daily basis hit with an impact that I did not expect, and it struck me once again how little I knew about the man I loved.

"Fury? A kiss before I go?" It was a plea, this time, rather than a command.

I moved to his side. Feeling more conspicuous than ever—this was really a good-bye kiss until we could figure out what to do—I shyly leaned my face up, meeting his lips. This time the passion was muted, and the longing deeper. There was a sadness that came through the kiss as well—laden with fear and loss and worry. I realized that he was afraid for me, and afraid of losing me, and that made my heart ache even worse.

Quietly, I pulled to the side. I had to maintain my courage, had to put our separation beyond what was coming. I couldn't go into this torn. As if reading my mind, Tam smiled then, and bopped me on the nose.

"Give them hell, my Fury. Go out there and tear up that portal and stop the pestilence that is threatening Seattle. If anybody can do it, you can." And with that, Laren motioned to Tam and they headed toward the door. Turning to Damh Varias before he left, Tam said, "My kingdom is in your hands. Treat her gently, treat her like she deserves. I'll contact you the usual way once I reach sanctuary."

Damh Varias bowed, very low. "As you order, milord. I am your faithful and obedient servant, always."

As the door closed behind Laren and Tam, Hecate motioned for me to return to the table. "Come. We must plan quickly, and then we must act."

I closed my eyes, shoving every ounce of anguish I had to the side. I returned to the table as Hecate laid out what needed to be done.

Chapter 19

As we crept out from the entrance to
UnderBarrow next to the World Tree, I was still
trying to wrap my head around what I needed to
do. My muscles had eased a bit. A good layer of
All-Heal saw to that, as well as some AntiBruise on
my face. Tam had arranged for a group of guards
to go with us. They were skilled in dealing with the
undead, and all of them were armed with silver
weapons. Silver was a scourge to the walking dead.

As we stepped into the now-raging storm, it
was difficult to see much farther than a few feet
ahead of us. But then, as my eyes adjusted to
the glowing light of the World Tree, I saw them.
Figures shuffling all too fast for my taste, away
from the base of the tree. And by shuffling, I meant
very quickly moving into the Sandspit. Several
were headed in our direction and I tensed, hand on
my thigh, ready to bring out my whip.

But Tam's men moved in, their swords flashing
as they waded into the snow, heading toward the
shambling corpses. I grimaced as the glint of their
swords flashed in the green glow, and the sound
of grunts and slobbered shouts echoed as the men
engaged. I was torn between helping them, and
circumnavigating the battle and heading toward
the World Tree.

Hecate decided for me. She led the way
around the fight, bringing to bear a silver wand.
It shimmered with a pale blue light, and as she
held it up, the light shone through the snowfall,
illuminating the way. While she couldn't close the
portal herself, she could fight off zombies, and her

very presence lifted our spirits. Tymbur swung in behind her, then Montran. Behind me were Jason and Greta, then Elan and Hans.

Another group of zombies closed in—about ten of them—and Hecate's wand flashed, the brilliance lighting up the entire area. As the light flared, the creatures staggered, giving Montran time to move forward and hold up a silver sigil. I recognized it as a symbol belonging to Hades.

*"From body to earth, the grave your home,
Return to your shrouds, never to roam."*

His voice echoed, stronger than I thought it could manage. The energy emerged from the sigil, concentric rings of a pale gray light, a toroidal vortex rippling out toward the zombies, flowing over them like a twister on its side. I watched, breathless, as the spell caught them up, churning them into the topsy-turvy funnel. I couldn't quite see what was happening to them, but it seemed a blur of body parts and then the funnel vanished, along with the zombies.

I let out a long breath. "That was impressive."

"Well, hope I don't need to cast the spell more than twice. That's about the most I can manage before recharging." Montran rubbed his head; he looked strained and his shoulders hunched forward. Even in the dim light and the swirling snow, the toll the spell had taken on him was apparent. Tymbur motioned for him to move closer to the group, taking his place.

"My magic is different, given I'm a Theosian, but rest for a bit. Save your energy in case we're in desperate need." He seemed protective of the young priest, and I suddenly noticed a resemblance between the two.

"Are you Montran's father?" I blurted out before I could check myself.

But Tymbur smiled softly. "No, Lady Fury. But I am his uncle, many times removed. My brother, who is long, long dead, had sons. And they had children. And so on, until Montran came along. I have seen many generations of my family slide past in the arms of time. As will you as you grow and age."

I blinked as his words penetrated. He was right, of course. Theosians lived far, far longer than they would have if they hadn't been altered by the Sandspit. I was barely into my thirties, but if I did have family—if my mother had survived or if I had siblings—I would have had to watch them age and die while I stayed young. The aging process slowed dramatically during the third decade. From now on, I'd only show my age in fits and spits as time went on.

The revelation unsettled me and I shook my head. "I can't think about that now. I have no family to leave behind." Which was true. If I had grandparents, I had never been to see them. If I had cousins, they hadn't come over to play when I was young. As far as I knew, I was the last of my line. Suddenly feeling more alone than I had since I watched my mother die, I fell into a deep silence.

Hecate seemed to pick up on my confusion. "Fury, we'll talk about this later. Focus on our task at hand." She leaned back, clapping me on the shoulder. Her snakes, who weren't affected by the chill at all, bobbed and tongued the air in my direction, but they didn't coil, nor did they seem agitated.

As the weight of her hand pressed down on me,

a flood of power and strength echoed through me, as if I had just plugged myself into an outlet.

"I'm good. Thanks." I caught her gaze and she smiled softly. The unsettled feelings that Tymbur's comments had stirred up faded away. I was where I belonged. Inhaling deeply, I shook them off and channeled my attention onto the World Tree. We were standing at the base of it.

The World Tree rose a hundred feet high, and there were rough stairs leading up the trunk, notched from the tree limbs, roughly hewn and difficult to navigate. We would only be able to travel in single file, and our destination was the second tier—a line of branches up the trunk about thirty-five feet from the ground. From here, we could see the gleam of the new portal, shining with a sickly crimson light, as the zombies slowly appeared, moving out of the vortex of light to begin their trek down the web of limbs leading to the bottom of the Sandspit.

They were coming at intervals of every couple minutes and I suddenly realized just how many of these creatures had to be in the streets by now. My heart began to sink. We would stop the influx of them by closing the portal, but until we hunted them all down, the infection would continue as they attacked the living. The magnitude of our task hit home.

"What do we do? How are we going to track all of them down?"

"Fury, focus on one thing at a time. We shut down the portal, then we worry about cleanup afterward. Do you remember what I told you?" Hecate stood back, handing me the components of the spell Athena had fashioned. There was a scroll and a small sphere that swirled with brilliant colors. Reason and war, bound together in a smooth glass orb. The surface was mirrored, shining in the dim light.

"How do I hold this so I don't break it before we get up there?" I was horrified that I'd make a mistake and ruin everything.

"Carry it in this bag—it won't prevent an accident, but it will cushion the orb well. Keep the orb and the scroll in an easy-to-access place." She glanced at my jacket. "You're going to want to take that coat off. It's too long to manage the Tree with. Too easy to get caught on a stray branch."

I shrugged out of it, my teeth chattering as the cold settled in. I was used to my legs being cold, but the snow seemed to settle into my bruises and I ached. I glanced down. My corset had no pockets and I didn't trust slipping the sphere into the pockets of my leather shorts. I didn't even know if it would fit. So I tied the loops of the pouch holding the orb through the loops of my belt, letting it dangle against my left thigh.

As instinct kicked in, I shed thoughts of everything and everyone except the task at hand. I could do this. I took on Abominations and sent them back to Pandoriam. I was the chosen of Hecate, I was her servant. I pulled my hair back, wrapping it into a ponytail and, ignoring the aches in my body, turned to my goddess.

"Milady, I am ready."

"Go, and be safe." She stood back. "I cannot venture up the World Tree with you, but I will do everything I can from below. Take care of her," she told the others. "She must reach her goal or your world is in danger and the Order of the Black Mist will win this time."

"Let's get a move on," Tymbur said. "Montran,

you and I go first. If one of us falls, the other will be there. Hans, you next. Fury, after him. Then Greta and Elan. Jason, can you fly up over the Tree and do what you can from up there?"

I will go too. I can carry messages to Hecate should need be. Queet suddenly swept around us.

Queet! I'm so glad you're here. Stay close. I'm afraid. I didn't want to admit it, not even to myself, but the truth was, as focused and ready to go into battle as I felt, the sight of the dead walking out of that portal was enough to freeze my blood.

I'll be by your side, Fury. I'm in fighting form again, so there may be ways I can help.

As we headed up the tree, Tam's men spread out, hunting down what zombies they could find around the base of the World Tree. There were still figures coming out of the portal, but Tymbur was leading us up a different route so that we wouldn't meet them head-on.

"I want to come in at them from the side," he said. "That way we can reach the portal without going through the onslaught of zombies that have already come through. See, we're climbing boughs that lead to other portals. But halfway up, another bough crosses over close enough to our destination that, with a little luck, we can jump the distance and be almost at the portal we're aiming for without having to fight off any zombies."

"Speaking of portals." I pulled up my Trace screen and scanned for Aboms. The last thing we needed was—*Oh hell.* An Abom had just entered our realm from the portal leading to Pandoriam. Wishing we could shut that one down while we were at it, I cast around, trying to see where the Abomination was.

Queet, there's an Abom loose on the Tree.

I can see him, Fury. He's four tiers up and two tiers over. I can guide you there, if you want.

I paused. What should I do? I had to close the portal leading to Tartarus. *Queet, hurry back to Hecate. Tell her about the Abom, and ask her what I should do. Hurry.*

He swept away without a word as I stiffened, trying to focus. *Keep to the mission at hand until ordered otherwise. Always obey your Elder God—* the two main rules set forth for Theosians.

"What's wrong?" Greta, who was behind me, leaned closer.

"You're good at body language, aren't you?"

"I saw you straighten. Also, the look on your face wasn't pleasant." The Valkyrie-to-be stared at me.

"There's an Abom that's just come through. Queet is talking to Hecate now about what I should do." I abruptly grabbed hold of a limb coming off of the big bough we were climbing as the stairs narrowed. We were headed toward an area where we would leave the steps behind shortly, and then we'd be reliant on our balance and the hope that the branches weren't too slippery from the snow.

"Freya preserve us." Greta shook her head, and turned around to pass the news to Elan.

A moment later, Queet swept up through the tree to hover beside me. *I talked to Hecate. The Abom seems perplexed by all the activity. He's studying the area. She said leave him for now, but be prepared in case he spots you and makes a beeline for you.*

Oh, that was a comforting thought, all right. I glanced over my shoulder. "Greta, tell Elan about the Abom. Also tell her that Hecate has ordered me to ignore him for now. But he's watching the area, and if he comes this way, people need to be prepared. We don't want to have him shove us off the World Tree into a pile of zombies below. Or worse."

She nodded, pausing to pass along the news. Ahead of me, Montran stopped. We had come to a fork in the branch where the steps turned to the left, toward the trunk, leading to a portal about five yards above us. The other fork led out to the end of the branch, and about fifteen feet separated us from the large branch we were aiming for.

"Hell, it was hard to tell below but it looks like the gap between the two is a lot wider than I first thought." Tymbur stroked his chin.

I shaded my eyes from the falling snow, staring at the distance between us and the other tree. "What do we do now? Turn around and go back?"

Tymbur scanned the tree. "There are a few branches further up that stretch closer. But they're thin and I don't know if they would hold our weight. What do you think? We can't jump, that much is obvious. But if we go back around the other route, we're going to meet the zombies as they come down from the portal."

"I've got an idea," Hans said. "I have rope. Have Jason fly across with it, then transform. He can tie it off there, and we'll tie it off here and create a single rope bridge. Then we can use it to monkey crawl across."

"Brilliant." I looked around for Queet. "Queet?"

I'm here. What do you need?

Find Jason. Tell him to hurry down here. We need him to fly across to that branch over there with a rope, then shift back and tie it down.

Right. I'm on it.

While we waited, Hans tied the rope tightly to

the main bough. Jason spiraled down, his hawk form sleek and beautiful with wings spreading wide, their feathers a deep rust color. His eyes were the same piercing green as they were in his human form. He cautiously perched on one of the nearby branches. Hans held out the rope and Jason took it in his beak, then launched himself off, flying to the other branch where he first draped the end of the rope over the limb so it wouldn't fall, then transformed back into his two-legged form. He shifted position to balance himself, then picked up the rope and lashed it tightly around the thick bough. Straddling the branch and leaning forward to be ready to help, he motioned to us.

Montran adjusted his robes so that they didn't interfere, then cautiously wrapped his ankles around the rope and, hand over hand, began to pull himself across the rope, glancing over his shoulder at the drop below. It was a good thirty feet to the ground, through a latticework of sharp branches, any one of which could easily impale someone falling through them. At one point, when he was almost across, his hands slipped and he flailed, grabbing for the rope as he began to fall backward, holding on only by his knees.

Jason shifted in a flash and he launched off the branch, flying beneath Montran to shore him up with his massive wingspan. Montran managed to catch hold of the rope as Jason strained to leverage him up, and a moment later, the priest managed to cross the rest of the way. Jason joined him, landing back on the branch as Montran reached the bough. Jason transformed again, in time to help him scramble off the rope and find a firm footing back further toward the trunk of the tree.

Tymbur went next, managing to cross without

incident.

As I secured Xan to make certain she wouldn't drop out of her scabbard, I glanced up at the falling snow. Winter had come for certain. It might be only late October, but the drifts weren't going to melt until spring. My breath forming white clouds in front of my face, I rubbed my hands together. It was a good thing I was Theosian and could handle temperature variations easier than humans or I'd be a frozen treat by now. Gritting my teeth against the chill, I wrapped my ankles around the rope and, grabbing hold of it with my hands, swung down below, scrunching across. I didn't look down, trying not to think about all of those sharp branches waiting below, keeping my eyes toward the top of the World Tree. Time seemed to stand still while I crossed the rope, but then I was at the other side and Jason was helping me onto the bough. He motioned for me to join Montran and Tymbur. Another few minutes and we were all together again. Jason shifted once more, flew to the other side, untied the knot on the rope, and then carried it back over.

"Where to from here?" I tried to make sense of where we were, but all I could tell through the fall of snow was that we were high up in the World Tree.

"We climb up this lattice of branches. They aren't technically part of the stair system, but they lead directly to the portal we want."

He pointed up. As we followed his direction, we could see the wide branch overhead leading away from the crimson portal.

I caught my breath. The portal led to Tartarus, where the Titan oversaw the souls of the wicked. At least those who had followed the Greek gods.

The energy pouring out of the portal was violent and filled with a hunger that hit me even standing well below it. I could feel the ache to devour, the hunger to feed roiling through the crimson gateway, and it nauseated me. Montran and Tymbur both looked just as pained as I felt.

"Are you okay?" I asked them.

Tymbur shook his head. "Tartarus and Hades do not dwell in the same worlds. Hades may be Lord of the Underworld, but his is a peaceful, quiet place where the dead go to rest. You know he rules over Elysium too."

I jerked up. "Elysium? Where the Devani come from?"

"They are only one element that lives there. They are the guardians of order there, and keep the peace in a peaceful land. But in Elysium, the Devani belong in a way that they don't over here." Tymbur lowered his voice. "One of my tasks, as a Theosian bound to the Lord of Death, is to keep watch and report on what goes on here. While I'm not privy to what Hades thinks of the Devani who live in this world, trust me, the situation is being monitored."

With that, Tymbur fell silent for a moment before continuing. "Tartarus is a dark and painful place, Fury. Hades does not rule there, nor does he delight in having to order the dead to venture there. I know you can feel the hunger leeching through that portal, but I feel it ten times more and it makes my very bones ache."

As he spoke, the portal flared again and another zombie staggered through. We were close enough to see the creature, and the sight made my stomach turn. Whoever he had been was gone in a mash of decomposition. The zombie no longer resembled anything quite human, save for the fact that he was walking on two feet, and had arms and a skull that showed through the rotting flesh. The light in the eye sockets burned with a vicious light, and again, a wave of hunger rolled off the creature as he began the journey down the steps toward the base of the World Tree. There were five others who were making the trek, and I wondered how Tam's men were faring in hunting them down. Once again, I hit a wall of despair when I thought of having to track them down through the city before they engendered a plague.

"Let's move." I nodded toward the zombie. "We have to shut down that portal."

Tymbur nodded and, without another word, began climbing the branches to the portal like he might climb a ladder. Montran scrambled to follow, and I waited till he was halfway up, then grabbed hold of the first limb. The climb wasn't difficult. Most of the danger rested in possibly slipping on the snow that had iced over the tree. But my boots had a firm tread on them, and I managed without a problem.

As I lifted myself onto the branch near Tymbur and Montran, my stomach clenched. The crimson mist of the portal flared, and before we could move, it opened and we found ourselves facing a very large, very hungry corpse.

Chapter 20

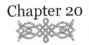

Tymbur pushed me behind him. "Move. Give us room to work."

As I stumbled back, catching a nearby branch to keep from falling over the side, Montran shifted to allow Tymbur the chance to move to the front. He pulled a short sword from the folds of his robes, startling me. I hadn't realized he was armed with anything beyond his magical implements. The blade gleamed, glowing with a soft light that flickered as Tymbur raised it.

"The light—"

"It glows when the undead are near, regardless of type." He zeroed his focus in on the zombie, who was grunting.

I watched with a morbid fascination as the creature lurched toward Tymbur, arms out as if to embrace him. The teeth and jaw bones showed through the ragged flesh, and they gnashed, as if trying to clamp down on Tymbur from a distance.

I edged over to the branch-ladder. "Greta, Hans, get up here. Zombie."

Greta, who was almost to the top, hauled herself up faster, swinging over the edge as Tymbur shouted from behind me. I whirled, scanning for him. *Crap.* The zombie had suddenly turned and was bearing down on Montran, who had been standing to the side. Montran was trying to scrunch as far back as he could away from the wild flailing of the creature.

Tymbur let out a shout as he plunged the sword toward the zombie, piercing its back, but it didn't turn. Instead, it just tried to keep moving steadily

toward the warrior priest. Montran had backed up
as far as he could. He was muttering something
under his breath. Tymbur twisted the blade, but
the zombie pulled off of it and stumbled forward,
slashing at Montran.

Montran shouted, trying to sidestep the attack,
but his foot slipped on the snowy branch and
before anybody could get past the zombie to him,
he went over the edge. He managed to catch hold
of the branch and hung there, swaying above the
dizzying drop.

The zombie seemed fixated on him, unsteadily
kneeling to reach for his hands. Montran screamed
as Tymbur lunged forward again, swinging the
short sword sideways through the air to connect
with the creature's neck. As it cleaved into the
rotting flesh, tearing muscle and sinew away to
expose bone, the zombie fought to pull itself away.
It neither screamed nor showed pain, which was
almost more frightening than the creature itself.

But as we watched, Montran gave a sudden
shout as his grip began to slip. I glanced down
at the branch below us. It was about eight feet
down and not very wide, but it was directly below
Montran. Without a word, I aimed and jumped.
I landed, teetering, and crouched, grabbing for
the nearest limb to steady myself. As I balanced,
I realized I wasn't alone. Jason had shifted and
flown down. Now, he was back into his human
form. Without a word, he grabbed me and lifted
me up. I reached out. I was facing Montran's
knees. He struggled, swinging back and forth as he
desperately attempted to regain his handhold.

I couldn't hold him if he slipped, but I could
steady him to give him time. I grabbed hold of his
knees, bracing them against me. Jason held me up,

trying to keep his own footing.

Montran relaxed into my arms, adjusting. He brought one hand down, wiping it on his robe, then switched hands, bringing the other down to dry it off. I gave him a shove, taking hold of his foot to place it on my now-burning shoulder. My body was protesting the weight and the stretching but I couldn't let him down. If I let go now, he'd fall.

Another moment and he had regained his hold. As I pushed, he scrambled up. I couldn't tell what was going on with the zombie, but apparently it wasn't preventing him from getting back on the branch. Once Montran was safe, Jason lowered me to the branch we were on. I suddenly realized I'd have to figure out how to get back up to them. But then the rope dropped down. I looked up. Hans was straddling the branch, motioning for me to wrap it around my waist. Grimacing, I did, even though the rope was cutting into the bruises in my side. The chill numbed me up but I'd be sore later. As he began to lift me up, Jason flew by me.

Once I was near the branch, I reached up and grabbed hold. Hans helped me scramble up. I looked around for the zombie, but all I could see was the crimson portal.

"Did you kill it?" I asked Tymbur.

He nodded, looking solemn. "But you need to hurry before the next comes through. Whatever you have to do, do it now, please."

I cleared my throat, so numb that even my bruises weren't fazing me by now. "Give me room." I moved toward the portal, fumbling to untie the pouch that Hecate had given me. As I opened it, letting the orb roll out onto my hand, the sphere felt like the most delicate of glasses—sparkling as the colors swirled within. I raised it up, staring in at the juxtaposition of fire and ice, of logic and chaos, of reason and war.

"What do you have to do?" Tymbur asked.

I stared at the orb. "I must use the scroll to step through into Tartarus and cast the sphere down to break it. Then I have to return before the portal shuts. I won't lie, this is dangerous."

Hecate had warned me when she instructed me how to use it. She had warned me that there was a chance I might be trapped if I didn't move fast enough, but I hadn't told anybody else that. I didn't want them trying to dissuade me. The threat we were facing was too great. Disaster loomed if we couldn't stop them from coming through. As it was, we were already facing a growing plague until we tracked down all of the zombies.

"Fury, are you going to do what I think you are?" Jason started to move forward, but Hans stopped him.

"She was given a task by Hecate. Let her do her job." Hans flashed me a grim look. He knew what it meant to be Theosian. To be the blade of the goddess. Or, in his case, the hammer of the gods. He understood that we didn't belong to ourselves, but to the Elder Gods, and it was up to them to do as they would with us.

Jason stared at him for a moment, then backed away. But he gave me a pleading look that said everything, and yet nothing.

"I have to do this. Trust me. Hecate wouldn't ask me if it wasn't absolutely necessary." And with that, I motioned everybody back. "Give me room." I pulled out the scroll and unrolled it. Athena had written a simple charm on it, but the paper itself almost leapt out of my hand, it was so charged.

I stood in front of the portal, raising the sphere as I read from the paper. The winds picked up, howling as if they could sense what I was doing, and I felt an ache so deep in my heart that I wanted to weep, as if the World Tree itself was grieving over what was befalling it.

"Between the realms, between the worlds, This spell invoke, this spell unfurl,
Let no paths cross, let no paths meet, Life from this vortex, now must flee.
In the name of Pallas Athena, I strike thy power from thee!"

The scroll burst into flames, the words vanishing into the fire. As the vortex flared from the spell, I jumped through.

For a moment, I thought I had entered the wrong portal. Everything was black. Pitch black, like the black of nightmares. It felt like I was falling, and then—I wasn't. As I reached out to steady myself, I felt flesh. Squirming hands, tentatively reaching toward me. I screamed and the world flared to light. The flames were everywhere, burning off ponds as though a wick had turned the pools of briny water into oil.

The blinding flash faded into a sooty, stricken landscape. I could see what had been touching me. Figures, both men and women, skulked around. Some looked like lumps of puddling flesh and still others were skeletal. Then the zombies came into view. They were shambling around, filling the air with their hungry groans. Everywhere, I sensed despair and anguish, and the screams were no longer human, but animal in nature.

I blinked, too terrified to move. Then, remembering what I had come to do, I cast the sphere down on the ground, falling to my knees as everything lurched when the glass shattered. New shrieks filled the air, the rumbling echoed by an earthquake that rippled in waves through the fire-torn land.

I staggered to my feet as the ground continued to shake. I had to get back through the portal. As I raced toward the vortex, trying to keep my balance, I became aware of a change in color in the portal. I skidded to a halt in front of it, but as I began to step through, some force tried to push me back. Damn it, someone was trying to shove their way through, and they were blocking my exit.

I shoved back at them, frantic, but whoever—*whatever*—it was, was strong.

"Get the hell out of the way!"

The portal was beginning to close. I only had seconds to escape. I backed up a couple steps and, running as hard as I could, I dove for the vortex, body slamming whatever it was out of my way. The crimson iris of the interdimensional door was swirling closed as my weight and speed drove through, bowling over whatever was in my way. I emerged back onto the World Tree just as the crimson faded and the portal vanished from sight.

I landed so hard on the branch that it knocked the wind out of me. But the next moment, something latched onto my throat. I tried to breathe, but it was cutting off my air. Scrambling against the unseen force, I realized that the Abomination had hold of me.

Queet!

I'm here! I see him. Fury, he's a powerful one and he isn't in-body. You're going to have to take him to the Crossroads if you hope to have a chance against him.

But there's no Crossroads here. I can't. I struggled, managing to catch a shallow breath as the Abom shifted positions. *Hecate—tell Hecate!*

Queet vanished as the Abom lashed at me with his psychic tether, trying to get his siphon to my crown chakra. I managed to slide my hand down to my thigh and slapped, grabbing hold as the whip came off in my hand. But as I raised it, I realized that the Abom was too close. We were entangled and there was no way for me to hurt him with the whip without bringing it back on myself.

Jason was shouting something. Through a growing haze caused by the lack of oxygen, I realized he and Tymbur were trying to help, but they didn't know how to deal with Aboms, especially when they weren't in-body. Jason had helped me a few times, but mostly to pick up the pieces when I was done.

As I thrashed my head back and forth, trying to evade the damned siphoning tube, there was a blinding flash and the world went white, lit up like the sun.

Again, I hit hard, and the impact shook the Abomination off of me. I blinked, trying to get my bearings, and then knew exactly where I was. There was the cauldron, and the sign—Hecate had bounced me out to the Crossroads.

"Okay, sucker, bring it on." I rolled to my

feet, ignoring every ache and pain that protested through my body. I brought my hand down so hard on my thigh I almost knocked myself over, but my whip was ready and in-hand.

I'm here, Fury.

Queet, thank gods. Where's his soul-hole?

It's at the base of his tailbone.

The Abom had taken the nebulous form of a human. Or rather, a *giant*. He was big and mean, and I had the feeling he was all too cunning. He wasn't corporeal, but rather condensed mist, as if encased in a body-shaped bubble.

That means I have to get around behind him. I need you to distract him, Queet.

On it.

Queet flitted around in front of me, then shimmered into sight. The Abom grunted, turning toward him as I dashed toward the nearby bank of bushes. There were a few benches in front of the hedgerow and scrub trees, and I leaped over one, ducking into the vegetation as Queet did his best to engage the Abom. From where I was hiding, I could see what was going on until I could make my way around behind the creature.

The Abomination was looking around for me, but then Queet dive bombed him. Spirits couldn't do much to Aboms except annoy them, but it served our purpose when the Abom swatted at him. I chose that moment to slip through the ever-present mist around the other side of the benches to come in behind the Abom.

My whip ready, I took aim toward his tailbone.

There it was! The glowing hole that I needed to attack.

Wound an Abom in their soul-hole and you'd send them back to Pandoriam. I raised my whip and brought it down hard, but the Abom shifted, turning. The fall of my whip hit him square across the face, slicing deep into the swirling clouds that made up his body. He shrieked—the blow hurt, even if it wasn't a killing-strike—and the Abom charged.

I danced back, teetering as my foot landed on a rock and threw me off balance. If I tried to recover, I'd be right in his line of attack. So I fell, rolling as I hit the ground. I brought my whip around low to coil around his legs at the moment he lunged.

With a roar, he tripped forward. As he toppled toward the ground, I whipped out my dagger and moved in, letting go of the whip to bring the blade down two-handed toward his soul-hole. The tip of the dagger penetrated and I fell on it, hard.

The Abomination shrieked again and then, with one quick whoosh, a fractured light pierced the Crossroads, flowing from his soul-hole. The Abom vanished and I dropped to the ground, exhausted. Taking out an Abom on the Crossroads always left me half-dead.

I could barely think...could barely hear...
Fury? Fury? I'm getting Hecate.
Queet? I think I'm dying.
No, you're not. You always say that, but you're not. I'll be right back.
And then the world went black.

"Fury?" The voice pierced the blackness, but it was so loud that it made me want to vomit. I couldn't open my eyes. There was light around me and right now, that light would get me so sick I wouldn't be able to handle it.

I tried to move my head, but everything whirled.

"Uhhh..."

"Can you hear me?"

I wasn't sure who "me" was at this point, but I let out another "Uhhh."

"We're taking you somewhere safe. The Abom's gone. You got him."

Another "Uhhh" was the best I could manage.

"Just rest. You're going to be all right. We've got you."

I wanted to ask if everybody was all right. If the portal had really closed. But there were no words. My tongue couldn't form them, and my throat felt like it was on fire. Every move jarred me hard, but I had no idea where we were. Who "we" even was.

And then, the jostling stopped and I sensed that it was dark around me. I tentatively forced one eye open to see that I was in a chamber somewhere. I thought it was UnderBarrow, but wasn't sure. There were a lot of people standing around, but I decided to forgo trying to make an attempt to identify them.

I breathed in and groaned. Every muscle in my body ached. Softly letting out my breath, I closed my eyes again, and slipped into blessed darkness.

Chapter 21

The next time I opened my eyes, I was in bed, and even though I ached like a son of a bitch, I was able to push myself up against the headboard. I glanced around. I was in UnderBarrow all right, in my bed in the room Tam had given me. Tam was sitting by my side while Jason and Hans were on the other side of the room. Jason was reading, and Hans was staring at the wall. As I groaned, they all scrambled to their feet.

"Fury? Are you all right? Can you talk?" Tam gently pressed his lips to my forehead.

"I thought you left already?"

"I couldn't go, not till I knew what happened with the portal. With you."

I winced. Even the slightest touch rippled through my body with some sort of pain. "I feel like somebody took a hammer to me."

Tam pulled me into his arms, kissing me deep, welcoming both his touch and the blessed relief that flowed from his kisses. It was as if he reached into me, caught hold of the pain, and sucked it out through his lips. As the shock of pain began to lessen, my head cleared. Another moment and he sat back, looking quite pale but smiling.

"Better?"

I tested, raising one arm, then the other. My muscles still ached, the bruising wasn't gone by any means, but I felt capable of thinking again and the sharp jolts had subsided to a dull ache that I could manage.

"Yeah, much better. Especially seeing you." I rested a hand on his arm. "What's today?"

Some days, after I took an Abom down on the Crossroads, I'd be out for hours. Sometimes even longer.

"About twelve hours from when you sent the Abomination home to Pandoriam. I'm surprised you're awake now." Jason sat on the foot of the bed, while Hans held onto the spiraling post that rose to meet the canopy.

"I guess I'm just getting used to feeling like a punching bag." I tried to joke, but tripped over the words as I flashed back to the scenes I had witnessed in Tartarus. The pain there had been so palpable that I had a feeling I wouldn't be able to blot it off my memory for a long time, if ever. Then, remembering everything, I let out a sharp breath, wincing as it caused a stitch in my side. "What about the portal? The zombies?"

"You closed it, thanks to Athena's charm. But I'm not going to lie," Jason said. "Seattle's in big trouble. We don't know how many zombies escaped into the streets. The council has declared martial law in all quarters. The Devani are out in droves, hunting for the zombies, but there are reports that enough managed to get free that we're facing a potential plague."

"It's worse than that," Tam said, so pale it was hard to look at him. "My compatriots from the Wild Wood sent word that there's a massive battalion of soldiers on the way to lock down the city. They don't want any of the zombies escaping to spread the infection. If they can't cleanse it of the plague..." His voice drifted off, but his meaning was clear.

"You think they might level it?"

"They could easily set up Bellingham as the new Seattle. Or even the Everett area. Move the ports. It would come at an enormous cost, but the fear of infection is nothing to wave away. The last thing the Conglomerate would want is a zombie infection."

"Then it looks like the Order of the Black Mist got at least some of what it wanted. Chaos and disorder." I pressed my lips together, thinking over the options. "We could go zombie hunting—"

"Not yet. We can't risk the Devani capturing you, and until they know how many of the creatures escaped, the government isn't going to let this drop. We have to leave the city for now, while we can. Because if they decide it's a lost cause, their method of cleansing will destroy everything left. They'll check every single person evacuating, and when they come to you and me, they'll take us down." Tam stood. "We need to leave as soon as you can travel. There's no safety here now for any of us."

"But Hecate! I can't..." I stopped as my phone rang. Tam handed it to me. It was Hecate. I put her on speaker.

"Fury? Tam told me what's going on. You need to leave. The Elder Gods are closing the Peninsula of the Gods right now. We won't be letting anybody in or out. You have a choice. You can come here, or you can go with your friends into the wild. I can find you without a problem. I don't need a phone to track you down, so don't worry about that."

I tried to take in everything that both she and Tam were saying. "But what about the Aboms? My job for you is—"

"Your job right now is to stay alive and out of the hands of the government. You also need to get away from the Order of the Black Mist. You managed to put a stop to their plans again, albeit the collateral damage has been done, and Lyon will still be hunting you down. You really can't afford to stay in the city. If you come here, we will protect you, but the wait may be a long one until you can leave."

I stared mutely at the phone, not knowing what to say. Then I turned to Jason. "What about you? About the Cast?"

"We're preparing to evacuate. Greta's gone to escort Shevron and Leonard here. I don't trust them on their own when there are zombies running around." He shrugged. "I guess Dream Wardens will be closed for a while. I went back to bag up whatever I could find that might help us. Elan and Laren are waiting for us at the boat."

"What about your people, Tam?" I turned a bleak gaze to him.

"UnderBarrow can withstand many things. As soon as I give the order, they'll seal our entrances from the outside and move the Barrow through, into the mist. As my people long ago separated from humans, so will UnderBarrow. I will leave Damh Varias in control and he will be my regent until I can return." The look on his face was so sorrowful that it made me want to cry.

My stomach still churning, I said, "I will go with you."

Hecate was still on the line and her voice came through loud and clear. "You should, Fury. Go with your family. Your friends are your brothers and sisters. I will be able to meet you in the Crossroads, and I will be able to find you in the Wild. Go into the Wild, to safety, for the world is once again shifting and things are going to get worse before they get better. In other cities around the world, the darker creatures are coming out, rising from the Underbelly at the behest of the Order of the Black Mist. Contact with several lands has been cut off. Bifrost has closed its gates to all outsiders."

I inhaled slowly, then pushed my way out of bed. "I'll go. I assume we leave as soon as possible?"

Tam nodded. "We've been waiting for you to wake. Elan went ahead to help Laren prepare the boat. Shevron and Leonard should be here by now. We need to go now."

"Hecate, don't forget me," I stuttered brokenly into the phone.

"Fury, you are one of my Chosen. You are my daughter. I will never forsake you. Trust me, I will be with you. And Queet can run messages if need be. He will go with you, too."

And then, she signed off.

We hurried then, gathering everything we could. A servant had already packed my things I had left in UnderBarrow. One of the healers came, spreading ointment on my bruises and giving me a drink that had the energizing effect of several lattes without all the jitters.

Tam and I were left alone when Jason went to

greet Shevron and Hans went to talk to Greta.

I turned to him. "We don't have much time."

"I want you too. Now, here." He pulled me to him, his lips meeting mine as I melted into his embrace, willing the kiss to go on and on. As his hands met my breasts, my hips, sliding between my legs, I explored his body. Every lithe muscle, I knew. Every curve and dip was familiar territory under my fingers. I could read his body with my eyes closed. Tam stroked my hip, playing over the whip.

"I love what you are. *Who* you are. You are my chosen mate. You are my furious passion." He nipped my lip with his teeth and then laid me back. I opened myself to his body as he bore down on me, penetrating the folds of my core.

As we moved in rhythm, my heart swelled. This man had awakened feelings in me I didn't know existed. I had thought I knew what love was before, but I now knew the difference between infatuation and truly giving your heart to someone capable of giving theirs back.

We made love, quickly, silently, and when we were done, we dressed and joined the others.

Like thieves in the night, we crept through the tunnels, Tam, Greta, Hans, Montran, Tymbur, Jason, Shevron, Leonard, and me. We snuck out to Elan and Laren's boat and, as the waves rocked us back and forth, I looked back at Seattle. Smoke was rising from various quarters through the snow that fell softly to coat a wounded city. Somewhere in the winding streets, a walking plague lurked and golden soldiers from Elysium drove their way through the city, free to use whatever force they chose to keep order for the corporatocracy.

Heartsick, we hid down in the magical hold as

Laren set sail. Seattle lay behind us. What waited ahead? There was no telling. But as we headed to the Wild Wood, I wondered if we'd ever be able to come back. To come home.

~End~

If you enjoyed this book and haven't read the first, I invite you to do so now. Fury Rising *is available in e-book and print. And I invite you into my other worlds. Stay tuned for the release of Bewitching Bedlam, Book 1 of my new Bewitching Bedlam Series, coming in January. You can read the prequel story—Blood Music—in* Taming the Vampire *right now!*

You might also enjoy the paranormal mystery series I just re-released this past month, the Chintz 'n China Mystery Series. All five books are now available in e-book and the first has been discounted to $2.99 permanently! Check them out: Ghost of a Chance, Legend of the Jade Dragon, Murder Under a Mystic Moon, A Harvest of Bones, *and* One Hex of a Wedding.

Fury Awakened, *Book 3 in the Fury Unbound Series, will be coming next year, along with a number of new releases! And be sure to sign up for my newsletter to ensure you always get updated on new releases. You can find out more about all my books on my web site at Galenorn.com and in the Biography at the end of this book.*

Upcoming releases:

January 2017: Bewitching Bedlam
(Bewitching Bedlam Series—Book 1)
March 2017: Souljacker
(Lily Bound Series—Book 1)
April 2017: Moon Shimmers
(Otherworld Series—Book 19)
May 2017: Fury Awakened
(Fury Unbound Series—Book 3)
July 2017: Crow Song
(Whisper Hollow Series—Book 3)

Playlist

I almost always write to music, and FURY'S MAGIC was no exception. Here's the playlist for the book:

Android Lust: Here and Now; Yaakuntik, Saint Over
AWOLNATION: Sail
Beck: Think I'm in Love; Broken Train
Black Angels: Indigo Meadow, Don't Play With Guns, Young Men Dead
The Chieftains: Dunmore Lassies
Clannad: Banba Óir; Newgrange
Clash, The: Should I Stay or Should I Go
Cobra Verde: Play with Fire
Crazy Town: Butterfly
David Bowie: Fame, Heroes
David & Steve Gordon: Shaman's Drum Dance
Death Cab For Cutie: I Will Possess Your Heart
Eastern Sun: Beautiful Being (Original Edit)
Eivør: Trøllbundin
Enya: Orinoco Flow; Cursum Perficio
Faun: Rad; The Market Song
Fluke: Absurd
Gabrielle Roth: Rest Your Tears Here, Mother Night
Garbage: #1 Crush
Gary Numan: Splinter, Here in the Black, Soul Protection

Gospel Whiskey Runners, The: Muddy Waters

Guess Who, The: No Sugar Tonight/New Mother Nature

Hedningarna: Ukkonen; Räven [Fox Woman]

Huldrelokk: Trolldans

Justin Timberlake: SexyBack

Kerstin Blodig & Ian Melrose: Kråka

Kills, The: Nail In My Coffin, You Don't Own The Road; U.R.A. Fever, Sour Cherry, DNA

Lorde: Royals

Loreena McKennitt: All Souls Night

Low with Tom and Andy: Half Light

Motherdrum: Big Stomp

Strawberry Alarm Clock: Incense and Peppermint

Tamaryn: Violet's in a Pool; While You're Sleeping, I'm Dreaming

Tangerine Dream: Exit, Dr. Destructo, Grind

Tom Petty: Mary Jane's Last Dance

Tuatha Dea: Tuatha De Danaan

Wumpscut: The March of the Dead

Biography

New York Times, *Publishers Weekly*, and *USA Today* bestselling author Yasmine Galenorn writes urban fantasy and paranormal romance, and is the author of almost fifty books, including the Otherworld Series, the Whisper Hollow Series, the Fury Unbound Series, the upcoming Bewitching Bedlam Series, and many more. She's also written nonfiction metaphysical books. She is the 2011 Career Achievement Award Winner in Urban Fantasy, given by RT Magazine.

Yasmine has been in the Craft since 1980, is a shamanic witch and High Priestess. She describes her life as a blend of teacups and tattoos. She lives in Kirkland, WA, with her husband Samwise and their cats. Yasmine can be reached via her web site at Galenorn.com.

Books by Yasmine Galenorn:

Fury Unbound Series:
Fury Rising
Fury's Magic
Fury Awakened (May 2017)

Bewitching Bedlam Series:
Blood Music (prequel novelette in Taming the Vampire)
Bewitching Bedlam (2017)
Maudlin's Mayhem (2017)

Whisper Hollow Series (in order):
Autumn Thorns
Shadow Silence
Crow Song (2017)
Morrígan's Blade (2018)

Otherworld Series (in order):
Witchling
Changeling
Darkling
Dragon Wytch
Night Huntress
Demon Mistress
Bone Magic
Harvest Hunting
Blood Wyne
Courting Darkness
Shaded Vision
Shadow Rising
Haunted Moon
Autumn Whispers
Crimson Veil
Priestess Dreaming
Panther Prowling
Darkness Raging
Moon Shimmers (2017)
Harvest Song (2018)
Blood Bonds (2019)

Otherworld: E-Novellas:
The Shadow of Mist: Otherworld novella
Etched in Silver: Otherworld novella
Ice Shards: Otherworld novella
Flight From Hell: Otherworld--Fly By Night
crossover novella
Earthbound

Otherworld: Short Collections:
Tales From Otherworld: Collection One
Men of Otherworld: Collection One
Men of Otherworld: Collection Two
Moon Swept: Otherworld Tales of First Love

Chintz 'n China Series:
Ghost of a Chance
Legend of the Jade Dragon
Murder Under a Mystic Moon
A Harvest of Bones
One Hex of a Wedding

Lily Bound Series (in order):
Souljacker (March 2017)

Fly By Night Series (in order):
Flight from Death
Flight from Mayhem

Indigo Court Series (in order):
Night Myst
Night Veil
Night Seeker
Night Vision
Night's End

Indigo Court: Novellas:
Night Shivers

Bath and Body Series (under the name India Ink):
Scent to Her Grave
A Blush With Death
Glossed and Found

Anthologies:

Silver Belles (November 2016)
Taming the Vampire (October 2016)
Once Upon a Curse (short story: Bones)
Never After (Otherworld novella: The Shadow of Mist)
Inked (Otherworld novella: Etched in Silver)
Hexed (Otherworld novella: Ice Shards)
Songs of Love & Death (short story: Man in the Mirror)
Songs of Love and Darkness (short story: Man in the Mirror)
Nyx in the House of Night (article: She is Goddess)
A Second Helping of Murder (recipe: Clam Chowder)

Magickal Nonfiction:
From Llewellyn Publications and Ten Speed Press:
Trancing the Witch's Wheel
Embracing the Moon
Dancing with the Sun
Tarot Journeys
Crafting the Body Divine
Sexual Ecstasy and the Divine
Totem Magic
Magical Meditations